"I SHALL ENDEAVOR TO BEHAVE MYSELF IN A MORE SEEMLY FASHION IN THE FUTURE"

He forced himself to smile down at her. "Since our party shall be at least another half-hour in the maze, ma'am, do you think it would be seemly to take a stroll?"

"Yes, I suppose there can be nothing amiss about a little stroll, so long as we remember to behave like near-strangers."

"You have my word." His lips curled up wryly at the corners. "May a near-stranger offer his arm?"

She couldn't resist smiling back at him. "Yes, of course," she said, tucking her arm in his. But the mere pressure of his arm sent her pulse racing, and, as if in response, a shiver ran right up his arm. "Oh, dear," she muttered in embarrassed acknowledgment of the tingle they both felt.

"You'll have to blame my arm, ma'am," he apologized. "It acts on its own. I'm afraid that there are parts of us that refuse to be strangers."

"So it seems," Jan admitted unhappily. "Oh, Max, what a *muddle* we are in."

Books by Elizabeth Mansfield

A Prior Engagement

Elizabeth Mansfield

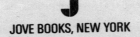
JOVE BOOKS, NEW YORK

A PRIOR ENGAGEMENT

A Jove Book / published by arrangement with
the author

PRINTING HISTORY
Jove edition / September 1990

ISBN: 0-515-10398-5

A JOVE BOOK®
Jove Books are published by The Berkley Publishing Group,
200 Madison Avenue, New York, New York 10016.
JOVE and the "J" design are trademarks
belonging to Jove Publications, Inc.

PRINTED IN THE UNITED STATES OF AMERICA

10 9 8 7 6 5 4 3 2

One

AT JUST AFTER eight in the morning Lady Hazeldine was awakened by the sound of a violin. Her ladyship groaned in disgust. This was, as any sane person would agree, a most ridiculous time of day for music practice. She opened her eyes and rolled them heavenward, asking herself and the gods above why she was cursed with a daughter who felt compelled to practice the violin at the crack of dawn! Then, knowing she was unlikely to get an answer either from herself or from heaven, she thrust her head under one of her pillows and tried to fall asleep again.

Down the hall in the music room (the room that Lady Hazeldine—because she'd had "more than enough music in my life, thank you!"—insisted on calling the upstairs sitting room even though it contained an elegant pianoforte and a huge bookcase full of musical scores), her daughter Jan was practicing finger exercises on her beloved violin. Jan hadn't intended to take up her instrument quite so early. When she'd first arisen, more than an hour earlier, she'd hoped to be able to venture out of doors for a brisk, soul-cleansing walk. She'd pulled aside her draperies and peered out, hoping to discover, if not a glimpse of sunshine, at least a small patch of blue sky. But she'd seen only grayness. *Hang it all,* she thought glumly, *we're going to have another one of those days! The clouds will hang heavy over those grim-looking London rooftops and spill down buckets of rain at the slightest provocation!*

It was the fourth consecutive day of chilling rain, as well

as the fourth consecutive day of Jan's depressed mood. This unfortunate conjunction of gloomy weather with gloomy spirits had been recurring with increasing frequency of late. There hadn't been a week in the three months since 1818 had begun without grim skies for London and grim moods for Jan. It was really too bad; a bit of sunshine this morning might have brightened her spirit and attacked her growing conviction that this spring (which her mother promised daily was "just around the corner") was not going to be any happier for her than the past springs had been. At this point particularly, her life seemed empty and purposeless, and she could see no signs promising future improvement.

There in her bedroom, standing at the window in night-dress and bare feet, she'd been about to sigh with self-pity when she stopped herself abruptly. "What is the matter with you, Genevra Hazeldine?" she'd asked herself under her breath, as she stared out at the winter-faded little garden and the wrought-iron fence that ringed her mother's townhouse on Welbeck Street. "Here you are, almost twenty-eight, and still childishly hoping that your life will change."

But she knew it wouldn't change. As her mother was wont to remind her several times a day, "It's all your own doing, my girl, all your own doing. You've jilted more men than I can count. You are utterly determined to defeat yourself at every turn."

Her mother was quite right. Something deep within her, something alarmingly self-destructive, always seemed to rise up and prevent her from seizing the opportunities to make for herself what the world deemed a "proper" life. She didn't understand her own behavior. It was as if there were a pernicious inner force keeping her from taking the one significant step that all the adult females of her class were expected to take: the step into wedlock. She'd stood on the brink of it seven years ago, but after she'd extricated herself from that experience, she never permitted herself to approach the brink again.

The mere recollection of that earlier experience added to her depression. There was only one thing to do when these moods of discontent took hold of her—play her violin. It was the one activity that made it possible for her to restore her peace of mind. That was why, despite the early hour, she'd dressed herself quickly, slipped out of her bedroom and run down the hall to the music room. She'd taken up her instrument (a fine Amati that had been her father's) and, after striking an A on the pianoforte, tucked the violin under her chin with the absentmindedness of long familiarity, and tuned up.

She'd been absentminded about her mother, too. Not thinking about the early hour or her mother's habit of sleeping late, Jan began her practicing. Before she knew it, she was wielding her bow with thoughtless energy. Thus, just down the corridor, her mother was finding it impossible to recapture sleep. Poor Lady Hazeldine opened her eyes, emerged from her cocoon of bedclothes, groaned again and swore aloud that never before was a mother so cursed. Shivering with cold, she leapt out of bed in irritation.

Jan, unaware of the small disturbance her playing was causing, continued to work on the exercises her father had transcribed for her years ago. Lord Hazeldine, deceased for more than a decade, had repeatedly emphasized to her the importance of daily finger exercises. Her father had been a fine violinist himself and, despite his busy schedule in the House of Lords, had always found time to practice and to give lessons to his daughter. When he was alive, the house had been filled with music. Every evening a group of musicians would gather in this very room, her father sitting among them as they played Handel and Mozart and new works by Spohr or Beethoven. Sometimes, after she'd become adept, her father would permit her to play with the group. Those occasions remained among her proudest memories.

Her father had not been a musical dilettante (as were so many of his peers) but a true artist. Not only had he mastered the violin but the pianoforte and the flute. In fact, Lord Hazeldine had been one of the organizers of the Philharmonic Society, the only one of that august circle who was not a professional musician. In her youth, Jan had spent many blissful evenings listening to the Philharmonic Society concerts.

Unfortunately, however, life changed radically after her

father's death. Jan's mother had little interest in music. Not only was she unsympathetic to her daughter's musical talent, but she was convinced that Jan used the violin as an escape from reality. "You have fiddled away all your years and all your suitors!" Lady Hazeldine was wont to declare. "If you end your days an eccentric old maid, you will only have yourself and your blasted violin to blame!"

At that moment, as if she'd materialized from her daughter's thoughts, Celia Hazeldine burst into the room. Not having taken the time to dress, she'd merely wrapped herself to the chin in a down-filled quilt. "Jan, *really*!" she barked.

"Mama!" Jan exclaimed, startled. Her bow froze on the strings as she stared at the apparition before her, a shapeless heap of quilting with only a nightcap showing above and a pair of slippered feet sticking out below. "What on *earth* is the matter?"

"Dash it all, Jan," the quilted heap snapped, "the clock's just struck *eight*! Couldn't you at least have waited until after breakfast before starting your deuced squeaking?"

Jan lowered her fiddle and, unable to hide a grin at her mother's ludicrous appearance, bit her lip. "Sorry, Mama. I didn't think. I'll stop playing at once. Go back to bed."

"As if I could get back to sleep now," her mother muttered, pulling the thick coverlet more closely round her. "My sheets will be icy by now. The damage has been done."

"I am truly sorry, my dear." Feeling quite ashamed of herself, Jan turned away and laid her fiddle gently back in its case. "I'm a thoughtless wretch."

Lady Hazeldine frowned. Watching her daughter stow away her bow with loving care, she was struck with shame herself. She'd made a to-do about nothing, and in so doing she'd spoiled her daughter's morning. Jan did so love to play her violin. Why was she, her mother, so unsympathetic to her daughter's one pleasure?

Celia Hazeldine peered at her only child from under the lacy edge of the nightcap that had slipped down low on her forehead, her anger melting away in a wave of affection. Her dearest Jan. Her husband had insisted on naming the girl Genevra, "for the lovely, musical, Italianate sound of it."

She'd objected, wanting a solid English name like Jane. Hazeldine wouldn't hear of it. He'd been the romantic, but she, the practical one, was never comfortable calling her daughter Genevra. She'd called the girl Jan from the first.

Jan, even at the advance age of twenty-seven, was still so strikingly lovely that it was almost impossible to be angry with her. Jan's face, with its fine skin stretched over delicately chiseled bones, was both strong and gentle, the strength coming from the slightly squared chin and the gentleness from the wide, softly gray eyes. There was something unusually expressive in those eyes, something that was eternally seeking answers. Jan seemed always to be questioning the validity of whatever she looked upon. That searching expression, enhanced by her high cheekbones and broad brow, gave her the look of an artist. Lady Hazeldine was convinced that it was Jan's air of artistic sensitivity that set her apart from the crowd.

Her ladyship studied her daughter ruefully as the girl packed away her deuced fiddle. She noted, with the shock of new awareness, that Jan's manner, too, had an artistic detachment. The girl seemed always slightly withdrawn, as if she were watching the scene before her with careful but uninvolved attention. Why had she, the mother, never noticed that before? It was probably this attentive detachment, coupled with the loveliness of her appearance, that drew so many men to seek Jan's approval. Not that her face, her tall slimness and her thick, lustrous brown hair wouldn't have been sufficient to attract the gentlemen, even without the added attribute of cool detachment. But the coolness gave her the luster of sophistication, an added inducement that attracted the gentlemen in the same way that icing enticed children to cake.

In short, Jan was lovely, sensitive, talented and intelligent. Any mother would be proud of such a daughter, Lady Hazeldine admitted to herself. So why was she always carping away at the poor girl?

Annoyed with herself at having disturbed her daughter's playing, Lady Hazeldine frowned again and turned to the door. "Oh, go ahead and play, if you still wish to," she said in gruff capitulation. "I'm up now anyway."

Jan grinned at the picture her mother made as her ladyship swept from the room, the quilt trailing along behind her. But as soon as the door closed, the girl promptly unpacked her fiddle and resumed her practicing, a trace of a smile lingering at the corners of her mouth.

As she sawed away at the rote exercises, however, her smile slowly faded. Her mind returned, as it usually did when she wasn't concentrating on the music, to the problems of her present life. She and her mother loved each other dearly, but they did not get on well together of late. They had different temperaments, different interests, different ideas of how to spend their days. But if Jan did not marry, she was doomed to spend the rest of her life in her mother's house, where, in time, their differences were certain to become more irritating to one another. Then why, she had to ask herself, did she not accept any of the offers that had been made to her?

In her mother's view, there wasn't a reason in the world why Jan should have reached this advanced age without being married. "There hasn't been a season, these past seven years, when you weren't considered the greatest beauty of the entire lot of marriageable females," her mother would declare with irritating frequency. "Everyone agrees on that. But good God, girl, you're almost twenty-eight! Your cousin Belinda, who's a whole decade younger than you, is coming out this season, do you realize that? This very season! She'll probably be announcing her betrothal before the year is out, while you'll still remain single. I can't believe it *possible*! My lovely Jan, to be again a leftover on the marriage mart! But unless you change your ways, that's just how it will be. For how long, Jan? How long do you think we can go on playing this match-making game?"

Jan had to admit there was not much more time. By the time a woman reached thirty, she had to don a cap and thus admit to the world that she was and would remain a spinster. The thought of that approaching day almost drove her mother wild. "How can you have fiddled away all your chances?" she raved almost daily. Jan had had, by her mother's count, eighteen perfectly suitable offers of marriage in her many seasons on the town, and she'd rejected every one of them. And what maddened her poor mother even more was that Jan was never able to give a good reason for the rejections. ''Any reason will do!'' her mother would cry. ''Even Philippa Thorpe gave her mother a reason when she turned down her Duke. 'The Duke wheezes when he talks.' It is as silly a reason as I've ever heard, but even a *silly* reason is better than *none*!''

Jan did, of course, have a reason, and it was a perfectly good one, too: Max. John Maxwell, the Marquis of Ollenshaw. Blasted Max. All her troubles dated from the time of her betrothal to him. But Jan would never admit that to a soul, to her mother least of all. Max, the deuced rake, had left a mark on her that seven years had not been able to erase. This spring would make eight years since she'd jilted him. And on days like this one, it seemed that the scar he'd left on her psyche would remain with her forever.

The thought of Max made her hands shake. Her bow trembled on the strings, causing an unpleasant disharmony. ''Dash it all,'' she swore aloud, ''how can I still permit his memory to affect me this way?''

She thrust aside the tedious exercises and launched forcefully into a Haydn sonata, hoping that the vigor of her playing would banish all thoughts of Max from her mind. After an hour of energetic music-making, she almost succeeded.

It was then that her mother strode back into the room. Now that she was fully clothed, Celia Hazeldine seemed much taller and shapelier than she'd appeared when wrapped in a quilt. She was not unlike her daughter in appearance, but where Jan was pale skinned and gray eyed like her father, her ladyship was swarthy and very dark of eye. Her graying hair, pinned back in a tight knot at the back of her head, gave her an air of dignity, but the firm line of her mouth and a certain calculatedness in her expression revealed a disposition more practical than artistic. As a matter of fact, Lady Hazeldine did not have an artistic bone in her body.

Heedless of her daughter's virtuoso performance and her own rudeness, Lady Hazeldine again interrupted Jan's play-

ing by breaking into speech at once. "Of all the announce-
ments in the world I'd prefer *not* to receive, *this* one tops the
list," she declared disgustedly. "I've just had a letter from
your Aunt Nettie. It seems that Belinda's *already* betrothed!
Not even out, and already spoken for. I don't think I can
stand it!" She sank down on the sofa and held out the letter.
"Even *she's* to be wed before you! If anyone had told me a
few years ago that the vacuous Belinda would precede *my Jan*
to the altar, I would not have believed it!"

Jan put aside her violin. "Belinda is not vacuous, just effusive. An adorable little prattle box, if I remember rightly.
Is she really *betrothed*? *Already*?" Eagerly, without (her
mother noted irritably) the slightest sign of envy, the girl
reached for the letter being held out to her and scanned it
quickly. "Well, Mama, this is very exciting! My little cousin
Belinda seems to have got herself quite a catch."

"Yes, confound it, that certainly appears to be the case."
Irritably, Lady Hazeldine snatched the letter back again and
glared at it. "Nettie says he's rich, handsome and charming.
Of *course* he is. What else was I to expect? Nettie would not
permit her daughter to accept less. Lucky Nettie. What more
can one wish for one's daughter?"

"What indeed?" Jan, in complete understanding of her
mother's feelings, slid down on the sofa beside her and said
gently, "Aunt Nettie must be very pleased."

"My sister was ever more fortunate than I," Celia Hazeldine said, sighing deeply.

"Come, come, Mama," Jan teased, taking her mother's
hand comfortingly. "It ill becomes you to be jealous of your
sister in her hour of happiness."

"I can't help it. I'd like to experience an hour of such
happiness myself. Why am I deprived of the pleasure of seeing *my* daughter wed, when she's more of a beauty than my
sister's daughter will *ever* be and has more brains and talent
besides?"

"Now, Mama, that's most unfair. Belinda is a charmer,
and you know it." She took the letter from her mother's now-
limp fingers and searched for something in it to lift her mother's spirit. "Ah, look here! Aunt Nettie asks us to come to

Bath for the month to celebrate with them. Shall we go, Mama? It might make a pleasant change.''

Lady Hazeldine shrugged. "I suppose we must. What a bore!''

"It won't be a bore at all. You can spend your days combing all the lovely shops in Milsom Street for bargains and your evenings combing the assembly rooms for eligible gentlemen to thrust in my face.'' She gave her mother a teasing smile before she rose and turned away to restore her violin to its case. "What more enjoyable way is there for you to spend the remaining month before the London season begins than to scout out some new eligibles?''

Celia Hazeldine eyed her daughter's back speculatively, a gleam of hope lighting up her face. "Yes, you're quite right. That's just what I shall do. I'll send for Dorrie at once and set her to packing our things.'' She pulled herself up and strode purposefully to the door. "Nettie says Belinda's wedding is to be held in June. That gives me three months to find an eligible for you.'' At the door she paused and glanced over her shoulder at her daughter. "If only you'd bring yourself to cooperate,'' she added, her voice wavering between her newborn optimism and the desperation that had come from long years of dashed expectations, "perhaps we can *still* beat my sister's precious Belinda to the altar.''

"Beat Belinda?'' Jan's head came up abruptly, and her back stiffened. "How, my love, did this innocent little trip to Bath suddenly become a competition?'' She whirled about, her teasing smile having changed to a look of irritated dismay. "I tell you, Mama, I won't be party to making this a race to the altar. Do you *hear* me, Mama? *Mama!*''

But her mother had long since made a hasty retreat.

Two

SPRING MADE NO appearance in the week that followed, nor was there a sign of it in all the hundred miles of countryside that Jan and her mother traversed on their way to Bath. A winter dullness still depressed the landscape, and the harsh wind that whipped past the carriage windows bore no hint of the warmth to come. But when the equipage trundled over the arched North Parade Bridge, and the two travelers could hear the laughing roar of the Avon River as it bubbled over the weir just below them, their spirits lifted. "I don't know why I suddenly feel so larky," Lady Hazeldine remarked. "I've always found Bath to be a stuffy, *petit-bourgeois* bore."

"Come down from your high ropes, Mama," Jan taunted. "You've cheered up because, for one thing, this chilly journey is over. And for another, because you know you'll enjoy every moment here. *Petit-bourgeois* or not, so long as Milsom Street has shops and the Assemblies have bachelors, Bath will please you."

"And Bath will please *you* so long as there are concerts to attend," her mother retorted.

"Yes. I'm quite looking forward to the concerts," Jan admitted.

They peered excitedly out the coach windows. Ahead of them rose the pinnacled tower of the ancient Bath Abbey, gleaming in amber-colored splendor in the late afternoon sunshine, with the rest of the city huddled closely round its base. From the high point of the bridge the travelers could see much of the city. Although Bath had declined somewhat from its heyday, when it had attracted the very cream of the Ton, it was still a city of remarkable architectural beauty. The rays of the setting sun threw the columns and pediments of the Palladian buildings in sharp relief, making the grandeur of streets, the squares and the magnificent Royal Crescent (a glowing, golden arc of columns in the distance) seem an elegant oasis of sophistication amid the rustic surroundings. Both Lady Hazeldine and her daughter smiled appreciatively at the view. They were glad they'd come. This was a city meant for refined pleasure, and the prospect of that pleasure warmed their spirits.

Less than two minutes after leaving the bridge, the carriage drew up before No. Two Pierrepont Street, the house that Lady Hazeldine's sister Nettie, Lady Briarly, had found for them. Lady Hazeldine had written to her as soon as she and Jan had decided to come. "We'll stay for a month," she'd informed her sister, "so please find us a suitable abode. A modest house, with no more than fifteen rooms, for Jan and I shall bring with us only a skeletal staff of six; but the neighborhood must be choice."

Lady Briarly, overjoyed that her wealthy, stylish sister had condescended to come to Bath, had rushed out at once and found the perfect place. "I've rented No. Two Pierrepont for you," she'd written back, "where no less a Personage than Lord Nelson once stayed. It is a Charming place, twelve rooms, very well Situated, a short walk to the Pump Room and just round the Corner from my rooms on the South Parade."

Celia Hazeldine found herself pleased by the first sight of the house. It was on one of the lovely, wide streets that Wood himself had designed, and its modestly pedimented doorway and graceful facade were models of understated elegance. The interior proved to be in keeping with the exterior; the modest-sized rooms that they could see from the central hallway appeared to be well appointed and tasteful. With a sense of happy anticipation, they followed Beale, the butler (who had arrived barely an hour earlier with the other staff members and the baggage), into the sitting room and removed their wraps while he made suggestions to them about the quartering of the staff and the disposition of the bedrooms.

Beale had barely launched into his report when the door knocker sounded. "Good heavens, who can be calling on us so soon?" Lady Hazeldine asked in annoyance.

"Who else can it be but Aunt Nettie?" her daughter reasoned. "She's the only one who was informed of the date of our arrival."

"But she couldn't have guessed the precise moment of our arrival, could she? Good God, the woman must have had someone watching our door!" Frowning in irritation, she thrust her hat into the butler's hand. "I'll answer the door, Beale. You stay here and continue discussing the arrangements. Jan, my love, do go over these matters with Beale, or we shall never settle in. I'll deal with Nettie myself."

It was indeed Lady Briarly at the door, with her daughter Belinda beside her. Nettie Briarly, a stout, cheerfully voluble woman who was two years younger than her sister but looked ten years older, embraced Celia fondly. "Cecy, my love!" she exclaimed as soon as she released her sister and stepped over the threshold, "I'm so glad you're here at last, so very glad!"

"So am I, Aunt Cecy, so am I," Belinda bubbled, kissing her aunt's cheek affectionately. "With you and my cousin Jan here, I have all I need to make my happiness complete."

Celia Hazeldine, while offering appropriate murmurs of congratulations to her newly betrothed niece, couldn't help staring askance at the girl. She was decked out in a showy blue lustring gown and an enormous bonnet with a high poke and a mass of feathers that fell over the brim in profusion. Both the gown and the hat were much too ornate for a simple afternoon call, but although Celia did not approve of the girl's taste, she could find no fault with her looks. Belinda Briarly had turned out to be a beauty.

Meanwhile, Nettie beamed at them both. "Isn't this the most wonderful pass? My little Belinda, not yet out and *already* caught herself the best matrimonial prize of the season!"

"Yes, quite wonderful," Celia agreed, her eyes taking

sharp note of all the changes that time had wrought in her little niece. Belinda was not tall, but her figure was softly rounded, and her face, quite pretty to begin with, was made outstandingly so by the confident glow that so often enhances the faces of the newly betrothed. But what struck Celia with the greatest surprise was that there was something about her high forehead, her full lips and the shape of her chin that was very like Jan's. In some ways the two girls could almost be taken for sisters.

Meanwhile, Belinda turned modestly pink at her mother's artless boasting. "Oh, Mama," she muttered in embarrassment, "*must* you?"

But Nettie paid no heed. "Now that you're here, Cecy," she rattled on happily, "we can truly celebrate Belinda's betrothal. All our friends have been wanting to hold routs and fêtes in her honor, but I've held them off. I insisted on waiting for you. And now we can tell them to go ahead! Isn't it all delightful? What an exciting time we shall have!" She stepped back and eyed her fashionable sister with approval. "My dear Cecy, you are looking splendid! Where did you ever find a gown in such a lovely shade of peach? I always say that there isn't anyone else in the world with such an eye for color as you."

Celia Hazeldine, never having had the least patience for her sister's ramblings, waved away the compliment in disgust. "Heavens, Nettie, how you do run on! You've as good an eye for color as I have. If you hadn't let yourself get so stout, you could wear this shade of peach yourself."

"I know, I know," Nettie agreed, laughing pleasantly. "You're right, my dear, of course. I intend to be quite firm with myself and lose a stone or two before the wedding. But never mind that now. First tell me how you like the house I found for you."

"How can I tell?" Lady Hazeldine said nastily. "I've had no opportunity to see it, what with callers arriving immediately we set foot in the door."

But Nettie, who was quite accustomed to her sister's sharp tongue, remained unperturbed. "Then you must let me show it to you," she insisted eagerly. "Come up with me and see your bedroom. It has a magnificent marble mantel over the fireplace, and you can see the Avon from the windows.'' She started for the stairs but, realizing that her daughter was hanging back, paused and looked over her shoulder. ''Well, come along, Belinda. Don't you want to see the bedroom, too?''

''No, thank you, Mama. I'd rather say hello to Jan, if I may. Where is she, Aunt Cecy?''

''Across the hall in the sitting room, giving Beale instructions on where the boxes are to go. Do go along and see her, my dear. She's been waiting eagerly for the opportunity to wish you well.''

As the two sisters climbed the stairs (Nettie Briarly babbling happily on about the virtues of the house), Belinda ran across the hall. ''Jan, Jan,'' she cried ecstatically, ''I've been wanting to see you this *age*!''

Jan, not yet finished giving the butler his instructions, turned in surprise at the sound of her name, but before she had a chance to take a step toward the door there was a flurry of flounces and feathers, and she found herself enveloped in a most enthusiastic embrace. ''Belinda, my dear!'' she exclaimed, trying to see over the gigantic bonnet that had suddenly lodged itself under her nose.

Beale suppressed his irritation at the interruption. ''Shall we continue this later, Miss Jan?'' he asked discreetly.

Jan nodded, throwing him a glance of amused helplessness over Belinda's feathers. ''Yes, Beale, later.''

Belinda stepped back and beamed at Jan adoringly. She'd idolized her elder cousin from infancy and now could barely contain her delight at seeing her again. ''Dear, *dear* Jan,'' she gushed, ''I don't know how you manage it, but I'd swear you're as beautiful as ever!''

''In spite of my advanced age, you mean?'' Jan laughed. ''But, my love, do take off that overwhelming bonnet and give it to Beale, so I can take a proper look at you.''

Beale took the feathered monstrosity from Belinda's hand and bowed himself out while Jan stared at her cousin in admiring astonishment. The changes that nature had wrought in the girl in the mere two years since their last meeting were incredible. Belinda had been a delightful, prattling, chubby little thing in her sixteenth year. Now, with her figure slimmed to luscious curves, her hair cut into short, feathery curls that framed a face that had matured to something beyond mere prettiness, and with her eyes sparkling with happy self-confidence, she'd become a real beauty. "But *you*, Belinda, are a *dream*!" Jan exclaimed. "So grown up, and so very lovely! I've never seen anyone so glowing!"

"Yes, I know." Belinda grinned, whirling about so excitedly that the flounce of her gown ballooned up like an umbrella round her ankles. "Isn't love marvelous? I've been in *transports* ever since it happened."

"Yes, I can see it shining in your eyes." Jan took Belinda's hand and drew her to the sofa. "Come, my dear, sit down and tell me all! From the very beginning."

"Do you truly want to hear it *all*?" Without waiting for an answer, Belinda perched on the sofa beside her cousin and drew up her legs under her with girlish eagerness. "Well, then, to start, you must know that my betrothed is the most wonderful man I ever met, and I am the most fortunate girl in the entire world."

"But of *course*." Jan grinned. "I never doubted it. How and where, you lucky creature, did you find him?"

"I met him right here in Bath, the very week we arrived. Mama's friend, Mrs. Kendall, introduced us during our first stroll round the Pump Room. We'd barely had a chance to look about us when Mrs. Kendall came running up to Mama and me, pulling this *breathtaking* gentleman by the arm. The moment I looked up at him I *knew*!"

"Love at first sight?" Jan teased. "My dear Belinda, don't you know how dangerous that is?"

Belinda nodded in quite serious agreement. "Oh, yes, I *do*! You mustn't think I didn't caution myself about the dangers," she admitted. "But can you credit it, Jan, that nothing troublesome has ever occurred? Not ever. The whole courtship has been the *smoothest* sailing!" She beamed at Jan in beatific bliss. "Never even a tiny little pebble on the proverbially rough road to true love."

"How very fortunate," Jan murmured, unable to keep from feeling a twinge of envy at her cousin's untroubled romance. But she promptly squelched the feeling. It wasn't Belinda's fault that she, Jan, had not had the same good fortune. She felt for Belinda the same affection she might have had for a little sister. She was truly happy for her. "But do go on with your tale," she urged. "You met in the Pump Room. And then?"

"Then he asked to accompany Mama and me to the Assembly that evening. I was so overwhelmed I could hardly speak a word. I was sure he would find me the greatest bore. But the very next morning, at the Pump Room, there he was again! When I realized that he was truly taken with me, it was easier to talk to him. And soon thereafter he began to court me in earnest. At first I feared that he was attracted to me because I reminded him of someone in his past, but soon he convinced me that he cares for me, myself." She looked across at Jan, her youthful self-confidence suddenly wavering. "He would not have asked to wed me otherwise, don't you agree?"

"Of course I agree, you goose," Jan assured her, taking her hand and squeezing it fondly. "How could he help loving such a charmer as you?"

Belinda giggled. "Right. How could he help himself?" Her confidence restored, she grinned broadly. "I know you think I've lost my head, but just wait till you meet him. You won't fully understand until you see him, my dear, for he's beyond description."

"Is he, indeed?" Jan smiled at the younger girl indulgently. "He's handsome, then?"

"Oh, yes, very! Tall, you know—he quite towers over me— and broad in the shoulders, as a man should be. He's beautifully powerful in build, if you know what I mean. Handles the reins most expertly, like the sportsman he is. But you mustn't think he's one of those sporting types who thinks only of racing and hunting. He's a Corinthian, but he's very clever with it all."

"Of course he's clever. I never doubted it for an instant."

"But wait, Jan, I haven't finished. He has dark, curly hair, cut in the Brutus style like a true Corinthian. And the most *wonderful* eyes. They are a sort of hazel, very light, and when he looks at you, you feel almost . . . naked, you know? As if he could look right through you. Yet if you feel the least bit embarrassed by his piercing stare, he'll promptly say something to make you laugh, and then, of course, you feel perfectly at ease with him.''

"Oh, my!" Jan gasped, half-teasing and half-awestruck. "He sounds almost too splendid to be real. Tell me, my love, does this paragon have a name?"

"Oh, haven't I told you that? He's John Maxwell, Lord Ollenshaw. And Jan, do you know what has Mama in transports? He's a *marquis*! Really! An actual *marquis*! But good heavens, Jan, you needn't stare at me so! You've never been one to set store by rank. And one of the things I truly love about him is that he's not in the least high in the instep. In fact, he doesn't permit his acquaintances to call him Lord Ollenshaw. Everyone calls him—"

"I know," Jan cut in, clenching her fists to control her trembling fingers and hoping desperately that her face did not reveal that her insides had just been struck a numbing blow. "Max."

Three

"GOOD HEAVENS, DO you *know* him?" Belinda asked in delight.

"We've met," Jan answered, barely knowing what she was saying. Her mind was reeling with confused thoughts and emotions. Max, betrothed to, of all people, *her own cousin Belinda*! The fact seemed beyond belief; it was as if some vengeful god was playing a cruel joke on her. But not only on her. On Belinda, too.

"But when did you meet him? Where?" Belinda prodded avidly.

Jan flicked a nervous glance at the girl's face. Belinda was peering at her in eager innocence, waiting for an answer. Jan had no idea how to reply to the question. How much should she say? How would Belinda feel if she learned that her beloved cousin Jan had once been betrothed to her beloved Max?

Jan's instinct told her to say nothing more. In any case, her brain was too benumbed with shock to be relied on to assist her in making a proper confession. The best thing to do right now, she decided, was to say as little as possible.

"Well, Jan?" Belinda persisted. "When?"

Jan blinked at her cousin stupidly. "I don't quite . . . I'm afraid I barely remember. It was so long ago, you see . . ."

"But you must!" Belinda shook her head in disbelief. "Max isn't the sort one easily forgets. Don't you even remember how handsome he is?"

"Yes, vaguely. Very handsome," Jan mumbled.

"You *do* remember him!" Belinda threw her arms about

her cousin in delight. "Then you already know whether or not I exaggerated in my description of him. I didn't, did I, Jan?"

"No, I don't believe you exaggerated. If my memory serves, he is . . . just as you described."

Belinda beamed. "Perhaps he'll remember you a little, too. When I introduce you, I won't say you've met. That way we'll see if you both recognize one another. Won't it be fun?"

"Oh, yes," Jan said numbly, "great fun."

Belinda babbled on happily. "How lovely that you're already acquainted! We shall be able to skip all those awkward beginnings and be good friends from the start."

"Good f-friends?" Jan shut her eyes, wondering dazedly if she should let herself swoon. Swooning was something she'd never done in all her life, but it seemed a distinct possibility now. Her head was swimming, and the whole room seemed to be spinning slowly about. All she had to do was to surrender to the feeling and let herself slip quietly to the floor. It would be a very good way to escape from this dreadful conversation. Surely Belinda must have noticed her state of perturbation. If she swooned, she could later explain that she'd simply been ill.

But Belinda did not notice anything at all. Wrapped up in her happiness, she was as unaware of Jan's feelings as a dinner guest would be about the mood of the cook. She prattled on merrily, making cheerful predictions about the coming reunion between her cousin and her Max. "It's deucedly annoying that Max had to go to London on business at just this time," she remarked, "but he'll return in three or four days. I can't wait for you two to meet again!"

Jan's eyes flew open as her mind leapt to attention. Had Belinda said that Max was far away in London? Of all the girl's babblings since mentioning Max's name, this last remark was the only one that didn't cut into Jan's soul. It was the one bit of news she could bear to hear. *Thank heaven!* she thought, heaving a grateful sigh. *At least I shall have a little while to come to my senses before having to face him.*

* * *

Jan had no idea how she got through the next two hours. In a fog, she responded to Belinda's enthusiastic questions, greeted her cheerful Aunt Nettie, helped to serve tea to the visitors, participated somehow in their conversation, agreed to plans for joining them the next morning in the Pump Room, and at last kissed them adieu.

As soon as the door closed behind them, Lady Hazeldine turned to her daughter, her brow wrinkled worriedly. "What on earth is the matter with you, Jan?" she asked. "You've been stumbling about as if in a daze. Is something amiss?"

Jan peered at her mother in befuddlement. Hadn't she been told the name of Belinda's betrothed? Aunt Nettie must have mentioned it. But once she'd heard it, she'd surely have reacted strongly. It would not be like the sharp-tongued Celia Hazeldine to refrain from making a to-do. At the very least, she'd tease her sister about it. (Jan could almost hear her: "Aha, Nettie! So your Belinda has betrothed herself to one of Jan's castoffs. I find that vastly amusing, don't you?") At the worst, she'd give Jan one of her thundering scolds. ("You see? It's just like you, Genevra Hazeldine, to have thrown away a catch like Ollenshaw. But Belinda was not such a fool, no indeed. Barely eighteen, but she's clever enough to snatch him up! It is only *my idiotic daughter* who hadn't the sense to keep him for herself!")

But her mother had not said any of those things. She was only showing concern for her daughter's state of mind. Was it possible that she still didn't know? Well, if she didn't, Jan had no intention of telling her. "No, Mama, nothing's amiss. I'm merely tired. The journey alone—"

"Yes, my love, I know. So many hours in that draughty carriage, and then a two-hour visit from my sister and Belinda. I'm utterly fatigued myself. Come, let's make an early day of it. We'll tell cook not to bother about dinner, and we'll simply retire for the night. Perhaps Dorrie has made up the beds by now."

"Yes, Mama, that is a very good idea. There's nothing I'd like better right now than bed."

They started up the stairs. "By the way, his name is Ollenshaw," Lady Hazeldine remarked out of the blue.

"What?" Jan asked, her whole body stiffening. "Who—"

"Belinda's betrothed. Nettie said his name is Lord Ollenshaw. I don't know why, but the name has such a familiar ring."

Jan gaped at her mother in amazement. *Is it possible*, she wondered, *that Mama doesn't remember?*

"The family name is well known, of course," her mother mused. "Everyone knows of the Derbyshire Ollenshaws. But I keep trying to recall—" Suddenly she gasped and wheeled about to face Jan *"Max!"* she exclaimed, remembering. "John Maxwell, Lord Ollenshaw. I say, Jan, wasn't he one of your jilts, years and years ago?"

"Yes, Mama," Jan answered carefully. "My first. Don't you remember him?"

"Not very well. Handsome devil, wasn't he?" She rubbed her forehead in frustration. " Oh, well, how can I be expected to remember? You've jilted so many." And with a careless shrug, she dismissed the matter from her mind and went up to bed.

Four

I HAVE NOT jilted so many, Jan said to herself as she threw herself on her unfamiliar bed. *Max was the only one, really.*

Her mother's sarcastic assessment of her character wounded her. She was not a jilt. There had been a few of her suitors to whom, in moments of weakness, she made promises, but she'd never actually become betrothed to anyone but Max. Her mother had no right to malign her in that way. Who besides Max had she really jilted? She supposed her mother would say Lord Sherbrook, for one. But although she'd *almost* accepted Sherbrook, she'd stopped herself just in time. The same with Richard Hughes. Tommy Halstead had mistakenly taken it into his head that she'd actually said yes and had written an announcement to the *Times,* so when she refused him it *seemed* like a jilt but was actually just a misunderstanding. And as for Sir Niles Clark, it was only his ridiculous rodomontade at his club—when he threatened to shoot himself—that made people think he'd been jilted; the truth was that the scene at the club caused a great deal more talk than their brief courtship warranted. Everyone in London had called her a jilt then, but it was patently unfair. And as for Geoffrey Pettifer, could she be blamed when, after her refusal, he'd sent his mother round to plead his case with her mother? As a result of that interview, Mama accused her of jilting Geoffrey, too, but it wasn't true. None of those instances was truly a betrothal, and therefore she should not—could not—be accused of jilting any of them. Max was the only one.

And in truth, she hadn't really jilted Max either. It was more the other way round. He'd betrayed her. She had no choice but to break it off. If one judged the matter by hurt feelings, then one would have to say that he'd jilted her. Here she was, still feeling the pain, while *he* was happily betrothed to a girl of eighteen. So who was the jilt and who the jilted?

She got out of bed and paced about the room in which she still didn't feel at home. Everywhere she looked was unfamiliar. The dressing table did not yet hold any of her things, most of her clothes were still packed, and although the view from her window—a tiny garden and the back of another house—was not so different from her view in the London house, it all felt strange. The only familiar items in the room were her nightgown, which Dorrie had laid out on the bed, and her violin case, which Beale had carefully placed on the chest of drawers. She would have been soothed if she'd been able to play some Bach for an hour or so, but she knew her mother would find the music disturbing.

Still in emotional turmoil over Belinda's news, Jan sat down on the window seat and, lifting up her legs and hugging her knees, stared out into the twilight. Over the roof of the neighboring house, just to the north, she could see the Abbey tower silhouetted in dark majesty against the faintly glowing sky. It was a lovely scene, and at any other time it would have pleased her immensely, but now she barely noted it. Her mind remained fixed on the past, on memories that had been stirred up by Belinda's announcement and that refused to be put to rest.

Memories. They swirled about inside her like a whirlwind . . . a windstorm of faces, sounds, feelings. Memories of Papa as he looked just before he died, just two weeks after her come-out. Memories of Mama, pushing aside her own grief to help her daughter conquer hers. Memories of balls and routs and galas that the passing years had fused in her mind to one varicolored blur. Memories of sounds—dance music, and laughter, and lonely nighttime sobs, and Mama's scolding voice, and, always, the sweet cry of the violin. And above all the other memories, the bright, searing, stinging memory of Max . . .

Five

THE MEMORY OF the ball at which Jan met Max was not a blur. Although eight long years had passed since, all she had to do was close her eyes to bring to mind every excruciating detail—the glittering chandeliers that lit the Edgertons' ballroom, the dozens of dazzling couples whirling about on the dance floor, the flounce of her blue lustring gown as it swished about her ankles during the waltz, the face of her waltz partner, William Coombe, as he stepped clumsily on the toe of her right foot during a turn, and, of course, every moment of what happened next.

She hadn't wanted to attend the Edgertons' annual squeeze at all. It was her mother who'd made her go. Jan was then only twenty and hadn't yet acquired the sophistication and savoir faire that would characterize her later. Nor had she yet learned how to say no to her mother.

Although she'd been "out" for two years and been pursued by a goodly number of suitors in that time, she still felt girlish. Her mind was more occupied with her musical studies than with her beaux. The reason for this preoccupation with music was caused, her mother claimed, by her father's sudden death. Lord Hazeldine had died shortly after Jan's come-out, and Jan, utterly heartbroken, had convinced herself that by continuing her violin studies with diligence she could keep him alive in her heart.

Lady Hazeldine, however, had no patience for what she called "morbid sentimentality." She was convinced that neither grief for Lord Hazeldine nor an obsession with music should be permitted to stand in the way of progress, and progress meant finding a proper husband for her daughter. "What on earth is the matter with you, Jan?" she'd ask at the slightest provocation. "How can a girl with your gifts remain unattached after two whole seasons on the town?"

Lady Hazeldine was extremely put out that her daughter— a girl so lovely, so talented, so perfectly reared, so eminently qualified to make a perfect match—had not yet done so. She was determined that such a match would come to pass. To that end, she pushed the girl to attend every social function of the season. Jan, not yet adept at rebellion, reluctantly but dutifully obliged.

So it was that she found herself at the Edgertons' ball at midnight, suffering from extreme boredom and a bruised toe. Weary from having danced every dance since the evening began, and fearing that the cloddish William Coombe would seek her hand again for the next waltz and wound her other foot, she slipped out of the ballroom and ran down the corridor to find an empty room in which to rest. She opened a door and, seeing a glowing fire within, stepped over the threshold. It was only after she shut the door behind her that she realized she'd interrupted an intimate encounter: across the room, a man and a woman, involved in an excessively warm embrace, sprang apart at the sound of the door. "Oh!" Jan cried, deeply embarrassed. "I'm sorry! I didn't mean to—"

"No, of course you didn't mean to," the woman said, putting a bejeweled hand to a breast that was heaving nervously over the low décolletage of her modish gown. "But you gave me quite a fright just the same. I thought you were my . . . someone else."

The gentleman, tall and darkly attractive in his impeccable black evening coat and gleaming white neckerchief, stepped forward as if to shield the woman from Jan's scrutiny. "Did you wish for something in this room, ma'am?" he asked, his voice deep and coolly unperturbed. "Perhaps I might be of assistance to you."

"No, no," Jan said awkwardly, backing to the door.

"Thank you, but it is of no importance. I only . . . that is, I just w-wanted to put my feet up."

"And so you shall," the woman said briskly, circling round her "protector" and crossing quickly to the door. "I was just going anyway." Her gown, of a stunning green silk, swished as she walked, and Jan couldn't help noticing that her underskirt had been damped to make it cling, and that her hair was too orange-red to be natural. This was obviously the sort of woman Jan's mother would have labeled "fast."

"No, please," Jan mumbled, "don't trouble. I can find another—"

The woman patted Jan's shoulder as she passed her, as one might pat a slightly annoying child. "No need. I must go. I've been gone from the card room too long." She looked over at the gentleman. "Later?" she asked pointedly.

The gentleman bowed. The woman threw him a small, intimate smile and departed, leaving the door ajar.

Jan stood rooted to the spot. It was awkward to remain there, feeling the gentleman's eyes on her, but it would be just as awkward to run out, for the redheaded woman might think she was being followed. Jan dropped her eyes, feeling the color flood her face.

She heard rather than saw the gentleman approach her. "May I help you to a chair, ma'am? This one here, near the fire, is just the thing, for there's a hassock near it for your feet."

"Thank you, but it isn't . . . I don't need . . ." Annoyed at herself for stumbling over her tongue like a schoolgirl, she took a deep breath and said carefully, "I think I should return to the ballroom."

"But, my dear, why on earth should you? If you've been danced off your feet—as you must have been if the young bucks have eyes in their heads—you should certainly take this opportunity to catch your breath. Here, take my arm."

Before she knew it, Jan found herself ensconced in an easy chair, with the gentleman lifting her feet up on the hassock, his hands on her ankles giving the act an exciting tinge of intimacy. While he was thus engaged, she took the opportunity to flick a quick glance at his face. He was quite the handsomest man imaginable, with the dark skin and light eyes that young women dream of. His lips might have been judged too full, but Jan rather liked the way one corner of his mouth turned up slightly and made his expression enticingly satiric. His brown hair was cut in the short, tightly curled manner of a Corinthian, and his superbly cut evening clothes showed his wide shoulders and muscular legs to advantage. She might have taken him for a Beau Brummell, but the casual way he carried his attire revealed him to be more the sportsman than the dandy.

Suddenly he looked up at her, and their eyes met for the first time. Jan's heart did a flip-flop in her chest, and she felt herself blushing again. This time, however, she did not let herself look away. She was not a green girl, she reminded herself, and she would permit neither his handsomeness nor the awkwardness of the situation to make her behave like one. "Thank you," she said, putting up her chin. "You've made me quite comfortable. I need not detain you any longer."

He straightened up and smiled down at her, a smile that was both teasing and admiring and that made her heart skip a beat. "Dismissing me, are you, ma'am? Not that I blame you. If I were an innocent young girl at my first ball, I would not wish to find myself alone with a—"

"Rake?" Jan supplied impetuously. As soon as the word escaped her lips she gasped, astounded at herself for her impertinence.

His smile broadened. "I was going to say 'stranger.' Do you really think me a rake, ma'am? Because you discovered me kissing a lady in the shadows?"

Since she'd already blurted out one frank response, she decided that there was no harm in adding another. "What else am I to think, sir?"

His smile altered, one corner of his mouth turning down in caustic contempt. "You *might* think, ma'am, that your knowledge of me is too brief and circumstantial to jump to such conclusions. Have you never heard that even criminals are given hearings before they are condemned?"

Jan lowered her eyes, reluctantly admitting to herself that the fellow had a point. "Well, whatever the case, your conduct is no business of mine, and I have no right to comment on it.''

''But I've given you the right by asking your opinion,'' he said, the acidity in his smile changing to an expression of utterly self-assured charm. ''I hope, however, that you will give *me* the right to defend myself. You, being a young girl at your first ball, may not yet have learned that a stolen embrace is not uncommon in these circumstances. Embraces at balls are completely commonplace, I assure you. In fact, many young ladies—though they may not be willing to admit it—don't consider a ball to have been truly satisfying unless they've indulged in at least one such embrace.''

Jan was not impressed by his glib excuse. ''I'll have you know, sir,'' she said with spirit, ''that you'll have to do better than that to take me in. I am *not* a little innocent at my first ball. I've been out for two full seasons, and *I have never*—'' She stopped herself abruptly, realizing that she was about to make an admission that was much too personal to reveal to a stranger. In truth, now that she thought about it, this entire exchange was inappropriate with a stranger.

''Never been kissed at a ball, ma'am?'' The gentleman peered down at her in mock astonishment. ''Not in two whole seasons on the town? I cannot believe it. The young bucks in your circle must be a group of clods and mooncalves.''

Jan was unaccustomed to badinage of this sort, but she sensed that its tone was too improper to indulge in any longer. This man, attractive though he was, was too fast for her. He was toying with her as if she were a green schoolgirl. It was time to stop him . . . to put him in his place. ''On the contrary,'' she declared, getting to her feet and turning a cold shoulder on him, ''the 'young bucks in my circle' are, to a man, respectful and well bred, which is more than I can say for present company. Good evening, sir.''

With head high, she moved quickly toward the door, feeling quite proud of the setdown she'd delivered. But before she'd gone three steps he came up behind her, grasped her arm and whirled her round to face him. ''Respectful and well bred, eh?'' he grinned, pulling her into his arms. ''What a pity!'' He lowered his head until their faces were only a breath apart. "In their well-bred respectability, they've cheated you, my dear. You are too lovely to have suffered such deprivation." Then quite abruptly, he closed the gap between his lips and hers.

It was the first kiss she'd ever experienced, and she found the sensation astounding, too astounding to do any of the proper things, like pulling herself away, slapping his face and bursting into tears. She just stood there, yielding slightly to the pressure of his arms, feeling deliciously soft and feminine pressed against his stiff-shirted chest. It was an utterly new feeling, and she was not a bit afraid until she became aware of the beating of his heart. Then a shudder—of fright, or of something else—ran through her body from her throat to her toes, and she pushed against him somewhat hysterically. But when he let her go, she had the oddest wish that he'd held her a little longer.

He was looking down at her with his irritatingly teasing grin. "You are supposed to slap me now," he instructed.

Jan stared up at him, breathless and bemused. "*Supposed* to?"

"That *is* the expected response when a man kisses a girl without her permission. But it's not a requirement. I'm sure we can dispense with it if you are not so inclined."

Jan, recovering herself, put up her chin with disdainful dignity. "We may as well dispense with it, sir, since I don't see what purpose it would serve. A slap from me would not be likely to cause you to amend your abominable manners, would it?"

An appreciative laugh burst out of him. "Not at all likely. You seem to have taken my measure, ma'am. I *am* abominable. Well, then, since you don't deign to punish me, I assume I have your permission to take my leave." He made a mocking little bow and, still grinning, turned and strolled to the door. "*Now*, my dear," he said over his shoulder, "after two full seasons on the town, you can finally say that you've had a truly satisfactory ball. Good night, ma'am."

So, arrogant as a peacock, he strolled out of her sight. And eight years later, sitting on the window seat of her bedroom in Bath, she could still remember it all—every word they spoke, his cocky smile, the turbulence of her blood during that rude embrace, the dizzying pressure of his lips on hers, and the shame she felt afterwards, when she realized that she'd permitted herself to be kissed by a man whose name she had yet to learn.

Six

SHE WAS TO learn his name a fortnight later.

She spent that fortnight vainly trying not to spin dreams of him, but she found herself unable to banish him from her thoughts. A girl doesn't easily forget the man who gives her her first kiss. But since the man in this case was obviously a rake, Jan tried to convince herself that the incident was not worth remembering. She was not the sort, she told herself, to be drawn to men of that ilk. Wickedness was not a quality she found attractive.

She discovered, however, that she possessed a hitherto-unknown romantic streak which, having been stimulated by the provocative scene at the Edgerton ball, became a powerful inner force that resisted all her efforts to dismiss the incident from her mind. Instead of forgetting him, she found herself wishing she'd meet him again.

There was not much likelihood of such a meeting. The rake apparently moved in much faster circles than she did. But she did see him again, and at a most unlikely place—a small musicale given by the mother of her friend Harriet Coombe. A small musicale was not the sort of entertainment that Jan would have expected a rakish Corinthian to seek out, nor were the Coombes the sort of family one would expect him to number among his friends.

The Coombes were certainly not fast. They were not even stylish. They were a conventional, somewhat stodgy family who were invited to the more fashionable salons only as an afterthought. Lord and Lady Coombe were well-to-do but, being too penurious to show off their wealth, they lived in self-imposed dowdiness. They had three offspring: their eldest daughter Mariella, who was dour and plain and, at the age of twenty-seven, already a confirmed spinster; their son William (the same clod who'd stepped on Jan's toe the night of the Edgerton ball), who was a bookish bore who constantly pursued Jan despite her many rejections of him; and their youngest, Harriet ("Harry" to her intimates), who was much prettier than her sister but so clumsy and ungainly that she'd become a kind of joke among the Ton. "If you've asked Miss Harriet Coombe to dinner," one hostess would advise another, "you'd better put your Ming vase in a safe place and use your second-best goblets." But Harriet had long ago endeared herself to Jan because of the cheerfulness of her disposition and her musical talent. They were the best of friends. Jan could never understand why the rest of society failed to see in Harriet what she saw.

But even if one were disposed to say kind things of the Coombe family, one had to admit that it was not a group to attract a Corinthian of the rake's style. Jan would never have guessed that Lord Coombe would even be acquainted with a rake, much less invite him to a musical evening at his home.

The Coombes' musical gala was a modest one, for Lady Coombe was both lazy and clutchfisted, and she was not one to put herself to the trouble of entertaining huge mobs. Only thirty people had been invited. And since her daughter Harriet was a skilled pianist, and her elder daughter played the flute, she'd weeks ago prevailed upon her daughters—and their talented violinist-friend Jan—to provided the musical entertainment. It was not only a method of keeping rein on the expenses; everyone knew the girls were superior musicians.

The three girls, understanding that the experience of playing for an audience helps a musician to develop, happily agreed to oblige Lady Coombe. When the evening came, they dressed themselves in similar rose-colored gowns, tied their hair back with rose-colored ribands, entered the music room and tuned up while the audience gathered.

The three young women had chosen to play trios by Haydn, Gluck and Mozart. Since they'd practiced diligently for weeks, the performance went very well. The audience was enchanted, for not only were the musicians pleasant to look upon in their matching gowns (the rose color becoming even to the sallow Mariella), but they exhibited a skilled musicianship that was far beyond the ordinary. So unexpected and pleasing was the quality of their playing that the guests demanded several encores.

As Jan drew her bow across the strings for the last, long, quavering note of the final encore, she glanced up from her instrument and found herself looking into the eyes of the very man who was on her mind: her rake. It was an eerie moment, for he was staring at her as if he'd never seen her before. His light hazel eyes were awestruck, as if he'd had some sort of heavenly revelation. This time she had to drop her eyes, for the intensity in his was disconcerting.

The guests surged round the musicians, congratulating them on their remarkable performance, but although Jan looked for her rake, glancing about the room from under modestly lowered lids, she did not see him among the throng. To make matters even more frustrating, William Coombe seemed always to insert himself in her line of vision, hanging about so close to her that a stranger might have thought he had a special claim on her attention. Jan would have liked to box his ears.

At last the guests began to move out toward the dining room where a buffet awaited them. Mariella, flushed with success, was eager to join them, and she took Jan's arm and began to urge her toward the door. William, however, blocked their path, holding out a tray of filled wineglasses. "Mama sent some negus for the three of you. She thought you might need some refreshment after your exertions."

Mariella shook her head. "It's food I'm after. Isn't anyone coming to the buffet?"

William approached Jan with the tray. "I'd be glad to escort you to the table, Jan," he offered.

But Harriet stepped in front of her friend protectively. "Leave Jan alone, William," she said curtly. "If you must escort someone, escort Mariella. Jan and I don't want your company."

William was not the sort to be so easily dismissed. "Let Jan speak for herself," he snapped, as Mariella, with an impatient shrug, swept out to the buffet. "Besides, don't either of you want a glass of negus?"

Jan, who had no liking for the insipid, sugary beverage, shook her head, but Harriet reached for one of the glasses, knocking over the other in the process. The thick liquid splashed on William's coat. "Dash it," he swore, "*now* look what you've done!"

"I'm sorry," Harriet said, hastily reaching for Jan's hand and pulling her toward the door. "You know how clumsy I am."

Leaving her brother disgustedly brushing away at his coat with a pocket handkerchief, Harriet pulled Jan behind her down the hall to a small sitting room that was luckily quite deserted. She led Jan across the room to a claw-footed love seat (tripping only once over her skirt and spilling only a bit of her negus in the process) and drew her bewildered friend down beside her. "Oh, *Jan*," she exclaimed, beaming excitedly, "did you *notice*?"

"Notice?"

"It was so thrilling I could scarcely *breathe*! Who would believe he could be so *stricken* with anyone?"

"What are you talking about, Harry?" Jan asked, perplexed. "If it's William you mean, you know I have no interest in encouraging him."

"Who cares about William? I'm talking about his *lordship*! Didn't you see how he *looked* at you?"

"Looked at me?" Jan felt her pulse begin to race. "Who?"

"*Who?*" Harriet echoed, staring at her friend agape. "His *lordship Ollenshaw*! That's who!"

"Ollenshaw? Who's—"

"Don't tell me you've never heard of him! Everyone knows of Lord Ollenshaw. William says he's the most dashing of Corinthians, a bruising rider and a crack shot, as well as being most adept with his fives. But better than all that, Mama says he has estates in Derbyshire and Cornwall and an income of twenty thousand a year! He'd be considered the greatest catch on the marriage mart if it weren't for his wicked reputation."

Jan found herself utterly fascinated. "Wicked reputation?" she asked, wide-eyed with curiosity.

Harriet leaned closer. "I'm not supposed to know about such things, but I manage to glean all sorts of interesting information from William. I've heard that Ollenshaw gambles recklessly, keeps an opera dancer in a flat in Bloomsbury, and recently fought a duel because of an affair with a married lady."

"Goodness me! A duel?"

"Yes. It caused a bit of a scandal, but since Ollenshaw only wounded the husband slightly, the affair was hushed up."

"How dreadful!" Jan shuddered, both revolted and fascinated. She wondered if the married lady in question was the same one she'd seen him embracing the night of the Edgertons' ball. "Do you know who the married lady is?"

"I believe her name is Wedmore. Yes, Lady Wedmore, but William says they call her *Red*more at the club because of her shocking hair."

"Ugh! It all sounds so horridly lurid."

"Doesn't it?" Harriet agreed, giggling. "But in spite of all of that, Mama says any matchmaking mother would be glad to see her daughter snare Ollenshaw."

"Good heavens!" Jan exclaimed, appalled. "Why would any mother want to tie her daughter to a man of such questionable character?"

"Well, Mama says that any man who's so handsome, well connected and wealthy can be made to change his wicked ways for love of a good woman. In fact, she positively fell into *transports* when Papa told us Lord Ollenshaw agreed to come tonight. Perhaps she hoped he'd take an interest in Mariella." Harriet shook her head, giggling at the thought. "As if a man of that ilk would ever toss so much as a *glance* at Mariella."

"Perhaps your mother hoped his lordship would take to *you*, Harry," Jan suggested.

Harriet shrugged. "When he walked in, after we'd begun playing, and he stopped stock still in the middle of the room and gaped, I thought for a moment it *was* me he was staring at. But no such luck, Jan. It was *you!* He stared at you all through the Haydn. It was as if . . . as if—" she wrinkled her brow in her effort to think of a way of describing what she'd seen in his lordship's face "—as if *he* were one of those fasting monks looking for spiritual salvation, and *you* were a statue of the Virgin he came upon on a mountain top!"

Jan had to laugh. "Really, Harry, aren't you being ridiculous? A statue of the Virgin indeed!"

"Oh, don't be so literal. You know what I mean. He seemed . . . awestruck! I think he's fallen in love with you at first sight."

"Now I *know* you're being ridiculous. It can't be love at first sight because it's already second—"

But at that moment, the subject of their whisperings came striding over the threshold, pulling Harriet's father along with him. As the two men came across the room toward them, Jan felt her heart begin to pound. Harriet gasped, dropping her half-filled wineglass in her excitement. The glass didn't break but rolled across the carpet spreading a trail of the sticky liquid behind it.

Lord Ollenshaw quickly bent down and, although his eyes were fixed on Jan's face, nevertheless managed to retrieve the wineglass. Harriet's father, quite immune to his daughter's losing battles with inanimate objects, paid no attention to the glass in his guest's hand and the stain on the carpet. He came right up to Jan and said with a booming laugh, "Excuse me, my dear, but Lord Ollenshaw insists on being presented to you. Positively insists. I told him I wanted to keep you for my son, but he would have none of it. So I find I must oblige him. Miss Genevra Hazeldine, may I introduce his lordship, John Maxwell, the Marquis of Ollenshaw."

Jan, holding out her hand politely, was again struck by the strange intensity of his stare. "How do you do, my lord?" she mumbled, wonder if she should acknowledge their previous acquaintance.

"Miss Hazeldine," he said, bowing.

"So, Max, now that you've coerced me into introducing

you,'' the jovial Lord Coombe teased, ''what will you do next?''

''I shall ask the young lady to accompany me to the buffet. Will you, Miss Hazeldine?''

Jan, coloring, looked hesitantly at Harriet, still seated beside her. ''I'm afraid, my lord, that I'm engaged with my friend at the moment.''

But Harriet, whose nature was utterly unselfish, was not one to stand in the way of Love At First Sight. ''Don't bother about me,'' she said, jumping to her feet. ''I have to go off to . . . to . . .'' Frantically seeking an excuse to depart, her eye fell on the wineglass in his lordship's hand. She snatched it from him. ''To get someone to see to the carpet.''

''Harry, *don't*—!'' Jan muttered desperately, getting up and taking a step after her. But Harriet, in spite of stumbling over her skirt again, was already disappearing out the door.

Lord Coombe chuckled at Jan's discomfiture. ''Looks like you're stuck with 'im, my dear. But don't repine. I couldn't leave you in better hands.'' And he put her arm in Ollenshaw's and took himself off.

Lord Ollenshaw did not look after his host, for his eyes were still fixed on Jan's face. She felt her color rise. ''Aren't you staring at me rather too fixedly, my lord?'' she asked with nervous bravado.

''Yes, I suppose I am.'' He blinked as if shaking himself from a reverie and smiled down at her. ''You needn't look so frightened of me,'' he assured her. ''I don't intend to assault you as I did before.''

''I should hope not, indeed,'' Jan retorted, determined not to let the information she'd just learned about him overwhelm her and turn her into a stammering schoolgirl.

''In fact, Miss Hazeldine,'' he remarked, releasing her arm and taking her hand instead, ''I intend to apologize most profusely for my behavior at our previous meeting.''

''Really? Why is that, my lord? Did you not instruct me at the time that by your action I experienced my first really satisfying ball?''

He winced. ''Did I say that? I was an arrogant gamecock, to be sure. I am more sorry about what happened than I can say. Rest assured, my dear, that if I'd been at all observant, I would have not subjected you to such, er, rudeness.''

"Observant? I don't know what you mean. Do you observe something in me now that you didn't then?''

For a moment he stared at her with the same disconcerting intensity that had unsettled her before. "Oh, yes. Yes, indeed,'' he murmured. "I didn't guess, at our first meeting, that I was assaulting an angel.''

"An *angel*?'' Her eyebrows rose, and she pulled her hand from his grasp. "What sort of jest is this?''

"No jest, ma'am, I swear. If you think I'm not in earnest, then you cannot know how you look when you play your violin.''

"How I *look*? Whatever can you mean?''

"There's something about you when you play that's quite extraordinary. Hasn't anyone else ever remarked on it? It is something so . . . so *pure* that it's almost unearthly.''

"Something that makes me look *angelic*?''

"Yes, my dear, decidedly angelic. The sight of you knocked the breath out of me. You are so absorbed when you play, so profoundly immersed in the music that you seem to . . . to give off a glow.''

Jan stared at him in disbelief. "What fiddle-faddle! If you are not bamming me, my lord, then you are being very foolish. There is nothing angelic about me, I assure you. Unless . . . can it be that you're particularly susceptible to trios? Music often creates a feeling of rapture that can dazzle one's judgment. Are you certain my 'glow' wasn't created by your response to the Haydn, my lord?''

"Quite certain. I felt no special rapture for the Haydn. I have no special feelings for music at all.''

"Then I can find no sensible explanation for your peculiar vision.'' She frowned at him, feeling a wave of irritation at this turnabout in his attitude toward her. Why was he attracted to what he imagined were her *angelic* qualities, when she was attracted to his *devilish* ones? "If you think me angelic,'' she said with some asperity, "I can only suppose that debauchery has befuddled your brain.''

He laughed. "For my repulsive past behavior, I deserve

that riposte, ma'am. And I admit that my brain *is* completely befuddled, but this time it's not from debauchery. It was the sight of you with your fiddle that undid me.'' He tucked her arm tightly into his and, smiling down at her with his heart-stopping grin, started for the buffet. "I am undone by your purity, you see. Truly undone.''

"*Undone*, my lord?" She hoped he would not notice, from the tremor of her arm on his, how her pulse was racing.

"Undone is the precise word." He gave a long, deep sigh. "I very much fear, Miss Genevra Hazeldine," he said, his tone of wry amusement tinged with an almost sad sincerity, "that I shall never be quite the same again."

Seven

THREE WEEKS LATER they were betrothed. Even now, so many years later, Jan could remember every word they'd exchanged the night he offered for her.

In retrospect she supposed it could have been called a whirlwind courtship, but it didn't seem so when she was living through it. That was because their relationship developed with the naturalness and inevitability of a bud flowering. During the weeks following the Coombe musicale, she saw him every day. For a day or two their manner toward each other and their conversations were properly formal. He was Lord Ollenshaw and she Miss Hazeldine. They bowed when they met, they strolled with her arm lightly resting on his, and he kissed her hand when he departed. Then, as inexorably as the dawn, they became Max and Jan; he took her hand, not her arm, when they walked; they concocted private little jokes at which they laughed constantly; they exchanged meaningful glances across crowded rooms; and, sometimes, when he found an opportunity, he kissed not her hand but her lips.

Although Max did everything he could to convince Jan that he did indeed find her angelic, he did not say anything of his intentions. He took her riding, escorted her to the opera, danced with her at Vauxhall, brought her flowers, and in dozens of other ways made it patently obvious that he was smitten. But he did not speak of his feelings. His failure to declare himself made Jan wonder, sometimes, just what his intentions were.

Jan was smitten, too. It was inevitable, she realized later, that an innocent such as she was then would be overwhelmed by a rake. Naive, inexperienced young females are always taken in by worldly wickedness. There were hundreds of romantic novels that would supply testimony to that effect.

But what thrilling weeks those were! He did not seem wicked at all. He was charming and attentive and showed her a world she didn't know existed. He taught her to drive a high-perch phaeton. He took her to a sparring match, where she was both horrified and fascinated by what he called the "art" of fisticuffs. He invited her to watch him race a tandem-and-pair at Newmarket, an event which brought her to screaming excitement and, when he won it, to a pride in him that was beyond words. Among the Corinthians he was heroic. In that world a woman would have to be both blind and unnatural to resist such a specimen.

On the other hand, he generously attempted to enter her world, too. He accompanied her to concerts and the opera and tried to become interested. Often, however, she caught him stifling a yawn or blinking sleep from his eyes. At those times she wondered if perhaps, in the long run, they would not suit each other. Wouldn't their different interests divide them in the course of time?

But her doubts were stifled by two strong factors. One was the sight of his face when she played her fiddle. He often begged her to play for him. When she did so, he gazed at her with such adoration that she was moved almost to tears. He might not have had a true appreciation of music in general, but it was obvious that her playing in particular made music seem splendid to him.

The second factor was the power of his embrace. On the rare occasions when they were alone—in his carriage, for example, when he could manage to escort her home from the opera without chaperonage or from a dinner party which her mother didn't attend—he would gather her into his arms and kiss her. She found those occasions thrilling beyond words. She could not imagine that there would ever come a time when the mere pressure of his lips on hers would fail to make her blood race.

It was at one of those times when they were alone in his

carriage that he at last declared himself. Only three weeks had gone by since the night of the musicale, but by this time Jan could scarcely envision a life without him. He was taking her home after a concert at Covent Garden. Suddenly he tapped on the roof of the carriage and ordered the coachman to turn into a side street and halt until given further orders. Jan raised her brows. "Max, you devil! What mischief is this?"

"No mischief. I think it's time we had a serious talk." He took her face in his hands, turned it up to his and stared down at her tensely. "I suppose you've guessed," he murmured, "that I love you, Genevra Hazeldine."

She felt a shiver run down her spine, for it was the first time he'd spoken those words. "I suspected it," she said, trying to be casual.

"Clever girl!" He brushed a vagrant curl from her forehead. "I don't suppose . . ." He took a deep breath. "Have you given any thought to your own feelings?"

"Yes. Yes, I have."

He frowned down at her, but his eyes glinted with a lover's confidence. "Then, dash it all, *say* something, my girl! Don't keep me hanging here in suspense."

"*Are* you in suspense, Max?" she teased. "I thought you sporting fellows were indifferent to matters of the heart."

"*Indifferent?*" He reached for her hand and pressed it against his chest. "There. Do you feel the pounding? Does that feel like indifference to you? Are you going to tell me you love me, vixen, or do I have to put my hands to your throat and choke the words out of you?"

Moved by the emotion she detected behind the badinage, she threw her arms about his neck. "Can you really be in doubt, Max? I'm no angel, but I sometimes think that even an angel couldn't resist falling in love with a handsome rake like you."

The smile in his eyes faded. "Don't love the rake in me, Jan. I'm no longer the man I was at the Edgerton ball. But you are, and always will be, an angel to me. I love you beyond anything I ever imagined. I don't deserve you I know, but if you'll be my wife, I swear I'll never do anything to hurt you or to make you sorry for this night.''

''Oh, Max!'' She hid her face in his shoulder. ''I'll never be sorry for this night, whatever happens. I do love you so!''

He kissed her then with a passion he'd never before revealed. She was shaken to her core as a wave of miraculous new sensations washed over her. She lay back in his arms, permitting herself for the first time to experience the embrace fully, without the least restraint. Slowly she found herself tensing, gripping him tightly round the neck, drawing closer and closer to him until she scarcely knew where she ended and he began. It was an embrace that seemed to her to symbolize their coming union—a union of body and soul. She wondered how she could ever have doubted that they would suit. She felt happier than she'd dreamed possible. At that moment she believed that she was the luckiest girl in the world.

After a while he let her go. ''I shan't be able to bear waiting for the banns,'' he muttered breathlessly. ''How soon may I speak to your mother?''

Jan's heart danced at his impatience. ''Tomorrow, if you wish.''

''What if she refuses me?'' He sat up abruptly, suddenly worried. ''She may not wish to have her daughter wed a man of my unsavory reputation.''

''Nonsense, my love,'' Jan assured him. ''You are a marquis with twenty thousand a year. They say that any matchmaking mother would be overjoyed to snare you.''

''They say that, do they?'' Max laughed as he tapped his cane on the roof to signal the coachman to proceed. ''I sincerely hope they're right. But I won't be easy in my mind until your mother calls me son-in-law.''

When she arrived home, Jan ran straight to her mother's bedroom and, lighting a bedside candle, shook her awake. ''He *offered*, Mama!'' she exclaimed, perching on the bed. ''I'm betrothed! Max is coming tomorrow to ask you for permission to wed me!''

''What?'' Her mother, dazed by sleep, propped herself up

on one elbow and peered at her daughter through the dim candlelight. "Is it Lord Ollenshaw?" she asked thickly.

"Who else?"

Celia Hazeldine nodded. "I'm not surprised. I thought the two of you were smelling of April and May. Very well, my love, I'll see him tomorrow. Meanwhile, will you please take yourself to bed and let me sleep?"

"You approve, then?" Jan prodded eagerly.

Her mother waved her off and burrowed back into the pillows. "Of course. Why shouldn't I? Anyone can see you're happy as a lark."

Jan leaned down and kissed her mother's cheek. "Thank you, Mama. I'm so relieved. Max and I were afraid his reputation would stand in the way."

"Reputation be hanged," her ladyship muttered, shrugging sleepily under her coverlet. "A man should be allowed to sow his wild oats during his bachelorhood. He'll settle down. Good night, my dear."

Jan danced down the hallway to her room. She opened the door and found Dorrie, their abigail, dozing in a chair near the window. "How can you all be asleep at a time like this?" Jan muttered in frustration.

Dorrie woke up with a start. "Oh, there ye are, Miss. I must've dropped off." She bustled out of the chair. "I've laid out yer night things an' turned down yer bed. Do ye wish some help with yer buttons?"

"Never mind my buttons," Jan said, taking the abigail about the waist and pulling her into a waltz. "I'm betrothed!"

"Are ye, Miss?" The abigail beamed, trotting along with Jan's dance steps as well as her short, stocky legs could manage. "Ain't *that* a bit o' good news!"

"And Mama approves!" Jan sang in three-quarter time. "I wish I could tell Max. He'd sleep a great deal better if he—" She stopped waltzing abruptly. "Why not tell him?" she asked herself. "It isn't yet midnight, and his house isn't far. Put on a cloak, Dorrie! We're going to pay a call!"

The abigail blinked at her mistress in utter disapproval. "Miss *Jan*! Ye can't mean it. It ain't a proper—"

"Oh, pooh! Who cares if it's proper or not? Besides, no one will know. The whole excursion should take no more than half an hour. If you don't hurry, Miss Prim-and-Proper, I shall go alone. And *then* what will people say if I'm discovered?"

With that threat to prod her, Dorrie permitted Jan to wrap her about with one of her own cloaks, and the two stole down the stairs and out to the street. It took them no more than ten minutes to traverse the distance between Welbeck Street and Ollenshaw House in Hanover Square, with Jan covering the distance in so blissful a mood that she was sure her feet never touched the ground.

She did not come down to earth until she saw the shocked expression on the face of Max's man. When he opened the door and saw her, the butler's chin dropped and his eyes almost popped from his head. "Bless me soul!" he exclaimed, horrified.

Jan was suddenly struck with a twinge of shame. Perhaps her surrender to the impulse to visit Max at this ungodly hour had been a mistake. She reddened in embarrassment, but since it was too late to undo it, she plunged ahead. "Never mind blessing your soul," she said to the butler defiantly. "Just show me to his lordship at once."

"I can't do that, Miss," the butler said, looking over his shoulder uncomfortably. "Not now."

"I assure you that his lordship will thank you. Just tell him it's Miss Hazeldine."

The butler threw another look—almost of desperation—over his shoulder. "I tell ye it's not a good time," he insisted. "Whyn't ye be a good lass an' come back t'morrow?"

"Don't be a fool!" Jan snapped in annoyance. "If I'd wanted to wait until tomorrow, would I have come tonight? Stand aside, man! I'll find his lordship myself!"

With that, she pushed the butler aside and strode into the hall. The entryway and the hallway beyond were dimly lit by candles in the wall sconces, but the rooms opening on to them were dark. She could see light, however, coming from a doorway down the hall. "Is he there?" she asked the butler, heading quickly toward the light.

"Yes, Miss, but—"

She did not heed him. She was halfway to her destination before he roused himself from his shock and ran after her. Dorrie, wringing her hands, followed.

"Max!" Jan clarioned as she neared the doorway. "I have the *best* news! Mama is delight—"

She'd reached the doorway, but what she saw inside caused the words to freeze in her throat. Max was standing in the center of the room. He was in his shirtsleeves, his neckerchief hanging open round his neck and his shirt half-unbuttoned. Also hanging round his neck was the redheaded woman he'd been embracing that night at the Edgertons'. The woman's head was turned toward the door in surprise, but her arms remained tight about him. The gown she wore was cut low in the back and had slipped from one shoulder, making her seem half-naked. Her skin glowed lewdly in the candlelight. To Jan, it was a scene redolent of lechery and lust.

Max's lips went white. "Good God!" he exclaimed. *"Jan!"*

Jan could not move. She felt the blood drain from her face, her heart, and all the blood vessels of her body. The sight before her had dealt her a blow so severe that her body reacted with shock before her mind fully grasped what she was seeing. It was a blow that sent her reeling, even though her body didn't move. Her brain was spinning, wheeling about crazily in her head, making her so dizzy she wanted to faint.

But she didn't faint. She stood in the doorway, frozen in place, as her mind slowly took hold of itself and thought became coherent. *Who is this woman?* her brain asked. The answer was immediately apparent. This was Max's *cher amie*, the married woman for whom he'd fought a duel. Harriet had told her the name—Wedmore. Lady Wedmore. That was the identity of the creature Max was holding—the detestable Lady *Red*more! Jan had pushed the tale she'd heard from Harriet out of her mind until this moment. She'd believed that the redheaded woman—and any other fancy piece with whom he'd dallied before—were part of his past, that he'd given them up when he'd found his true love. But she'd been mistaken. Evidently he'd not given up anything or anyone for love of her.

She didn't want to faint, she wanted to die! He'd lied to her. *Betrayed* her. Less than an hour ago he'd said he would never do anything to hurt her, and yet he'd done *this*!

Every thought brought a knife-sharp stab of pain, pain so excruciating she couldn't breathe. She had to get away from this place, this sight of the two of them staring at her in that horrid frozen embrace. She took one tottering step backward and then turned and fled. She never knew how she found the strength to run, but run she did, down the long, endless hall and out the door. She was not even aware of the commotion she left in her wake—footsteps . . . shouts . . . Dorrie bursting into tears . . . the butler shouting in alarm . . . Max dashing desperately after her crying, "Jan, *stop*! *Wait*! You don't *understand*!"

Now, seven years later, she would not let herself remember the days that followed. They had been the most painful days of her life. She'd had to steel herself to keep Max away. She'd had to find the courage to keep face before Mama and the world. It had been so brief a betrothal that she was able to convince her mother that it had all been a minor mistake. A trivial, correctable blunder. Nothing important. But in her heart she knew that she'd suffered a shattering blow and that recovery would be a long way off. If it weren't for the soothing effect of her violin, she might not have gotten through those days.

But she could not forget the day, three days after the fateful night, when she'd looked up from her music stand and found him standing in the doorway of the music room. He'd forced his way past Beale and followed the sound of her fiddle. He stood looking at her in that disconcertingly adoring way that, this time, constricted her heart. "Go away, Max," she'd pleaded. "Please."

His face was lined and weary. "Will you not even let me explain—?"

"There *is* no satisfactory explanation. I saw what I saw."

"Can you not conceive of a circumstance in which there is more—or less—than meets the eye?"

"No, I can't. Besides, explanations will only demean us both."

"I don't see why." He took a step into the room.

"Don't come in! I can't . . . !" She turned her back on him and leaned weakly on the pianoforte. "Explanations would not make any difference, you see," she said quietly. "I realize now that our . . . association . . . was a mistake from the first. We are too different to really suit."

"You mean," he said hoarsely, "that you cannot lower yourself to wed a man of my character."

She could not look at him. "Perhaps so."

"Yes, I understand. I always feared you were too good for me."

There was a long pause. She could hear nothing but the *thump-thump* of her heavy heart. Years later, she would regret what she'd said that day. After all the suitors, all the jilts, all the years of loneliness and pain, she would wonder if she'd perhaps been too hasty in convicting him without listening to his explanation. Years later her determination to hate him would erode. But at that moment, she believed that it was necessary for her to end this bond—despite the fact that her hammering heart was begging her to reconsider.

She heard him walk out of the room. Unable to help herself, she wheeled around. He, turning back for a last look at her, caught her eye. He gave a bitter smile. "Loving a rake is appealing in a romance but doesn't work so well in reality, does it?" With a shrug of defeat, he started for the stairs. "I should have known."

And that was the last she saw of him from that day to this.

Eight

JAN WOKE THE next morning feeling thickheaded and disordered. She opened her eyes slowly, wondering where she was and why she was so utterly miserable. As she took note of the streaks of sunlight on the unfamiliar ceiling and the sound of the Avon rushing over the weir just beyond the window, she knew she was not at home. Sunlight and babbling rivers were not the sights and sounds typical of London in early spring. Then, slowly, she remembered. *Oh, yes, I'm in Bath. We arrived yesterday, and I saw Belinda. And learned about Max.*

She got up and threw open the window draperies, faintly hoping that the view beyond the glass would reveal another place. It would be lovely if the events of yesterday proved to be no more than a bad dream. But alas, there to her right, looking solidly imposing against a bright blue morning sky, was the Bath Abbey tower. There was no mistaking where she was.

Ah, yes, I've come to Bath, tra-la. The words sang in her head with ironic bitterness. *Tra-la-la. Isn't it simply splendid? And it was all my own doing, too. I coaxed Mama to come. Sing derry-down-derry, let's celebrate my dear cousin's coming nuptials. How very delightful for us all!* Jan sighed deeply and sank down on the window seat. The situation in which she found herself was so devilishly compounded of awkward coincidences that it might have been written by a farceur. She herself could compose the opening song for the farce: *Heigh-ho the merry-o, my cousin is to marry-o. And whom is she to marry-o? The only man I ever loved. Heigh-ho.* It was farcical indeed. But she couldn't bring herself to laugh.

She had to decide, and quickly, if she should confess to Belinda that she and Max had once been betrothed. All her instincts cried no. It had been the briefest of betrothals, after all. In the grand scheme of things, it was an unimportant incident. Who but she was affected by it? Even Max had gotten over it; he'd found himself a new love. He'd probably not given her a thought in years! He would not like, any more than she, to have the matter made known.

If she told Belinda, the girl would undoubtedly tell her mother. Then Aunt Nettie would tell her friends. And soon everyone in Bath would know of it. How dreadful it would be, Jan realized with horror, to have her past whispered about, to be the subject of covert glances, wild speculation and snide gossip. No, she would not be able to bear it! The best course for her would be to keep silent and try to prevail upon Mama to return to London as soon as possible.

This decision made, Jan looked round for her fiddle and, still in her nightclothes, took it out of its case and began to play. She'd never needed the solace of music more than at this moment.

Later, however, after she and her mother had breakfasted and she'd dressed in a freshly pressed, lavender-sashed white cambric walking gown (in which she felt festive and pretty), she began to feel better. Max was not in town, after all, she reminded herself, and she had a few days in which to regain control of her feelings and concoct a scheme to avoid him. Perhaps she could even think of a way to prevail upon her mother to cut the visit short and return to London before Max came back. This hope, and the prospect of spending this beautiful day enjoying the diversions of Bath, did much to lift her spirits.

She threw a lavender shawl over her shoulders and strolled out with her mother to the Pump Room. During the short walk she couldn't help responding to the holiday spirit of Bath. Everyone who passed them on the streets nodded in cheerful friendliness. The springlike weather brought the res-

.idents and visitors out of doors in great numbers, the ladies as festive as the early spring crocuses, making the streets bloom with the colors of their feathered bonnets and their bright sprig muslin gowns.

The Pump Room (an enormous room three stories high, housing the pump in a windowed alcove and providing sufficient space for hundreds of visitors to saunter about while they drank their prescribed three glasses of the tepid water) was thronged with strollers, but Lady Hazeldine soon found her sister in the crowd. The sisters touched cheeks in greeting. "Where's Belinda?" Lady Hazeldine inquired.

"Over there with her friends," Nettie Briarly answered, pointing to a knot of young people gathered in the niche at the east end of the room in front of the famous Thomas Tompion equation clock. "Belinda is tremendously popular, you know. She's part of such a lively circle. Why don't you go and join them, Jan?"

"No, thank you, Aunt. I've—"

Her Aunt Nettie brushed aside her niece's refusal with an affectionate hug. "But, Jan dearest, you can't wish to spend your morning meandering about with your Mama and me. It's too dull for someone like you to be listening to gossip and sipping the waters. Do go over to the young people. Belinda will be so happy to make you known to everyone."

"But, you see, Aunt Nettie, I've brought a book."

Jan's mother glared at her but said nothing until her sister went off to the pump for a glass of Bath's famous medicinal waters. Taking advantage of their moment of privacy, Lady Hazeldine fixed her eyes on her daughter with marked disapproval. "Really, Jan, must you be so misanthropic?" she asked in an angry undervoice. "I won't have you spending your time here buried in a book. Why won't you join your cousin?"

"Because, Mama," Jan answered with that calm detachment that her mother sometimes admired but that, at times like these, set her teeth on edge, "you have only to take a look at my cousin and her friends to see that they are all veritable schoolchildren. If I joined them, I should feel like their governess. Besides, I'm eager to read this novel I brought with me. It's by Miss Burney, who wrote that charming story, *Evelina*, that you like so much.''

"Don't try to put me off, Miss! Did we or did we not agree that we would spend our time here finding some suitable bachelors for you?''

"We agreed that *you* would find them." Jan smiled at her mother and patted her hand. "Please feel free to do so, Mama. If you find anyone suitable, I shall be sitting there on that bench, waiting to make his acquaintance.''

Lady Hazeldine, who knew when she'd been defeated, turned away and strode off to sample the waters that so many Bath denizens swore were miraculously curative. *Would that they could cure the pains of motherhood,* she told herself in irritation.

Jan settled down on a bench just to the left of the front door. She opened Miss Burney's novel, *Cecilia*, but she'd not read a dozen pages when Belinda approached with three young ladies and two gentlemen in tow. Almost bursting with high spirits, Belinda introduced her cousin to her friends. The young ladies—a pair of sisters who were identified as the Misses Brett and their cousin, Mary Grindsley—were none of them older than eighteen. Jan tried to remember the three girls by name, but they were almost indistinguishable; they all had blue eyes and fair hair that they'd done up in identical fashion—masses of curls clasped tightly together at the temples and tumbling down over their ears to make a bouncy frame for their youthfully sweet faces. Jan, whose hair (tied back neatly in a bun at the back of her head) was in prim contrast to theirs, was convinced that she might indeed pass for their governess.

The two gentlemen, on the other hand, were not at all alike. One, Mr. Jack Grindsley, Mary's brother, was a callow youth of seventeen who adopted the Byronic in style and dress. His hair was long and wild, he wore a colorful scarf carelessly tied round his neck in place of a neckerchief, and when he exclaimed that he was delighted to meet the cousin of whom Belinda had spoken so often, the platitudinous words were uttered with far too much dramatic intensity. The other young man, whom Belinda introduced as Lord Liggett ("But everyone calls him Liggy,'' she giggled), was probably the oldest of the group, although Jan surmised that he was certainly no more than twenty. He was dressed to the nines like a fop, his coat distorted by exaggeratedly wide shoulders and satin-faced lapels, and his shirtpoints so high they reached to the top of his cheeks. The excesses of his costume, however, were in direct contrast to the modesty of his personality. The young nobleman was so shy that he colored a painful red when he was introduced to Jan. Though he gaped at her with instant adoration and stammered incoherently for a full minute, he was, in the end, unable to utter a simple how-de-do.

''Do stop nattering, Liggy,'' Belinda said, ruthlessly cutting off Lord Liggett's stammerings. ''We've come to invite you to join us, Cousin Jan. Since this is such a lovely day, we've decided to walk outdoors.''

''To the Sydney Gardens,'' one of the Misses Brett added, giggling so embarrassedly that, if one did not know better, one might think the Gardens were a naughty place to visit.

''Do come,'' urged the other.

''Yes, do,'' said Mary Grindsley, but since she glared at Lord Liggett as she said it (evidently furious that he was so obviously taken with Jan), Jan did not think her invitation was sincere.

Her brother made up in sincerity for his sister's lack of it. ''We *insist* that you come with us,'' Jack Grindsley said with a flourish. ''We shall not depart without you. That is my solemn vow!''

Lord Liggett said nothing, but fixed his bulging eyes on her pleadingly, ignoring Mary Grindsley's too-evident irritation with him.

''It is most kind of you to wish for my company,'' Jan said, ''but I beg you to excuse me I . . . er . . . promised my mother I would wait for her here.''

Belinda and her Byronic young friend argued against her decision for a few moments, but when they found her firm, Belinda kissed her cheek in a fond good-bye, and the group— led by Jack, whose ''solemn vow'' was promptly and conveniently forgotten—set off without her. Jan returned her attention to her book, but not before noting that Lord Liggett, as he trailed behind his friends, kept looking back over his shoulder at her with an expression of agonized calf love.

She'd read only two pages more when her mother reappeared. Lady Hazeldine was accompanied, not by her sister, but by a middle-aged gentleman with a half-bald pate, a slightly protruding stomach and a pair of kindly eyes behind the black-ribboned pince-nez perched on his nose. "Jan, I'd like you to meet a friend of your aunt. Sir Eustace Merriot, my daughter, Genevra Hazeldine."

Jan wondered, for a fleeting moment, if her mother was playing a spiteful trick on her, for this gentleman was certainly not the sort Jan was likely to consider favorably as a suitor. While Sir Eustace made his bow, Jan threw a questioning glance at her mother. Lady Hazeldine shrugged as if to say, "What did you expect?" She'd told her daughter often enough that girls who put off marriage until the ripe old age of twenty-eight, like beggars, cannot be choosers.

Jan, however, did not make judgments by appearances alone. She was perfectly willing to further the acquaintance. Therefore, she smiled at the baronet with the pleasant, unflustered detachment that was her style. "How do you do, sir? Do you know my aunt a long time?"

"For several seasons now I've taken rooms in the house adjoining hers," Sir Eustace replied with equal ease. "When she introduced me to your mother this morning, I was quite delighted. The name Hazeldine is well known to me, you see."

"Is it? How is that? Come sit down, Mama, and you, too, Sir Eustace, and then you may tell us all about it in comfort."

But Lady Hazeldine shook her head. "I must return to Nettie. She is holding my drink. Besides, Sir Eustace has already told me his story. I brought him to you because I knew you would find it of interest. So, if you both will excuse me." With a wave, she scurried off.

Sir Eustace sat down beside Jan. "It is not much of a story, I'm afraid, Miss Hazeldine," he said, his manner of speaking precise and scholarly. "I was somewhat acquainted with your father, that's all."

"Were you?" she asked, carefully polite. Many gentlemen

had attempted to win her friendship by claiming familiarity with her father.

The portly Baronet took off his spectacles and smiled at her with myopic innocence. "We once played together in a chamber group. It was at a musicale at Lord Holland's, if memory serves. The Prince was in attendance, and he was very generous in his praise of the performance."

Jan's interest was immediately piqued. "You are a musician, Sir Eustace?"

"Only an amateur, I'm afraid."

"Papa was an amateur, too," she said kindly.

"But a very gifted one." He wiped his spectacles with an immaculate pocket handkerchief and replaced them on his nose. "I felt very fortunate to be invited to play with his group. I am a flautist, and the program consisted of the Mozart Flute Quartets. Are you familiar with them?"

"Oh, yes, indeed." Any lingering suspicion of his motives was instantly dissolved by his obvious innocence and sincerity. She turned toward him, her face taking on the animation that a discussion of music always brought to it. "In fact I've studied the violin part of the D Major. It is very difficult, but such an enchanting piece, don't you agree?"

A discussion of the Mozart work ensued, and Jan could detect from his comments that, whatever his gifts as a flautist, were, his understanding of music was immense. In addition, he was modest and charmingly bookish. She quite liked him. It occurred to her that he would be a perfect match for Harriet. If only she could coax Harriet to come to Bath . . .

When the conversation lagged, Sir Eustace cleared his throat. "There is to be a concert at the Upper Rooms this evening, Miss Hazeldine," he said with sudden shyness. "I do not expect much from it—an Italian soprano whose name is unknown to me—but the evening concerts are generally superior to those we are hearing now from those mediocrities in the niche across the room. If you would care to attend tonight, it would be my pleasure to escort you. And your mother, too, of course."

"How very kind of you," she murmured. "I would have to ask Mama before I could give you an answer, but—"

At that moment there was a commotion at the front door. Jan would not have paid heed to it, however, had she not recognized Belinda's voice over the din of the room. Her young cousin was excitedly exclaiming, "Mama! Mama! *Look* who's come back *three days early*!"

With a gasp of alarm, Jan turned her head in the direction of her cousin's voice. Belinda and her entire entourage were bursting in, surrounding a tall gentleman like a gaggle of eager children welcoming a gift-bearing uncle. There was no mistaking the tall gentleman's identity. As Jan feared, it was Max.

Her heart began to pound alarmingly. *It's too soon!* she thought in terror. *I'm not ready!* She quickly turned her head back and pressed herself tightly back against the bench, hoping that she would be hidden from view behind Sir Eustace's bulk. But Sir Eustace had heard her gasp. "Is there something wrong, ma'am?" he asked in concern.

"Yes! No! No . . . of course not." She put a hand to her forehead to try to get hold of herself. "I . . . what were we saying?"

He peered at her through his thick spectacles with worried sympathy. "It was not important, my dear. Only about the concert tonight."

"Oh, yes," she mumbled abstractedly, wondering if she should peep over his shoulder to see if the group at the doorway had gone. If they had, she could slip out the door and run home before being discovered. "Yes," she repeated without knowing what she was saying, "the concert . . ."

"Something has distracted you." The kind Baronet took her hand gently into his. "Perhaps there is something I can—"

At that moment, to Jan's horror, Belinda came running up to them. "He's *here*, Jan! I'm so happy you didn't have to wait days and days to meet him!" She turned round to where her betrothed was exchanging quips with her friends, and, detaching him from the circle, pulled him forward. In her excitement, she took no note of how his smile suddenly froze and his eyes widened in shock. "Lord Ollenshaw," she said blithely, "my cousin, Genevra Hazeldine. Jan, *here* is Max!"

Nine

FOR WHAT SEEMED an eternity, Jan and Max stared at each other. In reality, however, only a moment passed. For Jan, time seemed to slow down to almost a standstill. In that hideously endless moment, a series of confused images etched themselves indelibly on her consciousness. First there was Max's face. It seemed to change without moving; without the alteration of a single muscle, his expression of smiling confidence became a look of acute, total shock. If there was emotion behind that shock (was he glad to see her? did some remnant of the old affection flare up behind his eyes?), it was impossible for Jan to recognize, for although his light eyes darkened, they were utterly unreadable.

Focused though she was on Max's face, other images filtered in through the mist of tense misery that fogged her mind. There was Belinda, smiling delightedly as she looked from Max to her cousin, blissfully unaware of the dramatic undercurrents. There was Aunt Nettie, whose eager arms were open to embrace her prospective son-in-law. There was Jan's mother, gazing with a look of envious appraisal at Belinda's "catch." There was Jack Grindsley, hanging closely at Max's elbow like an eager sheepdog, trying to get the attention of the man who was obviously his idol. There was the noisy, excited babble of the rest of Belinda's friends in the background. And making the dreadful embarrassment of the moment even worse for Jan, there was her own awkward discomfort at being discovered engaged in apparently intimate conversation with the portly, almost elderly Sir Eustace, who was sitting close beside her and still holding her hand in protective custody.

But even if one part of Jan's mind kept time locked in that frozen moment, another part was a very accurate timekeeper, and it prodded her into awareness that time was indeed passing. She was keeping Max (who appeared to be shocked into immobility and was probably feeling who-knew-what sort of agony) impaled there before her. Jan knew that she had to say or do something to acknowledge Belinda's introduction, something to free them both from this horrid trap. Through the fog of her emotions, she made herself smile up at him. "Hello, Max," she managed.

He bowed stiffly. "How do you do?" he murmured dazedly.

Belinda giggled. "Is that all you have to say, you clunch?" she teased flirtatiously. Then she turned to Jan. "I believe this oaf has forgotten you after all."

Max, who'd had no warning, as Jan had had, to enable him to prepare for this encounter, clenched his fists. "Forgotten her?" he muttered thickly. "I'd be more likely to forget my name."

Belinda blinked at him, confused. "What?" she queried. Although not fully understanding what she'd heard, she nevertheless leapt to a comfortable conclusion and clapped her hands gleefully. "You *do* remember her, then?"

Max's eyes glittered angrily as a host of bitter memories assaulted him. "Oh, yes, the face is quite familiar," he muttered, staring down at Jan fixedly. "If you give me a moment, I might even remember the pain."

This confused Belinda even more. "Max, you tease!" she chided. "I don't understand you. *What* did you say?"

"He said," offered Jack Grindsley, "that if you give him a moment, he'll remember her name."

But Jan had heard Max more clearly than Grindsley had, and his words cut through her like a knife. Unwittingly she tightened her hold on Sir Eustace's hand with so viselike a grip that the Baronet threw her a startled look.

"Of course he remembers her name," Belinda said to Jack in disgust. "I just told it to him."

There was a momentary pause, but it was prevented from becoming awkward by the tactful intervention of Sir Eustace. "No one who's met Miss Hazeldine even once would ever forget her," he said smoothly, rising to his feet but keeping Jan's hand tightly clasped in his. "I am Eustace Merriot, Lord Ollenshaw. I regret interrupting this reunion, but I must remove Miss Hazeldine from your midst. She'd just informed me, when you arrived, that she is feeling unwell. I was about to escort her home."

"Oh, *Jan!*" Belinda cried in disappointment. "How dreadful! Is it something serious?"

"No, nothing at all alarming," Jan assured her. She threw Sir Eustace a look of gratitude and, still gripping his hand, let him help her to her feet. "It is merely a headache. An hour or so of quiet rest will surely bring a complete recovery."

"How very unfortunate that you should feel ill at this moment." Her cousin pouted. "Just when you and Max were about to become reacquainted."

Sir Eustace did not permit Jan to reply but deftly maneuvered her out of the press and toward the door. Somehow (although Jan was too flustered to take note of how he managed it) he led her past the pouting Belinda and the white-lipped Max. Somehow he reassured Lady Hazeldine that she need not feel concern and that her motherly assistance was not at all necessary. Somehow he collected his beaver hat and Jan's lavender shawl. Somehow he made Jan's adieus to all of the crowd. And he did all this without pausing in his purposeful movement toward the doors.

When the pair at last reached the street, Jan heaved a deep sigh of relief. If Sir Eustace noticed it, he made no remark. He merely walked with her to the house on Pierrepont Street, asking no questions and making no conversation. Jan was grateful for his silence; her emotions were still too tumultuous to permit her to make polite chatter.

By the time they arrived at the door, she'd recovered enough of her normal calm to deal with the situation at hand. "I don't know how to thank you, sir," she said with sincere warmth. "You are most gallant. Your tact in removing me from the Pump Room was remarkably artful. How did you guess that I wished to escape?''

''It was not difficult.'' The Baronet took off his hat and, tucking it under his arm, smiled down at her with sympathy. ''I couldn't help noting your distress when Lord Ollenshaw came in. And then, when I saw his expression when he recognized you, I understood the whole.''

''The *whole*?'' She gave a little, self-mocking laugh. ''Even I don't understand the whole.''

''I'm sorry. I used the wrong word. I didn't mean that I guessed the circumstances. I only meant that it became clear that something troublesome had occurred between the two of you in the past . . . something that caused you both to feel discomfort at this unexpected meeting.''

''Yes, your assessment is quite on the mark. I suppose, after your inexplicable kindness to me, you've earned the right to hear the particulars, but—''

''Not at all, Miss Hazeldine. You owe me no explanations, no particulars, no details of any kind. Nor do I wish any. It's no one's affair but your own.''

''Thank you for that, sir. Then all I shall do is express my thanks to you once more for removing me from a scene that might have proved embarrassing to everyone.''

''You're very welcome, my dear. But *I* should thank *you*. Being part of such youthful melodrama made this old fellow feel quite young again.''

Jan gave a little, disbelieving snort of laughter. ''Old fellow, indeed!''

''Oh, yes.'' He sighed. ''Old enough to be your father.''

She cocked her head and studied him with a look of blunt appraisal. ''Either you are too disparaging of yourself or too flattering of me, sir. I might believe you old enough to have fathered my eighteen-year-old cousin, but I am almost a decade past eighteen.''

He adjusted his spectacles and peered closely at her. ''Impossible!'' he declared firmly. ''I refuse to believe it. But I'll make a bargain with you, Miss Hazeldine. If you're willing to believe me too young to be your father, I'll permit myself to believe that you're twenty-eight. And now, ma'am, if

I may be permitted to change this fascinating subject to a more pressing one—may I call for you and your mother at eight tonight to escort you to the Assembly Rooms?''

Jan's face clouded. She would have liked to attend the concert this evening, but Max would probably be there. She did not have the courage to face him twice in one day. "I think not, Sir Eustace, although I do thank you for inviting us. I'm supposed to have a headache, remember. It would not be seemly for me to recover so soon."

"As you wish, of course," the portly fellow said dubiously, "but if I were you, I would make the push to go."

Jan, who had started up the steps to her front door, paused and looked back at the Baronet. "Why, Sir Eustace?" she asked. "Why should I 'make the push'?"

"Because it's important to your growth to do so."

"To my *growth*?" She raised her brows curiously. "I don't know what you mean, sir."

"I mean, my dear," he explained, replacing his high-crowned beaver on his head, "that, in order to permit the continuing healthy development of your character and spirit, you should not put off facing the demons of the past. If you do, they will never cease to haunt you." And with that advice he tipped his hat and trudged off down the street.

Ten

Lady Hazeldine did not remain long at the Pump Room after Jan departed. Her alarm over the state of her daughter's health had not been fully allayed by Sir Eustace's earlier assurances. Jan rarely took ill and almost never had headaches, so her ladyship could not imagine what had gone wrong with the girl. She felt so uneasy that, as soon as she could politely take her leave, she bid a quick good day to her sister and the others and hurried home.

But her fears faded away as soon as she came in the door and heard the sound of violin music. If Jan was well enough to play, she said to herself in relief, the girl's headache could not have been very serious. She ran up to her daughter's bedroom, opened the door quietly and peeped in. Jan was standing near the window in nothing but her petticoat, silhouetted by the fading daylight. Her feet were bare, and the hair she'd coiled at the top of her head had come loose and was barely hanging on in tousled disarray. She'd evidently started to dress for dinner but, succumbing to an urge to play her fiddle, had stopped in the midst. Lady Hazeldine did not know enough music to recognize what her daughter was playing, but she could see that Jan was completely intent on the music, for the girl's eyes were shut, and her body swayed gracefully with the movement of her bow to the rhythm of the sad refrain. Celia Hazeldine, unaccountably moved by the sight, stepped back to steal away, but Jan heard her. The girl's eyes flew open. "Mama?" she asked, the note she was playing turning slightly sharp before it faded to silence.

"I'm sorry, my love. I didn't mean to interrupt. You were so absorbed."

"No I wasn't. You didn't interrupt, Mama, really. My mind was miles away. Do come in. Did you wish to speak to me about something?"

"I only wanted to assure myself that you were not ill," her mother admitted, stepping over the threshold. "Are you quite all right?"

"I'm fine, Mama."

"That's a relief. What a scare you gave me this afternoon! But if you weren't unwell, why did you run off so precipitously from the Pump Room?"

Jan put aside her fiddle. "I thought my precipitous departure would delight you," she said mischievously.

"Why on earth should it delight me?" Lady Hazeldine asked as she undid the ribbons of her bonnet.

"Because, Mama, I left on Sir Eustace's arm. Didn't you wish for me to do so? You chose him for me, did you not? I therefore assumed you wanted him as my new suitor, and so I accepted his escort just to oblige you."

"Fiddlesticks!" Her mother frowned at the girl suspiciously. "You're not expecting me to believe that you would seriously entertain the notion of permitting Sir Eustace Merriot to court you."

"Why won't you believe it? Your choice has turned out to be most satisfactory."

"Come now, Jan, stop teasing me! He is too old and too stodgy for you, and you know it. I only brought him to you to prove my point—that at your advancing age it will grow harder and harder to find suitable beaux."

"But I find Sir Eustace very suitable, Mama. He's not only musical, which none of my other suitors ever were, but he's kind, sensitive, thoughtful and wise. What more can a girl ask of a suitor?"

"She can ask," Lady Hazeldine retorted, "that he be as young, handsome, rich and charming as Ollenshaw." She tossed her straw bonnet on the bed and sank down beside it, all the while studying her daughter narrowly. "I'd forgotten, over the years, what a catch that fellow Ollenshaw is. Whatever possessed you, Jan, to discard him?''

Jan flicked a curious glance at her mother's face. "Don't you remember anything about it, Mama?"

"No. Isn't it strange? I've racked my brain to try to recollect the details of that episode, but I can't. I don't believe you ever made me privy to them. Sometimes, Jan, I have the suspicion that you are much too secretive."

"There was nothing to be secretive about, dearest." Jan sat down beside her mother and took her hand with soothing affection. "What is it that you think I'm holding back from you?"

Lady Hazeldine softened at this gesture of tenderness. "Only your reason for throwing the fellow over, my love," she said, reaching out and smoothing back a strand of Jan's tousled hair. "I never did understand why you did it."

Jan sighed. "There wasn't anything to understand, Mama. The termination of my brief alliance with Lord Ollenshaw came about in quite the usual way. Like so many rash young lovers, he and I were completely besotted by the romantic fiddle-faddle of a blooming attraction. But then, when the first bloom faded, we had the usual rude awakening, and good sense prevailed. The fortunate thing about it was that the awakening occurred so quickly after the betrothal.''

"Yes," her mother agreed dryly. "The next morning, if I remember rightly. That was a quick awakening indeed."

"It was not as quick as it seemed. I suspected all through our courtship that his lordship and I didn't really suit."

"Yes, you've said that before," Lady Hazeldine said impatiently, "but you haven't yet given me the reason. What I want to know is *why*. *Why* didn't you suit? He seems to suit Belinda well enough."

Jan's eyes fell before her mother's intent gaze. "It was so very long ago, you know, Mama. Max . . . Lord Ollenshaw . . . is older now, and perhaps less . . . less reckless."

"Are you saying you jilted him because he was *reckless*? That's a strange reason. Do you mean he *gambled*?''

Jan began to feel uncomfortable. She had never told a soul about the redheaded woman and, even now, had no wish to malign Max's character. If she'd never wished to make public the fact that he was an adulterer, which he *was*, she certainly didn't wish to accuse him of being a gambler, which he *wasn't*. "No, Mama, certainly not," she said with all the conviction she could summon. "He was a rather wild sportsman in those days, that's all. He much enjoyed racing and boxing bouts and many other such things that I had little interest in. And he knew nothing of music or—"

"Music!" Her mother made a gesture of disgust. "I might have known that music would be at the bottom of it." Forgetting how moved she'd been at the sight of Jan with her violin just a few moments before, she jumped to her feet and glared down at her daughter. "That deuced violin has made a *freak* of you, Jan Hazeldine! To jilt a man because he isn't musical is as silly as jilting him because he wheezes. I shall *never*, as long as I live, forgive your father for making a musician of—!"

A tap at the door stilled her tongue. Irritated at the interruption, she turned and threw open the door. Standing just outside was the butler, Beale. "There's a visitor downstairs, your ladyship, waiting in the drawing room to see Miss Jan," he said.

"Visitor?" her ladyship demanded. "Who has come calling at this hour? Any female who calls herself a lady should be dressing for dinner."

"It's a gentleman, my lady. Lord Ollenshaw."

Jan's heart clenched painfully in her chest. "Lord . . . *Ollenshaw*?" she echoed in alarm, coming up behind her mother.

The butler nodded. "He says he will detain you for only a moment, Miss Jan."

Lady Hazeldine, who'd taken due note of the sudden pallor of Jan's cheeks, peered at her daughter through narrowed eyes. "Well, don't stand here gawking, girl," she ordered excitedly. "Throw on a robe and go down. Don't you wish to know what the fellow wants of you?"

"But I *can't*!" Jan gasped, her hands flying to her hair. "I'm not—" Then, meeting her mother's eyes, she realized she'd revealed too much. She lowered her arms slowly as the blood came rushing back into her face.

Lady Hazeldine stared at her daughter, a sudden thought bursting on her like a blow. *The girl is still in love with him!* came a silent cry within her breast. For a moment she couldn't move, so shaken was she by this discovery. But now that the idea had occurred to her, she knew she was not mistaken; the truth of it was suddenly so obvious that she wondered how she could have been so blind for so long. That one fact—that Jan was still in love with Ollenshaw—explained everything about her daughter's behavior for the past eight years!

Clenching her fingers so that no one would see how they trembled, Lady Hazeldine took herself in hand and turned quickly to the butler. "Go and tell his lordship that Jan will be down directly," she ordered, her voice almost steady.

"Mama, *please*," Jan urged as soon as they were alone, "don't *look* at me so! You mustn't make too much of . . . I didn't mean to . . ."

"You didn't mean to reveal to me that you're still attached to him—is that what you're trying to say?" her mother asked gently.

Jan dropped her eyes. "That's what I'm trying *not* to say . . . You are jumping to wild conclusions just because I didn't want Ollenshaw to see me with my hair so . . . so . . ."

"Untidy?" Lady Hazeldine supplied.

"Yes, untidy."

Lady Hazeldine wanted to weep for her daughter, but she kept her emotions under tight control. "It is untidy. Come, my love, sit down at your dressing table and let me do it up for you."

"*You*, Mama? You want to do up my hair?" She threw her mother a startled look. "You haven't done my hair since—"

"Since you used to wear it in plaits." She urged her daughter onto the dressing-table bench and smoothed the loose tendrils of hair from the girl's forehead with fingers that shook. "I used to love to plait your hair when you were a child," she said, choked.

She pulled out the pins that were barely holding Jan's heavy topknot in place and let the hair tumble down her back. It was such lovely hair, as silky and shiny as when Jan was a child. The mother smothered a sigh. Her daughter—her poor, beloved Jan—had been suffering over that deuced Ollenshaw all these years. And she, Jan's own mother, had never even guessed! How *unkind* she'd been to her daughter through it all! How thoughtless! All the scoldings she'd dispensed, all the ravings and the naggings and the urgings for the girl to get herself betrothed. If only she could take them all back!

She picked up the hairbrush and began to brush out the long strands. The hair curled round the brush like something alive. She brushed it into one thick swirl and draped it over Jan's shoulder. "Why don't you just leave it this way? It looks so lovely."

Jan, meeting her mother's eyes in the mirror, winced. Her mother *knew*! She dropped her head in her hands and groaned. "Oh, Mama, *don't*—!"

Lady Hazeldine knelt down beside the bench and enveloped her daughter in a tight embrace. "My poor baby," she murmured tearfully, rocking her daughter in her arms. "My poor, sweet darling."

Jan, having kept her pain to herself for so long, was quite overwhelmed by this unexpected display of sympathy. She lowered her head to her mother's shoulder and burst into shuddering tears. She hadn't realized how much she'd needed this sort of tenderness. Her mother's display of affection seemed to break through a staunchly barricaded wall inside her, and a rush of feeling poured out.

But after a long moment, aware that Max was waiting for her downstairs, she tried to bring her emotions under control. "Now, M-Mama," she said firmly, pulling herself erect and taking a deep breath, "you m-mustn't place too much importance on this. You *mustn't*."

"Mustn't I?" Lady Hazeldine took Jan's face in her hands and began to wipe away the girl's tears with her handkerchief. "If that make-bait, Ollenshaw, can make my daughter cry like this—!"

Jan gave her mother a tremulous smile. "It's *you* who's made me cry, dearest. It was your unexpected mothering that opened the floodgates. You were quite irresistible."

Lady Hazeldine smiled mistily back at her. "Oh, pooh!" she declared.

"Truly, Mama, this little cry has had a very soothing effect on me. I feel much better. But you must believe me when I tell you my outburst had no real significance. I'm quite over Lord Ollenshaw."

"Of course you are," Lady Hazeldine said in ironic agreement. "The waterworks meant nothing."

"The waterworks came about only because I saw him today so unexpectedly. If he'd stayed away a few more days, as Belinda said he was supposed to, I would have had time to prepare myself properly."

"Oh, yes. Belinda. I was forgetting." Lady Hazeldine pulled herself to her feet. "How a man of sense can choose Belinda after being in love with you is more than I can—"

"Mama," Jan cut her off warningly, "let's have none of that. Max belongs to Belinda now. You must never even *think* of him in association with me."

"Then what's he doing calling on you here, may I ask?" Lady Hazeldine pulled a ruffled, rose-colored dressing gown from the wardrobe and helped Jan into it. "What do you suppose the fellow wants with you now?"

"I have no idea," Jan admitted, growing tense again. She stared at herself in the mirror. "Do my eyes look red, Mama?"

"Not noticeably. You look lovely. Put on these slippers and go down. Let the bounder see what he's lost."

"Really, Mama, you are being silly! He's not likely to regret losing me when he's won a beauty like Belinda for himself. You must make up your mind, dearest, that Max is not for me." She got up and strode bravely to the door. But there she paused. "Do you really think I should show myself with my hair loose like this?"

"Yes, I do. Wearing your hair down makes you look eighteen again. He's bound to find you beautiful. I know, I know, you needn't say it: you don't want him to find you beautiful. But even though Ollenshaw is not for you, it won't hurt to give him a pang or two over what might have been.'' And, giving the swirl of hair one last pat, she pushed her daughter out the door.

Eleven

"I'm sorry to have kept you waiting so long, my lord," Jan said from the doorway.

He'd been standing in the window embrasure, staring out at the street. He turned about slowly. "It wasn't so very long." His face was shadowed by the light from the window behind him, but her familiarity with his facial expressions made her almost see his sardonic smile. "It didn't feel much longer than the passage of two or three seasons."

She came into the room. "Time has not sweetened your acid tongue, I see," she remarked.

"No. In that much, at least, I haven't changed." He crossed the room to her and peered with blunt appraisal at her face. "But the eight years have touched lightly on you, ma'am," he said. "You are more beautiful than ever."

She studied him with a bluntness equal to his. "While you, on the other hand, have grayed at the temples."

He shrugged. "Time is not as kind to everyone as it is to you."

"Nonsense. The gray becomes you, as no doubt you are perfectly aware."

"I am not at all aware of it," he said irritably. "Do you think I bother about such vain concerns? Yes, of course you do. I suppose there will never come a time when you fail to think of me as a rake and a coxcomb."

Jan felt ashamed of herself. "I'm sorry. I didn't mean . . ." She bit her lip and turned away from his burning glare. "I'm sure, my lord, that you didn't come to call on me for the purpose of renewing old quarrels.''

''No, I didn't. I came to talk to you about Belinda.''

A wave of utterly irrational disappointment surged through her. ''About *Belinda*?''

''Yes. What else did you suppose I'd want to speak to you about?''

She swallowed her disappointment and flicked her hand at him dismissively. ''Nothing else, of course,'' she answered brusquely. ''But perhaps, my lord, we should seat ourselves before we begin.'' She lowered herself gracefully onto a chair, arranged the ruffled flounce of her dressing gown over her ankles and gestured for him to seat himself on the sofa at her left. ''Now, sir, what about Belinda?''

He leaned his elbow on the arm of the sofa and studied her curiously for a moment before he spoke. ''Why the devil, Jan, didn't you tell her about us?''

''Tell her about *us*?'' she asked, playing for time while she gathered her wits.

''Yes. Us. You and me.''

''But . . . what do you think I should have told her about us?''

''About our betrothal, of course, if an alliance of a few hours can be called a betrothal.''

Jan didn't know how to answer. ''I . . . I don't understand what you're asking of me, my lord,'' she mumbled, wondering how on earth she could defend herself against the obvious accusation in his tone.

''It's a perfectly simple question, ma'am. You arrived yesterday, I've been told, and had a long conversation with Belinda, is that right?''

''Yes, but—''

''And at that time, ma'am, you discovered the name of her betrothed, did you not?''

''Yes . . .''

Max leaned back in his chair and crossed his legs comfortably. ''I assume that the name was familiar to you? John Maxwell, Lord Ollenshaw? You'd heard it before?''

Furious at his arrogant self-confidence, she glared at him. "Yes, you make-bait, I remembered the name."

"And you also remembered our betrothal, brief as it was, did you not?"

"You know perfectly well that I did."

"Then why, ma'am, did you not tell Belinda?"

"Well, I . . . I . . ." She put a shaking hand to her forehead, trying to reconstruct her reasoning. "I don't know, really. I had my reasons. Several reasons. For one, I suppose I was trying to be protective."

"Protective? Of whom, ma'am?"

She whirled on him furiously. "Confound it, Max, must you keep calling me ma'am in that odious way?"

"Yes, since you were being equally odious and calling me sir and my lord. Of course, I did hear you call me 'make-bait' a moment ago, so I suppose I can relent and refer to you by your nickname."

"Thank you," she retorted dryly. "I should be much obliged."

"Then, if we may return to the subject, Jan, I would like to understand your motives. Whom were you protecting? Me? Belinda? Yourself?"

"All three, I'd say." She drew in a long breath, wondering how it was possible that he'd succeeded in making her feel like a criminal for something she'd done with the best of intent.

"Protecting us from what, may I ask?" he persisted.

"From embarrassment, of course."

His brows rose in surprise. "Embarrassment? Whose embarrassment? I, for one, would not be embarrassed if Belinda learned of our betrothal."

Now it was Jan's turn to be surprised. "Wouldn't you?"

"Of course not." His wonderful grin made a sudden appearance. "I'm rather proud of it, you know. It's to my credit to have won the hand of Ice-Maiden Hazeldine, if only for a few hours."

She gaped at him in horror. *"Ice-Maiden Hazeldine?"*

"Hadn't you heard that sobriquet? I've heard it often

enough at my club. Ice-Maiden Hazeldine, who lures men to the point of offering and then icily rejects them.''

"I don't believe it!" Jan snapped. "This is your vulgar idea of a joke!"

Max shrugged. "It's not *my* idea. I could never think of you as an ice-maiden. Something of a prude, perhaps, but certainly not an ice-maiden."

She threw him a glowering look. "You're having a wonderful time at my expense, aren't you, you dastard! Is this your way of wreaking a belated revenge on me?"

"Not at all. You have always misconstrued my motives. I haven't the least desire for revenge. The purpose of this visit is only to determine why you chose to keep our past a secret from Belinda and, if your reasons are not strong, to convince you that a full disclosure is the wisest course."

"Are you quite serious, Max?" she asked suspiciously. "I don't see the wisdom of that at all."

"Don't you? Why not? Isn't honesty always the wisest course? One would think that you, of all people, would wish to be honest with Belinda. If she learned the truth of our past, you would then be free to inform her about me. Don't you think you should warn her about the flaws in my character—flaws which were grave enough for you to find me unacceptable?"

Jan got up and took a few nervous steps round the room. Then she turned and fixed him with a level look. "To be honest, Max, I did think of that. But after so many years it's quite possible that the . . . the flaws you refer to no longer exist. Therefore I didn't think it fair to disclose them."

He stared back at her for a moment and then dropped his eyes. "That is very kind of you," he said with perfect sincerity, all traces of sarcasm gone from his voice, "but I don't think Belinda would be persuaded to reject me even if you *did* disclose the whole."

"Yes, you're probably right," Jan agreed, wondering why she hadn't seen the truth of that for herself. "Just because you were not faithful to me is no reason for her to suppose you would not be faithful to her." She returned to her chair and seated herself, leaning forward in earnest appeal. "But I have other reasons, Max. Belinda is so happy. Quite flying in alt, it seems. Don't you think her happiness might be a little impaired to learn that her cousin and her beloved were once, er, attached?''

"I don't see why it should matter to her. The attachment is many years in the past, after all,'' Max argued.

"Nevertheless, learning of it may give her a twinge.''

He shook his head. "A twinge is not so dreadful. In fact, if she's really 'flying in alt' as you say, it might be a good thing for her to touch down to reality from time to time. If you ask me, Jan, your arguments thus far are not very convincing.''

"Yes, I can see that.''

"Especially when they are measured against the moral rectitude of being honest.''

She gave a little gurgle of laughter. "Things *have* changed if *you* are put to lecturing *me* about moral rectitude.''

"I have no intention of posing as ethically superior to you, Jan. God knows that can never be the case. But even *I* am not such a bounder as to wish to enter wedlock with a lie of this nature standing between me and my bride.''

There was no mistaking his sincerity. Her throat clenched painfully as the word "bride'' smote her ears. She, Jan, was to be his bride, too, once upon a time. Why hadn't he tried a little moral rectitude *then*? But there was no point in asking herself, or him, such a question now. It was all too late. "You are quite right, Max,'' she said quietly. "I have no argument against that.''

"But you do have other arguments. You said you had several.''

"Yes. I have one more. It is my strongest, but perhaps I shouldn't state it. I have no wish to encourage you to erect moral barriers between yourself and your br—Belinda.''

"No. Go ahead and make it. I may as well hear them all.''

"Very well, then, here it is. Does it not seem to you that if Belinda—and thus everyone else in her circle—learns of our 'past,' we may find it awkward to be in each other's company?''

"*Shall* we be in each other's company?''

"I'm afraid so. My Aunt Nettie, Belinda's Mama, has planned any number of fêtes and is bound to include us both. I don't see how we can avoid each other. Mama has rented this house for a whole month, and though I may be able to persuade her to cut our stay short by a week or two, I don't think I can hope for any more. I believe we must anticipate that I shall be forced to remain at least a fortnight in Bath. In that time we shall, of necessity, be brought face to face quite often. Would it not be easier to meet each other as mere acquaintances rather than endure being scrutinized by one and all as erstwhile sweethearts?"

"Yes, I see your point. I suppose everyone *would* be scrutinizing us, human nature being what it is." Now it was his turn to get up and pace about the room. Finally he stopped before her chair. "*I* don't care about the scrutiny, my dear, but evidently you do. Would pretending to be mere acquaintances make this awkward situation easier for you?"

"It most certainly would," she admitted, coloring.

He sighed. "Then you have me. I have no refutation for that point. Very well, my dear, I shall do it your way and keep the secret. I only hope that Belinda may not accuse me, some time later, of guile and deception."

"Oh, I don't think that will happen."

"Why not? It happened before."

She stiffened. "Do you mean . . . *me*?"

"Who else?"

She gasped in outraged offense. "Do you *dare* to suggest, my lord, that refraining from revealing our *insignificant* betrothal to Belinda is the same sort of deception as . . . as the *heinous betrayal* you perpetrated upon *me*?"

"I'm only suggesting, *ma'am*," he retorted coldly, "that the nature of 'betrayal' is often in the eye of the beholder. Belinda may very well exaggerate the heinousness of the crime against her, just as you did the one against you."

Jan leapt angrily to her feet. "If you are still pretending that I *exaggerated* the evidence of my own eyes, then your morals haven't changed at all!"

"I never claimed they did," he said icily.

Finding herself close to tears again, Jan turned her back

on him. "I d-don't care to discuss this, my lord. Not now and not ever."

"Nor do I." There was a momentary pause. "Am I to assume, from this outburst, that you've changed your mind about telling Belinda what a rotter I am?"

She clenched her fists and forced herself to calm down. "No, you may not assume anything of the sort. As you pointed out, there would be little purpose in my telling Belinda. She would not be persuaded to reject you anyway."

"Then, ma'am, after all this squabbling, where the deuce *are* we?"

She turned round to face him. "We had agreed to keep up the pretense of being near strangers, had we not? Do you wish to renege?"

"No. I'm willing to go through with it, since it seems important to you."

"Thank you. I am grateful to you. I should find our situation unpleasantly awkward otherwise."

"Very well," he said brusquely, "it's agreed. And since there's no need to belabor the point any further, I'll bid you good night." He turned and strode to the door.

"Dash it all, Max," Jan burst out, following him, "you needn't behave as if you are making a great sacrifice for my sake. You'll not be lying to Belinda but merely postponing the truth. It's only a matter of remaining silent for a fortnight or so. As soon as I make my escape from Bath, you can tell Belinda all. It won't be too late, then, for you to make a clean breast of things, will it?"

He paused and looked back at her over his shoulder. "I suppose not," he said dubiously. "And I suppose I can endure a fortnight of pretense."

"Thank you, Max. I truly think this is the best way to handle what could be a very sticky situation."

He nodded. "So we'll have to treat each other as barely recalled acquaintances, eh?"

"Yes. Exactly. Like near-strangers, we must keep a cool distance."

"A cool distance." He expelled a long, surrendering breath. "I suppose it can be contrived." His expression was troubled, but he managed a little grin as he added teasingly, "But you must remember not to blow up at me when I call you ma'am instead of Jan."

"I'll be careful. We must both be careful."

He lifted her hand and bowed over it. "Good day, ma'am," he said with exaggerated formality. "Thank you for receiving me."

"You're quite welcome, my lord," she said, bowing with equal ostentation. "I shall ring for Beale to see you out."

"There's no need. I can find my way."

Nevertheless she followed him to the entryway and waited while he picked up his hat and cane from the table near the door where Beale had placed them. She couldn't help noticing that his brow was still furrowed. "There's no need to fall into a pucker, Max," she said soothingly as he opened the front door. "It will all be for the best."

"I doubt it."

"But why? Surely you don't believe this brief withholding of our story from Belinda will cause any real damage to your troth."

"That," he said, clapping his tall hat on his head in disgust, "is the most minor of concerns."

"Then what is the major one?"

He threw open the door. "It may be easy for *you* to behave with cool distance toward me, *ma'am*," he said over his shoulder, giving her a long, last, glowering look from under knit brows, "but for *me* it will be the very devil. You may take my word on it."

Twelve

A COOL DISTANCE. Lovely!

John Maxwell, the Marquis of Ollenshaw, walked slowly along the North Parade after the interview with Jan, a mocking smile disfiguring his countenance. Did Jan really think it would be as easy as all that for him to keep a cool distance? The girl was impossible. How could he keep a cool distance when the mere sight of her stirred up this roil of feelings in him? Did she have any idea of the residue of emotion their brief affair had left with him?

Max had always considered himself a plain, blunt man. He was not given to subterfuge. He did not like to indulge in complicated introspection. He was not comfortable thinking about the subtleties of his interior life. He liked simple explanations, clear alternatives and straightforward solutions.

He was a sportsman, and the rules of sports were the rules of his life. In sports, one had a clear, clean objective, and one tried to reach it by the strength of one's efforts. If one were strong, fair, and trained in the required skills, one could win the game. Any game. Even life's game.

The trouble was that every time he had anything to do with Miss Jan Hazeldine his life became convoluted. The simple rules of sports did not hold. There was something about her—something deep and subtle and quite beyond his grasp—that shook his usual self-confidence.

Sighing, he became aware of the sound of rushing water below him. He was on the Parade Bridge. To cross would take him in the wrong direction, yet he was not ready to return to his rooms. He walked to the edge of the bridge and leaned over the balustrade, staring down at the dark, swirling waters that shimmered with reddish flecks from the light of the setting sun. The dramatic turmoil of the river perfectly suited his mood.

Damnation, he cursed under his breath, *am I going to let Jan Hazeldine shake me up again?* Before he'd met and fallen in love with her he'd been the most confident of men. He remembered being very sure of himself, pleased with life and his place in it. He ran his estates with easy competence. He was adept at riding, fencing, shooting and boxing. He had many friends. Women threw themselves at him. He awoke each day without a care.

Then, without warning, love had burst upon him. One ordinary evening he'd looked up at a girl playing a violin, and since then nothing in his life was the same. He never fully understood just what had undone him, but there was something about her, that angelic purity perhaps, that had made him feel unworthy. Perhaps it was the aura that music gave her, but whatever it was, it had seemed to him that Jan existed on a higher plane than he. When he began to view the world through her eyes, he suddenly saw himself as the self-indulgent Corinthian rake she'd seen at their first meeting. But knowing her—loving her—changed him. Things like music and poetry, that in his circle were considered unmanly, suddenly became meaningful to him. But more important, she made him sensitive to the nuances of human feelings.

It was a strange experience; he'd never felt *inadequate* before. Yet inadequate though he was, she fell in love with him, too. She found things in him to admire. She seemed as proud of his talents as he was of hers. He permitted himself to believe, for a while, that their differences were complementary—that they each enriched the other. For a very brief time they were miraculously happy together.

Then came the night that Jan appeared at his door so unexpectedly and found the overbearing *Red*more woman hanging on his neck. It was a mere misunderstanding, and he couldn't believe, at first, that it was enough to drive them apart. All that was necessary to set things straight was an explanation—a simple explanation. He would simply explain that he'd been trying for months—even before he'd met Jan—to end the brief and meaningless liaison with Lady Wedmore but that the woman had refused to accept defeat. The scene Jan witnessed had been Lady Wedmore's final attempt at a reconciliation, an attempt he'd firmly rejected. He'd done nothing that night, or in all the weeks since he'd met Jan, to feel ashamed of. Surely, he told himself, he could make her understand . . .

But in the end, he never even *tried* to explain it to Jan. After he forced his way in to see her, but before he could explain, she said those words—those searing words that burned away his resolve: *This was a mistake from the first . . . we are too different to really suit.* Hearing them, he simply gave up. He realized at that moment that it wasn't the Wedmore incident that had driven them apart. It was Jan's admission that they existed on different planes. Despite the pain it caused him, he couldn't refute her. He couldn't argue against something that he'd feared from the first was the absolute truth. He knew from these words that she'd never change her mind, no matter how hard he tried to persuade her.

Looking down at the waters of the Avon, the memory of the dreadful misery of their separation came back to him. Something within him died when he lost Jan, some sense of self. It was a long time before he could wake in the morning without feeling a clench in his chest. It was years before he fully recovered. And even though the time finally came when he found a measure of contentment, and his friends said he was his old self again, he knew it was not true. He never returned to his old self. For one thing, he'd lost the feeling of youthful invulnerability. For another, though he still enjoyed his sporting activities and the other facets of his life, they were less fulfilling. He went to concerts now, and read Byron, and spent many hours in his own company. No, he was not his old self. And he knew that he'd never love another woman with the same intensity he'd once felt for Jan.

When he met Belinda he'd been consciously looking about for a wife. A man in his position was expected to marry and carry on his "line." Belinda Briarly was, he believed, a happy choice. Though she was very young, she was quite lovely and had a cheerfulness that was infectious. What made her most appealing, however, was the adoring way she regarded everything he said and did. Now, staring down at the rushing river below him, he wondered about his motives. Had he been drawn to Belinda merely because she idolized him? Was it a sort of antidote for Jan's rejection? The question was deeply troubling.

Blast it, he thought, *why did Belinda have to be related to Jan?* It seemed as if fate were taking a malicious pleasure in toying with him. Not only had it turned out that Belinda and Jan were first cousins, but fate had brought Jan right here to Bath. Of all the ironic torments fate could devise, this was the worst. And Jan wanted him to keep all this secret! To pretend that they had no shared past—that they were all but strangers. To keep a cool distance. Ha!

But all at once he stopped himself. *Good God,* he thought in self-disgust, *can I, a man of almost forty and a Maxwell of Ollenshaw, be indulging in a bout of childish self-pity?* A surge of virile revulsion swept over him. He was not a weak-kneed poltroon, after all. He was a man of some inner strength, and for a man of strength this sort of cogitation just wouldn't do. Standing erect, he adjusted the set of his hat to a more jaunty angle and set off for home. As he strode back toward his flat in the Crescent, he determined to banish forever this mawkish tendency toward self-conscious introspection. What was past was past. Dwelling on it did not change anything. Besides, as recently as yesterday he'd been quite content with the present. He'd be damned if he'd let Jan cut up his peace again. He'd agreed to her little plan, so he was stuck with it, but he would not let the situation get the better of him. Not only would he go along with her subterfuge, he'd play the role to the hilt. Now that he thought about it, pretending a complete indifference to her might even give him some perverse enjoyment. It could only be for a fortnight or so, she'd assured him. For a fortnight, he could endure it. For a fortnight he could endure anything.

Thirteen

THEIR AGREED-ON PLAN was put into practice that very evening, for when Jan explained to her mother what had passed between herself and Max, the two women decided that the sooner the scheme was put into execution the better. They therefore sent a message to Sir Eustace that they would appreciate his escort to the concert that evening after all.

They made a hurried scramble into evening dress and downed a hasty dinner, but even so they arrived at the Upper Rooms a bit late. At the entrance to the main hall, they could hear that the soprano, a Madame Rinaldi, had already launched into her first aria. Nevertheless, Sir Eustace introduced the ladies to the master of ceremonies, who gave them a hearty, if whispered, welcome. Then they tiptoed to their seats on the rearmost bench.

The enormous room was dimly lit to ensure that all eyes would be drawn to the front, where several large candelabras had been set up round the pianoforte to light the full-bosomed soprano. It did not take long for Jan to realize that the music would not be to her taste. Madame Rinaldi was the sort of singer who was known in musical circles as a "Vauxhall Soprano"—that is, one who catered to popular tastes rather than to the demands of true musicianship. Popular taste demanded a great deal of trilling and a generous supply of shrill high notes; these Madame Rinaldi was well able to provide. When one of her high notes went painfully sharp, Jan exchanged an amused look with Sir Eustace, who was as aware of Madame Rinaldi's deficiencies as she.

Since the music did not hold her attention, Jan let her eyes roam over the room. It was an enormous room, with a coved ceiling supported by lovely Corinthian columns, and it boasted five magnificent crystal chandeliers which, when fully lit for a ball, could make the whole room sparkle. Even now, with only a fraction of their candles burning, they emitted a lovely glow.

All at once Jan spotted her aunt, her cousin and Max seated a few rows in front of her. Even though she fully expected them to be present, the sight of them made her heart race. They were bound to meet at intermission, and she wondered how Max would manage to follow through on his promise to pretend to a mere acquaintanceship. The fact that he'd expressed such reluctance earlier only increased her nervousness.

Jan tried to pay attention to the singer, but she found her eyes drawn to the betrothed couple in front of her. They were sitting companionably close, their shoulders touching. Jan felt a stab of jealousy and was immediately ashamed of herself. *What else did I expect?* she asked herself. *After all, they are betrothed.* But the feeling of jealousy would not go away, and she began to wonder why Max had said that this game would be easier for her than for him. Why would she find it easier, when it was *he* who was so happily in love with a beautiful chit of eighteen, while *she* was a lonely spinster whose only choice of escort was a portly gentleman in his fifties?

After a few moments, Belinda, as if she felt Jan's eyes on her, looked round and discovered that her cousin and aunt were present. She beamed in delight and immediately whispered the glad tidings to her mother and Max. Nettie Briarly turned round and wiggled her fingers at them, but Max faced resolutely front. Somehow, his lack of response made Jan feel very sorry she'd come.

At the intermission, the two parties inevitably came together. Lady Briarly beamed at Sir Eustace in not-very-subtle delight at discovering that he was escorting her niece. "I see you've won yourself the second prettiest lady in the room," she said, tittering.

Lady Hazeldine, furious at what she considered a disparagement of her daughter, glared at her sister and changed the subject by declaring that Nettie's dark-red gown made her look like an overgrown beet.

Belinda, meanwhile, holding tightly to Max's arm, drew him happily to Jan's side. "Here we are, together again," she gurgled. "Isn't it delightful?"

"Yes, indeed," Max agreed, bowing over Jan's hand. "How nice to see you again, ma'am."

Jan dropped him a hasty bow and turned nervously to her cousin. "Are you enjoying the concert, Belinda?" she asked distractedly.

"Oh, yes. Very much. Madame Rinaldi has such a beautiful voice, hasn't she? But Max does not care for her, I'm afraid."

"Oh?" Jan could not resist quizzing him. "Don't you like music, my lord?"

"Not much, I'm afraid." He looked down at her with an amused glint. "There was a time when I was quite besotted by violin music, but it's an obsession that I seem to have outgrown."

"Indeed?" Jan answered politely, but to make it plain to the dastard that she did not like his taunts, she trod firmly on his toes as she turned away.

The party moved slowly down the aisle to the door on their way to the tea room. Sir Eustace, taking Lady Hazeldine's arm, offered his other arm to Jan, but the girl shook her head. "Thank you, sir, but I hope you will excuse me," she demurred. "I don't care to take tea now. I'll remain here and look over the program until you all return."

Sir Eustace was reluctant to leave her, but Lady Hazeldine assured him that he didn't have to worry about her daughter. "My Jan," she bragged as she led him away, "has always been as independent as the wind. You cannot tell her where to go or what to do with herself. She quite prefers to be left to her own devices."

It turned out to be a longer intermission than Jan had expected. She read over the program twice, and still the audience had not returned to their seats. She was beginning to think she should have gone down to the tea room with the others, when Max came strolling down the aisle. He had a half smile on his face and a full wineglass in his hand. Holding the glass carefully, he slid along the bench until he was beside her. "Some wine, Miss Hazeldine?" he asked.

Jan glanced round the room nervously, but only a few uninterested strangers sat on the benches or lounged in the aisles. "Are you insane?" she hissed. "Suppose someone who knows us saw—"

"Belinda sent me," Max explained, offering her the wine. "She insisted that somebody provide you with some refreshment. Lord Liggett, whom we discovered mooning about in a corner of the Octagon room—hoping, he said, for a glimpse of 'the magnificent Miss Hazeldine'—was desperate to perform that small service, but I think Belinda had no confidence in his ability to carry a full wineglass such a distance without spilling it all over himself. Therefore I was the one she chose to carry out her little errand. How would it have looked if I'd refused?"

Jan, relieved, eyed the glass askance. "What is it?"

"Ratafia. Belinda wanted to send you up a glass of negus. I almost blurted out that you hate negus, but I caught myself just in time. However, I did manage to switch to the ratafia when no one was looking."

Jan frowned at him. "You are looking smugly pleased with yourself, my lord. For someone who was so reluctant to engage in this, er, subterfuge, you seem to be enjoying yourself mightily."

"I'm surprised myself, but I am." He flashed his winsome grin at her. "This scheme of yours is turning out to be a diverting challenge. After all my misgivings, I'm beginning to think that—if I protect my toes, of course—the next few weeks may prove to be more entertaining than a French farce."

Fourteen

IT RAINED SO hard the next day that no one ventured out. This gave Jan a period of respite from the tensions of her situation. She used the time to practice her fiddle, to finish Miss Burney's delicious novel, and to write a letter to her friend Harriet urging her to come to Bath. She'd made up her mind that Harriet and Sir Eustace would make a perfect pair, not only for their mutual love of music but because they were both so gentle and good-natured. However, she did not hint in her letter that she was playing matchmaker. She knew enough about human nature to understand that such "arranging" was not good strategy for romance. It would be better for Harriet and Sir Eustace to discover for *themselves* that they were suited. So she merely wrote to her friend that it would be

> such fun to have your company. We'll be able to do all
> sorts of amusing things together: attend concerts and
> musicales at the Upper Rooms; see a play at the Theater
> Royal; take long, healthful walks through the Sydney
> Gardens; and play duets on rainy afternoons. Do come!

While she waited for a reply, the rain continued to fall. It fell for three long days, during which the social life at Bath seemed to come to a standstill. The Pump Room was virtually deserted, and only the most determined and hardy souls made their way through the downpour to the Upper Rooms in the evening. But Aunt Nettie sent word that, rain or no, her family dinner party would be held as planned.

But during those three days Nettie Briarly's plans to hold a small family dinner party to welcome her sister and niece to Bath began to expand. Originally Nettie intended the dinner to be a casual, intimate affair, with only the four family members and Max (who, she explained to her sister, was almost a member of the family anyway). But then she decided that Sir Eustace should be invited, too, in order to promote what she thought was a budding romance between him and her niece. "It will be only a small, casual family gathering," she warned Sir Eustace in her note to him. Sir Eustace was not put off by her modest disclaimer. He, like everyone else in Bath, was tired of being imprisoned in his rooms by the endless rain, and he promptly accepted Lady Briarly's invitation.

Soon after the invitation was sent to Sir Eustace, word of the dinner party somehow reached Lord Liggett. The awkward fellow paid a call on Lady Briarly in spite of the drenching downpour and managed to wangle an invitation for himself by subjecting the hostess to some mysterious sort of persuasion which, since he could barely utter a complete sentence, even Nettie was never afterwards able to explain.

When Belinda learned that Lord Liggett was to attend her mother's dinner party, she insisted that the rest of her "circle" had to be invited, too. "You can't leave them out, Mama," she cried, "for if Liggy hasn't told them of it by this time, he soon will. And then they will surely be offended." Thus the guest list was expanded to include the two Brett girls, Mary Grindsley and her brother Jack.

Lady Briarly sat down with pencil and paper, added up her list and discovered that her small family dinner now required eleven places at the table. Since any hostess worth her salt knows that eleven is an awkward number, Nettie Briarly promptly sent a note round to her friend Mrs. Kendall (who was Bath's most notorious gossip and therefore an interesting dinner conversationalist) to round out the guest list. Mrs. Kendall, who had been without company for two whole days and who could not bear being devoid of society for even one,

closed her eyes to the lateness of the invitation and accepted
with alacrity.

Nettie was not in the least dismayed by the expansion of
her guest list. ''Twelve is not an enormous number for a
dinner party, Celia,'' she assured her sister. ''We can still be
casual and modest. The evening will be, just as I promised
you, a quiet, simple affair.''

But Lady Hazeldine knew that her sister treated any gathering at her home as a major event, and that this affair would
more likely be grand than simple. Thus she was not surprised
to discover, when she and Jan alighted from their carriage in
front of the Briarly house, that the two footmen who held
umbrellas for them and ushered them into the door were in
full livery, that Nettie had set out her very best china and
plate on the flower-laden table, and that the menu was lavish
enough for a visit from the Prince. (The first course included,
among a dozen side dishes, both turbot with a lobster sauce
and braised goose, while the pièce de résistance of the second
course was a magnificent roast surrounded by a brace of par-
tridge fillets à la Pompadour and garnished with mushrooms
Provençale, candied turnips and glazed onions. The diners
could choose from six wines to accompany their food, and
the feast was crowned with a dessert so rich that it was ap-
propriately called the ''Antioch Ruin.'') When the ladies rose
from the table, Lady Hazeldine remarked to her daughter in
a careful undervoice that her sister Nettie was so lost to common sense that she could not tell the difference between sim-
plicity and ostentation.

When the gentlemen joined the ladies in the drawing room
(a large, square room generously supplied with sofas and
chairs and boasting a grand pianoforte situated in the niche
created by the room's huge bow window), they found Mary
Grindsley already at the piano, preparing to accompany one
of the Misses Brett in song. The gentlemen took seats among
the ladies and listened in glazed-eyed stupor as Miss Brett
performed the familiar ''Drink to Me Only with Thine Eyes.''
Miss Brett had a sweet, clear soprano voice but no ear, so
she sang her little song in serene oblivion of the fact that half
of the notes were off the mark. When she finished, she

blushed with innocent delight at the polite applause and only reluctantly relinquished her place near the piano to her sister. The other Miss Brett performed "Lover's Roundelay," with an equally unwarranted serenity.

As soon as Miss Brett ended her song (and was rewarded with equally polite applause), Sir Eustace, not wishing for an encore, hastily suggested that the young lady at the piano might be willing to sing for them. Mary Grindsley colored, shook her head and jumped quickly from the piano bench. "Thank you, sir, but I don't sing," she said with a nervous giggle and, taking a seat beside her brother, tried to look unobtrusive.

"Of course you do," her hostess declared fondly, even though she'd never heard the girl sing. Nettie, not in the least musical herself, was nevertheless pleased that her guests had chosen this form of after-dinner diversion. Music was a more elegant *divertissement* to crown the evening than cards, and she beamed with pride at the apparent success of this spontaneous entertainment. "Isn't it wonderful that we have so many talented young ladies gathered here?" she remarked to Mrs. Kendall. "My Belinda also sings, you know, and my niece is a very skilled violinist."

"Oh, yes, Jan is truly gifted," Belinda exclaimed with enthusiasm. "Did you know, Max, that Jan plays the violin?"

Jan tensed, but Max took the question in stride. "No, I hadn't heard that," he said, his eyes twinkling mischievously at his brazen lie. "I should not have guessed, Miss Hazeldine, that an instrument like the violin would suit you."

Jan, perversely annoyed at Max's apparent enjoyment of their little subterfuge, put up her chin. "No, my lord? Why not?"

Before he could respond, Mrs. Kendall, who had been absently adjusting the turban she'd set on her iron gray curls, suddenly pursed her narrow lips and interjected herself into the discussion. "A very difficult instrument, the violin, is it not?" she inquired, her long nose wrinkling in disapproval. "Not many young ladies attempt it, I'm glad to say. I do not believe that people of importance approve of young ladies taking up the violin."

"Rubbish!" Celia Hazeldine snapped. Despite the fact that she herself did not always approve of her daughter's devotion to her musical studies, she would not allow anyone else to disapprove. Jan *was* a gifted violinist, and Lady Hazeldine would never permit anyone to say otherwise. She certainly would not permit Mrs. Kendall's foolish comment to go unchallenged. "Why shouldn't young ladies play whatever instrument suits them?"

But Belinda didn't wish to pursue that argument. She was, instead, intrigued by Max's earlier remark. "What instrument," she asked him, "would you have guessed would suit Jan better than the violin?"

Max studied Jan for a moment in speculation (and with what Jan thought was shameless effrontery) and then turned to Belinda. "I should have guessed, my dear, that your cousin's instrument would be the harp."

"The *harp*?" Sir Eustace asked curiously. "Why on earth the harp?"

Lord Liggett, whose high shirtpoints prevented him from turning his head, leaned forward in his chair and coughed for attention. "Because she . . . she looks so an-an-*an*-gelic!" he managed, and sat back in self-satisfied triumph.

The others all laughed, but Max held up his hand. "No, don't laugh," he said. "Lord Liggett has got close to the truth of it. One needn't be angelic, necessarily, to play the harp, but it would suit Miss Hazeldine precisely because of her air of unworldly, rather detached purity. You're her mother, Lady Hazeldine. Don't you agree?"

Lady Hazeldine, who was well aware of the undercurrents of this conversation and its devastating effects on her daughter, fixed him with a cold stare. "Jan doesn't need a harp, my lord," she retorted. "She looks angelic enough with her violin, as you—and Mrs. Kendall, too—would surely agree if ever you'd seen her with it."

Sir Eustace beamed at her. "Well said, your ladyship! Well said!" he cheered. "I'm certain that's true. One day soon you must persuade your daughter to play for us. I'm sure we'll discover that with her violin she both *looks* and *sounds* angelic."

"Here, here!" Lord Liggett chortled.

All eyes turned to Jan, but she merely smiled and shook her head. "My violin is safely at home," she reminded them, "but my cousin's voice is right here. Do get up and sing for us, Belinda, and put an end to this silliness."

Belinda promptly acquiesced. She sat down at the piano and accompanied herself in a lively rendition of "Cherry Ripe." Her voice rang out clear and true, and the merry spirit she infused in the words made her performance all the more attractive. The applause that burst forth when she finished was both fervent and sincere.

"Do *you* sing, Miss Hazeldine?" Jack Grindsley asked, evidently prodded by Lord Liggett to put forth the question.

"Well, no, Mr. Grindsley, not really. The violin takes too much of my time to—"

"Nonsense," her mother said irritably. She did not like seeing her daughter hide herself in the background. "Of *course* you sing. And you can accompany yourself on the pianoforte, too."

Jan stiffened in chagrin. "Please, Mama—" she objected.

"Of course she does," Nettie insisted affectionately. "I've heard her sing many times."

"That was years ago, Aunt," Jan reminded her, unhappily aware that she was behaving stubbornly and that Max was watching her in her predicament with unholy amusement.

"Don't be so missish, Jan," her mother ordered. "Get up and sing for us, do!"

"I'm too old to be missish, Mama," the girl said, gently firm. "It's merely that I haven't sung or played the piano in ages. I'm no longer accustomed—"

"I can accompany you, if you'd like," Sir Eustace offered kindly.

"*Please,* Miss Haz . . . Haz . . ." Lord Liggett began, but meeting her eye, became so overwhelmed with his own temerity that he could go no further.

"Yes, please sing for us, Jan," Belinda begged.

"Come, Miss Hazeldine, say yes," Mary Grindsley chimed in, accompanying her words with her persistent giggle, "or else they'll be asking *me* again, and I can sing no better than a frog."

"I can vouch for the the truth of *that*," her brother Jack said, chuckling.

Mrs. Kendall leaned over to Sir Eustace. "I cannot like young ladies who need so much urging," she whispered loudly enough to be heard all over the room. "Such behavior indicates a surfeit of modesty, don't you agree? The Duke of York once remarked to me that too much modesty in a girl is like too much sugar in tea. It spoils the taste."

"I rather like a lot of sugar in my tea," Sir Eustace said coldly, shifting his chair away from hers and closer to Lady Hazeldine's.

But Jan was in complete agreement with Mrs. Kendall. She, too, didn't like young ladies who enjoyed being repeatedly urged to perform. If she'd had her violin, she would have played without any urging at all. But now she seemed to have little choice. Not wishing to appear more disagreeable than she had already, she sighed in surrender. "Very well, I'll sing something if Sir Eustace will indeed play for me."

"Oh, good!" Mary Grindsley squealed in relief.

"S-S-Splendid!" Lord Liggett cheered.

There was a burst of applause, and they all moved their chairs a little closer to the piano, except for Max, who got up from his chair and unobtrusively edged toward the door. He'd never heard Jan sing and, fearing he would find her voice as captivating as he'd once found her violin playing, decided to leave the room to prevent himself from being subjected to too much emotion.

As she moved to the piano, Jan caught a glimpse of him. It seemed clear to her that he was trying to make an escape without being noticed. She didn't blame him. He'd probably had more than enough of this amateurish musicale. It was the others in the room whom she didn't understand. They were looking up at her with an inexplicable air of hushed expectancy. Was it her reluctance to sing, she wondered, that made them so eager to hear her? *Well,* she thought, *they'll soon discover that my singing is nothing out of the ordinary. Max is quite right to wish to escape.*

Like the near-professional musician that she was, she tried to concentrate on the problem at hand by firmly dismissing Max from her mind. She turned to Sir Eustace, who was already seated on the piano bench, and made a few suggestions of songs that might be in his repertoire. After a brief conference, the song "Youth's the Season Made for Joys," from *The Beggar's Opera*, was agreed upon. Sir Eustace played the introductory bars. Jan took a deep breath and began to sing.

It was a simple ditty, the tune melodiously melancholy and the words bittersweet:

> *Let us drink and sport today,*
> *Ours is not tomorrow,*
> *Love with youth flies swift away,*
> *Age is naught but sorrow . . .*

Jan was too seasoned a performer to let her nervousness show. Her voice, a soft mezzo, flowed out flawlessly, velvety rich, and in deep contrast to the high-pitched sopranos who'd preceded her. It was not a loud, operatic voice, but the timbre was mellow, the pitch was pure and the feeling it expressed was touchingly sincere. At the very first note, the listeners were captivated. Lady Hazeldine leaned back in her chair and shut her eyes, trying not to let her pride show in her face. Nettie, who was not so ignorant of music that she couldn't recognize the lovely quality of her niece's voice, glowed with pleasure. Lord Liggett's mouth hung open in wordless adoration, his friend Jack pressed his clenched fists against his chest in poetic ecstasy, and the four young girls, more admiring than envious, all watched the singer in wide-eyed acknowledgment of the superiority of her performance. Sir Eustace glanced up repeatedly from the keys to steal a look at the face from which these melodious notes were issuing. Even Mrs. Kendall was so much moved, not only by the richness of the singing but by the words of the song, that she had to wipe away a tear from her cheek. And Max, just as he'd feared, was caught at the threshold as if by a rope, and he couldn't go another step. He turned reluctantly and stood leaning on the doorjamb, his eyes riveted on the singer, unable to tear himself away.

As Jan began the last few lines,

> *Time's on the wing,*
> *So dance and sing,*
> *In life there's no return of spring*

she caught sight of Max's face. He was looking at her with that expression she remembered so well—exactly the same mesmerized look he'd had when he'd first seen her play the violin all those years ago. Her heart constricted in her chest, and her throat tensed. Sir Eustace, hearing her voice falter, covered up for her by playing the ending chords loudly. It was fortunate that he did so, for at the words ''no return'' her voice cracked, her breath utterly failed her, and she could not sing the last two notes at all.

Fifteen

THE DAY AFTER the dinner party the sun reappeared. Jan, still shaken by the experience of the night before, asked to be excused from accompanying her mother to the Pump Room. She spent the morning playing her violin, but she didn't concentrate on the music. Her mind was occupied with trying to find answers to a number of questions that had loomed up in her consciousness since last evening. For example, she couldn't understand why Max seemed to take such pleasure from the enactment of their little subterfuge when he'd been so vehemently opposed to the subterfuge at first. Was it because he was still the rash, brazen rake he used to be and relished taunting her?

Her own behavior was a puzzle, too. In some deep, secret part of her, she relished the game they were playing just as much as he. But if she had any character at all, she should keep him at arm's length. She had no business engaging in flirtatious little games with him.

But there was a question that nagged at her with more insistence than the rest. All night she'd asked it of herself, and all morning, too: what was the meaning of the look on his face when she sang? Was it possible that he still loved her? And if he did, didn't that mean he was being unfaithful to Belinda in his heart?

Hours passed, but no answers came. Even playing her fiddle did little to soothe her. Finally Jan gave up and wandered idly down the stairs, looking for something else to distract her mind. She'd almost reached the bottom of the stairway when her mother strolled in the door. "Ah, Jan, my love, there you are! My dear, you will not *credit* how you were missed this morning. All of Nettie's dinner guests sought me out to ask for you."

"Did they? Why?"

"They all wanted to compliment you in person on your performance last evening."

"Compliment me?" Jan frowned at her mother in disbelief. "Why should they want to do that? My performance was dreadful. An embarrassment. I want nothing more than to forget it."

Celia Hazeldine paused in the act of removing her gloves. "What nonsense! Your performance was superb."

"*Superb?* I couldn't even finish!"

"If you're speaking of that little stumble at the end of your song, you're being much too critical of yourself," her mother declared, taking off her bonnet and placing it, with her gloves, on a side table. "Even Sir Eustace, who, as you know, is a fine musician with excellent taste, found your singing admirable. He said he preferred your voice to Madame Rinaldi's by far. *By far* were his very words."

"Sir Eustace was being polite, Mama. If it weren't for his quick support of me in those last notes, I wouldn't have been able to hold my head up."

"By the time you reached those last notes, you goose, everyone was so enchanted with your singing that the little falter didn't matter."

Jan shook her head ruefully. "It mattered to me."

Lady Hazeldine waved the remark away with a cheerfully dismissive gesture of her hand and slipped an arm about her daughter's waist. "Stop talking fustian, and let's have a bite of luncheon. I have news that will cheer you up considerably." She guided the girl toward the dining room. "Jan, my love, you'll never believe who's just arrived in Bath!"

"Who?" Jan asked with only dutiful interest.

"Someone of your acquaintance," her mother taunted.

"Someone of *my* . . . ?" She gaped at her mother in sudden surprise. "Good heavens, it's not . . . ! Can it be *Harriet*?"

Celia Hazeldine paused in the act of ringing for Beale and threw a mock frown at her daughter for spoiling her surprise. "However did you guess?"

"Because it was I who asked her to come." The news gave Jan's spirits a decided lift. "But why didn't she answer my letter? Where is she? Isn't she staying with us?"

"No, because Lady Coombe and her brother and sister are all with her."

"Oh, dear," Jan muttered. "I didn't count on William. *That* addition to our circle could prove irksome. Where are they all staying?"

"With an elderly aunt of Lady Coombe's on Lansdown Road. Harriet said to tell you that they'd planned to come even before she received your letter, so she didn't write, hoping to surprise you."

"Well, I *am* surprised. I hoped she'd come, of course, but I never expected her to be here so soon."

Beale presented himself at the dining room door at that moment. Lady Hazeldine put aside the subject of Harriet while she informed the butler that they were ready for luncheon. And in the bustle of seating themselves at the table and starting on their soup, the matter slipped her mind. But when the light luncheon was almost over, she remembered that she'd had a question to ask. She looked over at her daughter curiously. "Why on earth did you invite Harriet to come, Jan? Were you afraid you'd be short of company in this overcrowded town?"

"No, that's not it, although I shall certainly relish the companionship. I have an ulterior purpose in getting her here. I'm taking on myself a role that *you* love to play, Mama: acting as matchmaker."

"Matchmaker?" Lady Hazeldine lifted her brows. "For Harriet?"

"Yes. You mustn't breathe a word of this, Mama, for it will spoil everything, but I think Sir Eustace Merriot would be perfect for her."

Lady Hazeldine froze in the act of lifting her teacup to her lips. "Sir *Eustace*?"

"Yes, who else? Why are you so surprised, Mama? They

have so much in common, don't you think so? The sweetness of their characters, their love of music—''

"That's ridiculous," her mother snapped, putting down her cup and rising magisterially from her chair. "They won't suit at all. If he's too old for you, he's too old for her."

Jan was taken aback by her mother's tone. "I never said he was too old for me," she said defensively. "*You* did."

"Well, he *is*," her ladyship said curtly, adding as she strode out of the room, "and to consider him right for Harriet is the silliest thing I've ever heard!"

But Jan did not take her mother's objection to heart. It made no sense. She'd heard of many ladies approaching thirty who were *glad* to wed men in their late forties. Even if Sir Eustace were as old as fifty, the match would not be considered strange. Age was not the most important consideration; personalities were. And if the two personalities in question made a good blending, the difference in their ages was not so terribly important.

Barely an hour later, Harriet herself came to call. The two friends greeted each other with delight, but since they'd seen each other in London less than a fortnight before, the reunion needed no protracted conversation to bring them up to date. Once Jan recognized that Harriet was wearing an elegant new red-and-blue-striped spencer and expressed enthusiastic admiration for it, and Harriet made a similar to-do over the charm of Jan's deeply flounced green cambric walking dress, they felt they'd bridged their brief separation.

Harriet, eager to explore her new environs, urged Jan to take a walk with her. Jan asked her mother to join them, but Lady Hazeldine, still apparently disgruntled, told them to go off on their own. "I'll see you at the Pump Room later," she said with unaccustomed brusqueness.

The afternoon was crisp and bright, with fat little clouds scudding across a sapphire sky. The two young women linked arms under Jan's green parasol and set out. The air was fragrant with the scent of lilac, and the spring breezes tugged deliciously at the flounces of their skirts and loosened little tendrils of hair round their faces. As they strolled past the Parade Gardens and across the Avon via the North Parade

Road, they talked animatedly. But in all the conversation Jan did not mention Sir Eustace to her friend. She did not want Harriet to suspect her of engaging in matchmaking plots; she hoped that they would run into Sir Eustace later in the Pump Room, where she'd be able to introduce them with innocent nonchalance. The prospect made her smile inwardly. Playing matchmaker, she decided, was going to be fun.

But there was something else she had to tell Harriet; her friend had to be warned about Max. Harriet, of all people, would remember her brief liaison with Max, for Harriet had been privy to the romance from the first. Although Jan had not told her friend the reason for the end of it, she knew that Harriet suspected something of the residual effects. Harriet had many times hinted that she was aware that Jan had not forgotten Max. It would be best, therefore, to inform Harriet of the identity of Belinda's betrothed. Otherwise Harriet might be taken so greatly by surprise that she might blurt out the very secret that Jan and Max were trying to keep hidden.

Just as she was about to launch into the subject, however, she and Harriet turned onto Pulteney Road and came face to face with Sir Eustace. Jan could hardly believe her luck! Here was her opportunity to make him known to her friend in the most comfortable, casual manner. She introduced Harriet to the Baronet with well-concealed excitement. Sir Eustace made his bow, Harriet her curtsy (stumbling over her feet in her typically awkward style), and the deed was done.

The Baronet seemed perfectly willing to linger, so Jan asked if he were free to walk with them. "We're going to the Pump Room," she explained, "but we're going to take the long way round so that Miss Coombe may see some of the sights."

The Baronet cheerfully offered his escort, and they proceeded up toward Sydney Place. Harriet tripped only twice, and each time Sir Eustace caught her arm and kept her from falling. He did it with such ease that the incidents were barely noticeable.

By the time they were ready to turn down Great Pulteney Street and recross the river, their conversation had become delightfully companiable. They'd progressed from remarks about the weather to comments on the scenery and finally to their common interest in music. Jan was in transports about how well her matchmaking scheme was developing.

When they finally entered the Pump Room, they were conversing like old friends. Jan felt encouraged enough about their ability to converse with each other to leave them on their own. Murmuring that she wanted to find her mother, she excused herself and left them to fall in love.

She found her mother seated near the pump among a small circle of ladies. Lady Hazeldine, on her arrival at the Pump Room with Nettie earlier, had discovered Lady Coombe and Harriet's elder sister Mariella trying out the waters and had introduced them to her sister. Now the four of them were chatting amiably together, exchanging stories they'd heard about the miraculous cures (and notable failures) of the fabled but ill-tasting water they were sipping. Jan kissed both of the new arrivals and took a place beside her aunt, peeping only occasionally over her shoulder to see how Sir Eustace and Harriet were progressing. After a while, however, as the afternoon crowd increased in number, she could barely see the pair through the press of people parading about the room. Meanwhile, William Coombe (who'd been wandering about on his own, boldly appraising through his quizzing glass all the young ladies who sauntered by) discovered that Jan had joined his mother's group and, to Jan's annoyance, promptly attached himself to her. "You should be proud of yourself, ma'am," he whispered in her ear with obnoxious fatuousness. "You're the reason I deigned to accompany my family to this retreat for the elderly."

"I?" Jan asked with upraised brows.

"Yes, you. I'm only here because Harry said *you* were here."

"I don't see why my presence here should have had any effect at all on your decision to come," Jan said flatly, not wishing to give him the slightest encouragement.

"Come now, Jan, in this last refuge of the old, the halt and the lame, you must be grateful for any lively company. You're glad to see me, you know you are. Admit it."

Jan glared at him. For years now, because of his refusal to

take her rejection of him seriously, she'd been put to the necessity of repeatedly cutting down the fellow's pretensions. She was quite tired of it. "I am very fond of Bath," she muttered in a cold undervoice, hoping that none of the others sitting in the circle were paying any heed to them, "but even if Bath *were* as you describe it, William Coombe, I would not find your presence here a welcome addi—"

"Jan, my dear," Lady Coombe cut in, "where have you hidden my Harriet?"

"I left her in the care of one of my friends," Jan said, jumping up from her chair. "I'll be glad to find her, your ladyship, and bring her to you."

"I'll go with you," William Coombe offered, starting up from his seat.

"Thank you, William, but that's not necessary," Jan said, firmly pushing him back on his seat by pressing down on his shoulder. "I know just where she is."

William had no choice but to subside in defeat as Jan swept off in a whirl of her ruffled skirts. She found Harriet just where she'd left her, but Sir Eustace was gone. In his place were the Brett sisters and Lord Liggett. The Brett girls were chatting animatedly to her about the evening's schedule at the Upper Rooms, but Jan could see that Harriet looked upset. "Harry, my dear," Jan greeted, "I see you've found some new acquaintances."

Lord Liggett jumped to his feet, reddening with pleasure at the sight of her. "Miss Haz . . . Haz . . ." he began, stuttering in his eagerness.

"Good afternoon, Miss Hazeldine," one of the Misses Brett said with a welcoming smile.

"Sir Eustace introduced us to your friend," the other Miss Brett explained.

"Yes, I surmised as much," Jan said. "But I'm afraid I must take Miss Coombe away from you." She took her friend's hand and urged her to her feet. "Come, Harry. Your mother is asking for you."

Harriet bid them a rather dazed good-bye and, clutching Jan's arm tightly, walked off with her. "Good heavens, Jan," she exclaimed in a hissing whisper, "wherever did you go for so long?"

"Was I long? I'm sorry, dear. But I thought I'd left you in good hands. What's happened to—"

"Why didn't you *tell* me, you mawworm?" Harriet demanded accusingly.

"Tell you? About these youngsters you just met? I will, my dear, of course. But first I want to know where Sir Eus—"

"Not about those idiots you found me sitting with!" Harriet interrupted impatiently. "About Lord *Ollenshaw*!"

Jan stopped in her tracks. "Ollenshaw? How did you hear—"

"I *met* him! It was a dreadful shock, I can tell you."

"Met him? Here? Good God!" She peered at Harriet in alarm. "You didn't . . . Heavens, Harry, you didn't *speak* to each other, did you?"

"Not exactly. It was a most peculiar encounter. Your friend—what's his name? You know whom I mean: the Baronet you left me with. Well, he introduced me to your cousin, Belinda Briarly, and *she* introduced me to her betrothed. I declare, Jan, I could have fainted on the spot when I saw who it was! But Ollenshaw himself was as cool as ice. 'I believe Miss Coombe and I have met before,' he said. Then he bowed over my hand and winked. I don't know what he meant by it, but I followed his lead. I merely said, 'Yes, I believe we have.' And then, before the conversation could proceed, they went off somewhere and left me with those three."

Jan expelled a relieved breath. "Good for you, Harry. You did very well."

"Did I? I'm happy to hear it, but dash it all, Jan, what is all this about? Is Ollenshaw to marry your *cousin*? Why didn't you *tell* me?"

"I was about to tell you this afternoon, but we met Sir Eustace before I had the chance. I shall confide it all, I promise. But first, my dear, you must tell me what's become of Sir Eustace. Where has he gone?"

"I don't know. As soon as your cousin's friends surrounded us, he made his excuses and left."

Jan felt a surge of disappointment. "I suppose he had an appointment," she mumbled, trying to keep her matchmaking hopes alive in spite of what seemed to be a decided set-back. "But tell me, Harry, what did you think of him?"

Harriet shrugged. "Of your friend, the Baronet?" she asked with complete indifference. "A very pleasant gentle-man. Very pleasant. But if you don't mind, I'd rather talk about something more interesting. What on earth is going on between you and Ollenshaw?"

Sixteen

HARRIET'S INDIFFERENCE TO Sir Eustace did not change in the next few days. Nor could Jan discover in Sir Eustace anything but mere polite interest in Harriet. Jan wondered what could possibly be wrong. Harriet was certainly young enough for the Baronet, quite pretty and musically very talented. And he was wise, gentle, reliable and even witty. Why weren't the sparks igniting between those two?

Sir Eustace continued to escort Lady Hazeldine and Jan to the Upper Rooms and to other social gatherings at which Harriet often joined them, but Jan could never discover any particular desire in either one of the pair for the companionship of the other. It wasn't that the Baronet was taken with Jan herself, for there were no signs of an infatuation in that direction. He obviously enjoyed her company, but he treated her more as a friend than a suitor. When Jan left his side, he seemed to prefer to spend his evenings sitting alongside Lady Hazeldine and the other dowagers rather than to bestir himself to seek out Harriet. And Harriet, for her part, seemed perfectly content to exchange foolish chatter with Belinda's set rather than to discuss something serious, like music, with Sir Eustace. It was a source of frustration to Jan. She began to believe that her mother had been right; she had no talent for matchmaking.

Meanwhile, her own problems were not solving themselves either. Jan saw Max almost every day, and every day her unhappiness grew. Max's mere presence in Bath made her feel tense. To some people, the presence of a little tension in their lives was as invigorating and necessary as oxygen in their lungs, but to Jan the tension was more like alcohol than oxygen—it caused profound disturbances in her blood. She had counted on peace and tranquillity here in Bath, but she was finding, instead, conflict and unease.

Every day another incident occurred to cause her pain. A typical case occurred one afternoon a few days after Harriet's arrival. Jan and her mother were crossing High Street on their way back from a call on the Coombes when they came upon Nettie Briarly, walking toward the Pump Room with Max and Belinda. After the appropriate greetings were exchanged, Nettie cheerfully informed them that her daughter and Max were merely seeing her to the Pump Room door, after which they intended to go off on their own pursuits. She then turned to her sister. "Why don't you join me, Cecy," she suggested, "and let Jan go off with Belinda and Max?"

"Oh, yes! Do come with us, Jan," Belinda begged with what was obviously a sincere desire for her cousin's company rather than mere politeness.

But Jan had no wish to intrude on the couple. "No, thank you, Belinda, though it was kind of you to ask. 'Two's company, three's none,' as the old saying goes."

"Oh, you needn't be afraid of being *de trop*," Belinda assured her. "We are off to meet Lord Liggett and the Bretts."

"They are only going to stroll through Sydney Gardens," Nettie explained.

"Yes," Belinda said. "It promises to be very pleasant. We shall even attempt to make our way through the maze."

"Thank you, Belinda, my dear," Jan said, still adamant, "but I'm much too old to find it amusing to go lurching through the maze."

Max snorted. "If *you* are too old for it, ma'am, what shall you say about *me*?" he asked dryly. "Surely you know that I'm several years your senior."

"How would I know that, my lord?" Jan asked, frowning at him warningly.

"It is obvious to anyone with eyes." He threw her a teasing grin, proclaiming clearly that he had no intention of heed-ing her warning. "You look a mere girl, while I—as *someone* pointed out to me just the other day—am becoming an old codger with gray in my hair."

"Old codger, indeed!" Belinda said, bristling. "The gray in your hair is the merest touch, and quite attractive, if you ask me. Isn't it attractive, Jan?"

Jan felt herself redden. "Lord Ollenshaw does not need my approbation of his looks when he has such an enthusiastic spokesman as you, Belinda, to speak up in his behalf."

Max was amused at her discomfiture. "But that still doesn't explain, Miss Hazeldine, why you are too old for the maze while I am not."

"You, my lord," Jan retorted, "are a sportsman, kept young by your insatiable love of games. You'll probably make a sport of going through the maze, competing vigorously to see which one of the party will make it to the exit in the shortest time, or some such thing."

"You are implying, of course," he taunted, "that a love of games is not keeping me young, as my gray hairs prove, but keeping me childish."

"I did not imply anything of the sort," Jan declared defensively. "How can you find that in what I said?"

"The fact that you are 'much too old' to go through the maze makes it implicit that I, who am years older, must be acting childishly if I choose to 'lurch my way' through it."

"I think," Nettie interjected in her inevitably cheerful style, "that you are both quibbling about nothing. People of *any* age can enjoy walking through the maze, although I, I admit, do not do it for fear of losing myself in the byways forever."

"Come along with us, Jan," Belinda entreated. "You needn't go through the maze if you don't wish to."

"Yes, for goodness sake, go!" Celia Hazeldine ordered. "An afternoon in the fresh air will do you good."

"But, Mama," Jan objected, trying, by a glance of desperation, to indicate to her mother her dislike of the project, "you will wish for my company on the walk home, won't you?"

"Not at all," her mother answered, ignoring the hint. "I'll go to the Pump Room with Nettie."

Nettie propelled Jan to Max's side and pushed her arm in his. "Go along with the young folk, my dearest girl, and don't give us another thought."

Thus, a short while later, Jan found herself in the park, walking between the two indistinguishable Brett girls, while Max and Belinda paraded in cozy intimacy in front of her and the smitten Lord Liggett (not having the courage to insert himself between either of the Bretts to take Jan's arm) trotted along behind.

The Brett girls carried on a lively discussion about the color of Liggy's waistcoat, one of them asserting it was Copenhagen blue, while the other insisted it was Delft. This required a great deal of looking back over their shoulders at Liggy and giggling, which made the young lord utterly discomfited. At last, to settle the argument, the Brett girls turned to Jan and asked her to make the final judgment. "I am no expert in these matters," Jan replied. "My eye hasn't been trained for such fine color discriminations."

The Miss Brett on her right nodded understandingly. "I have heard," she said kindly, "that when one develops one of the senses, like an ear for music, the other senses may be neglected."

"Yes," agreed the other. "One can't expect a person to have both a musical ear *and* an artistic eye. Don't you agree, Liggy?"

"The f-fact is," Lord Liggett said, his face reddening in his excruciating effort to speak, "that M-Miss Hazeldine is gif-gif-*gifted*! The rest of us ha-have—" here he paused to fill his lungs with air, and then spilled out the rest of his sentence on one breath "—have no such gifts in *any* of our s-senses!"

"Hear, hear!" Max cheered, turning round and grinning at Lord Liggett approvingly. Not only did his approbation make Liggy blush with pride, but it made Jan's pulse quicken, for it proved that Max had not been as absorbed in a tête-à-tête with Belinda as she'd thought. He'd been listening, at least with one ear, to the conversation behind him.

When they arrived at the maze (an intricate labyrinth of passageways edged by impenetrable hedges six feet high), Jan repeated her assertion that she had no wish to walk through it. Liggy at once offered to remain outside with her, but Max would have none of it. "I must be the one to remain outside," he declared, "if only to prove to Miss Hazeldine that I am not so childish as she supposes."

Jan wanted nothing more than to wring his neck. "I don't think you at all childish to wish to keep your betrothed company in this adventure," she said, smiling at him so broadly that she was sure he'd recognize the meaning behind it. "I wouldn't *dream*, my lord, of keeping you from her side."

"Oh, pooh!" Belinda said with the indifference that comes from supreme self-confidence. "Max may stay out with you if he wishes. I can see that a run through the maze might be considered somewhat childish, but I like being childish sometimes. Do stay out here with Jan, Max. Liggy will be a more than adequate escort. You'll see us through the labyrinth, won't you, Liggy?"

Without further ado, Belinda took Liggy's right arm and the Bretts his left, and the poor young lord was dragged, willy-nilly, into the maze. When they were out of sight, Jan looked at Max worriedly. "You are skirting danger, Max. Do you *want* to give our secret away?"

"You're being much too uneasy, my dear," he assured her. "Nothing I've said or done has given anyone the least suspicion."

She turned away in disgust. "I think you are making a game of this, as you make a game of everything."

"It's one way of seeing life, Jan. Sometimes I think all of life is a game. I'm beginning to realize that you take life much too seriously."

She shook her head. "I don't know of any other way to take it. But I'm too upset to wish to philosophize just now. Besides, you are using your Corinthian philosophy as an evasion, to keep from explaining your actions. I want to understand your motives." She fixed her eyes on him accusingly.

"You purposely maneuvered the situation just now in order to stay out here with me. Why, Max? Didn't I make it clear that it was not at all necessary?"

"Not necessary to you, perhaps, but it was to me. Did you think I'd *enjoy* shepherding three giggling prattleboxes through the labyrinth? I was anticipating the whole experience with dread. You provided me with an irreproachable excuse to extricate myself."

Jan frowned at him. "You evidently enjoyed the company of *one* of the 'three giggling prattleboxes' enough to become affianced to her." She couldn't resist pointing this out, although she knew she had no right in the world to criticize or question his choice of a bride.

"Yes, so I did," Max responded with easy assurance, his manner showing no sign of having taken offense at her question, "but Belinda does not giggle nor prattle so much in my company as she does in the company of her friends."

"I see. I am much relieved to hear it, for the sake of your future happiness."

His right eyebrow rose questioningly. "Why, ma'am, are you concerned for my future happiness now, when it is *not* your affair, while you gave it no concern eight years ago, when it *was*."

Her eyes fell. "I'm sorry, Max. I had no right to . . . to say what I did. But I've always been concerned for your happiness, even when . . . even when—"

"Even when you were in the process of destroying it?" he supplied dryly.

She lifted her chin in quick anger. "In my view, it was quite the other way round, my lord. You destroyed mine."

Max stared at her, his heart clenching inside his chest like a fist. Until this moment, he *had* been playing a game. Jan's presence here in Bath had added zest to what had been, until she came, a very dull stay for him. Max had little in common with Belinda's circle in Bath, and he'd been enduring it only because it would have been unbecoming in a soon-to-be-bridegroom to keep running back to London (as he'd done once or twice before) as if he wished to escape from his bride-to-be. Therefore he'd indulged himself in twitting Jan, first because he enjoyed it, and second because he did not think the consequences would be in any way significant. He was safely and irretrievably betrothed, after all, and Jan, who had had so many suitors in the past eight years that she couldn't possibly retain any serious feelings toward him, would be, he thought, quite unaffected by his teasing. But she'd just declared that he had destroyed her happiness. He could hardly believe his ears. "*Did* I destroy your happiness, Jan?" he asked softly. "I never thought—"

She wheeled on him. "Never *thought*? Did you think I faced the severance of our . . . our ties with *indifference*?"

"Well, you've broken ties with so many. After a while I came to assume it was your nature to break ties."

"Yes, of course," she said coldly. "Ice-Maiden Hazeldine."

"I am not the one who named you that," he reminded her. "But, if, as you now seem to be claiming, you were not indifferent to our . . . ties, then why did you break them at all?"

"You seem to be forgetting, my lord, that you gave me ample cause."

"A cause trumped up in your own mind, ma'am," he snapped, reacting with his habitual anger to the old accusation.

She tensed, girding her loins for a riposte, but before she uttered a word, she stopped herself. "What are we doing?" she asked, putting up a hand as if the simple gesture might keep their unquiet past from invading the present. "There is no point in going round and round the old circles."

"No," he agreed sourly. "No point at all."

"This is just the sort of thing I was warning you about at this start of this . . . this exchange. We shouldn't allow ourselves to indulge in this sort of thing. It would have been awkward indeed if Belinda had emerged from the maze and found us at each other's throats."

"You're right, ma'am. I shall endeavor to behave myself in a more seemly fashion in future." He forced himself to smile down at her. "Since our party shall be at least another half hour in the maze, ma'am, do you think it would be seemly to take a stroll?''

"Yes, I suppose there can be nothing amiss about a little stroll, so long as we remember to behave like near-strangers.''

"You have my word." His lips curled up wryly at the corners. "May a near-stranger offer his arm?''

She couldn't resist smiling back at him. "Yes, of course,'' she said, tucking her arm in his. But the mere pressure of his arm sent her pulse racing, and, as if in response, a shiver ran right up his arm. "Oh, dear,'' she muttered in embarrassed acknowledgment of the tingle they both felt.

"You'll have to blame my arm, ma'am,'' he apologized. "It acts on its own. I'm afraid that there are parts of us that refuse to be strangers.''

"So it seems,'' Jan admitted unhappily. "Oh, Max, what a *muddle* we are in!''

Seventeen

JAN'S TENSION AND unhappiness were heightened markedly by two events that occurred the very next day. The first came to pass when Lady Hazeldine received word that her sister was not feeling well enough to walk out to the Pump Room. She and Jan decided to pay a call on the ailing Nettie. By the time they arrived, however, Nettie had already improved. That morning, she explained, she'd suffered a very queasy stomach, but after taking a dose of calomel dissolved in hot lemon water (her favorite remedy when the Bath waters failed her) and resting in bed until noon, she'd begun to feel better. She was now sitting up and taking nourishment. Lady Hazeldine and Jan couldn't help noticing, however, that now it was Belinda who was feeling upset.

Under her aunt's questioning, Belinda admitted that she was nervous about Max, whom she'd been expecting since noon. "He promised to drive me to Bradford-on-Avon, you see," she explained nervously. "I told him I'd like to shop for that special cloth they manufacture there. But he's now more than two hours late!" Max had never before kept her waiting, and the girl was convinced that a dreadful accident had befallen him.

When Max finally did arrive (with sincere apologies for the delay, caused by a broken wheel on his curricle), Belinda threw herself into his arms with such charmingly tearful relief that Jan was quite moved. Belinda sincerely loved her Max. That fact was as plain as pikestaff. And it was also plain that Max responded with equal affection. From the moment he arrived, he took nothing but the most distantly polite notice of Jan, but he soothed the weeping Belinda by gathering her gently into his arms and murmuring comforting words into her ear. By the time he ushered her out to his waiting carriage, Belinda was radiant. This time she did not ask Jan to join them.

Jan was so beset with jealous longings that she almost couldn't bear it. She hadn't realized until this moment how weak her character had become. If anyone had told her, even yesterday, that she could be so jealous of her cousin that it was like an ulcer in her stomach, she would have denied it vehemently. She had to do something to end this torture. "Mama," she begged when she and Lady Hazeldine left the Briarly house, "can we not cut this visit short and go back to London?"

"I don't see how we can," Lady Hazeldine responded, not unsympathetically. Ever since her discovery of her daughter's secret, she'd kept a close eye on Jan. She knew, more than her daughter imagined, how much the girl was suffering. And her heart ached for her daughter. But her ladyship believed that the suffering would not be assuaged by a return to town. She'd thought the matter over carefully, and she'd decided that it would be better for Jan to see with her own eyes that Max was beyond reach. She hoped that Jan, by observing the betrothed couple daily, would grow accustomed to the fact of their betrothal and become hardened to it. Sighing inwardly, she took her daughter's hand and squeezed it comfortingly. "Nettie is making so many plans," she said temporizing. "It would hurt her if we departed now."

"Yes, I suppose it would," Jan admitted. "But when—"

"In another week, after the ball Mrs. Kendall is giving for Belinda, I shall drop a few hints to Nettie that we are thinking of leaving for home. If she takes the suggestion with good grace, we can make arrangements."

"Very well, Mama," the girl said glumly.

Lady Hazeldine released her daughter's hand and took her arm in an affectionate hold. "Come, my love, let's stroll up Milsom Street. A little shopping will cheer us both. Perhaps

we can find a proper pair of evening gloves for you. The pair
you brought with you is showing its age."

Jan listlessly agreed, and they walked slowly in the direction of the street where the best shops in Bath were found.
In due time the gloves were purchased, as well as a length of
lace for the ruff of Lady Hazeldine's new roundgown. "And
now the milliner's," her ladyship suggested with a forced
vivacity. "Not that you or I stand in need of new bonnets,
but it's always cheering to try them on. It's just a little way
up the hill."

"You go ahead, Mama," Jan said. "I'd like to stop in at
Duffield's."

"Duffield's?"

"Are you not familiar with Duffield's, Mama? It's the cir-
culating library across the street."

"Ah, yes. Of course. But don't loll about there forever,
my dear. I'll be waiting for you."

The ladies separated, and Jan spent a pleasant quarter hour
browsing through Duffield's excellently stocked bookshelves.
She finally selected a recently published novel by Sir Walter
Scott, called *Old Mortality*, and the most recent of Miss Burney's works, *The Wanderer*. With these in hand, she crossed
back to the other side of Milsom Street and started up the hill
after her mother. She had not gone ten steps, however, when
her eye was caught by a woman a few yards ahead of her.
The woman was stylishly dressed in a bishop's-purple jaconet
gown with very full sleeves and a coal-scuttle bonnet of such
height as to call immediate attention to itself. But it was not
the bonnet that riveted Jan's eye. It was the dyed-red hair that
she glimpsed beneath it.

No, no, it couldn't be, she told herself. *It is a mere coincidence. There must be hundreds—perhaps thousands—of
women in England with dyed-red hair.* But her heart began to
pound in her chest, and her knees almost buckled beneath
her. The woman's form, the way she walked with that provocative swing of the hips, the flagrant stylishness of her
clothes, all were reminiscent of that repugnant creature—what
was her name?—Lady Redmore. No, Wedmore.

But Jan knew she was being ridiculous. *Jan Hazeldine,* she

scolded herself firmly, *get a grip on yourself!* Max would not bring his inamorata—even if, after all this time, she still was his inamorata—with him to Bath. Even *he* would not be so dastardly. She would not let herself indulge in such repulsive imaginings. She was seeing the woman from the back, after all. Just because she'd caught a glimpse of red hair . . .

Unable to stop herself, however, she hastened her step, hoping to catch up with the woman in front of her. She was quite conscious of the baseness of her thoughts and the indelicacy of her behavior, but she couldn't help it. A quick glance at the woman's face was absolutely necessary for her peace of mind. If the woman was *not* Lady Wedmore—and Jan was almost certain that it couldn't be—she would be reassured. Humiliated, but reassured.

She had almost caught up with her when the woman stopped to glance into the window of the linendraper's shop they were passing. Jan was very much afraid she would see nothing but the woman's back. But just as Jan drew up to her, the woman turned. Jan found herself face to face with the creature. There was no mistaking who it was. Jan was staring into the ice blue eyes of Lady Wedmore.

Good lord! she thought, *what ought I do now?* Should she utter a how-do-you-do? Should she give the lady a cut direct? Should she merely nod and pass on? But before she could make a choice of action, Lady Wedmore solved the problem for her. She cast Jan a cold but utterly indifferent glance, turned and continued strolling up the hill. There had not been an iota of recognition in her eyes. Although she had seen Jan twice before—and on occasions of significant embarrassment—Jan's face had not made any impression on her.

Jan stared after her, trembling. Lady Wedmore might have no recollection of her, but for Jan it was quite the reverse. That face, those cold eyes, that dyed-red hair were ineradicably impressed on her memory. And though the detestable woman was able to walk away from this encounter without the slightest perturbation, what was left of Jan's peace of mind was now completely destroyed. Revolting as the thought was, it was plain that Max had brought the creature here. Jan had begun to believe that he'd really changed, that he'd become the mature, sensible, responsible, *faithful* man she'd always wanted him to be. But here was the evidence that he was still the lustful rake he'd always been. Tears filled her eyes, and an old, familiar ache tightened her chest. *Not again!* a voice inside her wailed. *It isn't fair to have to go through this again when he's not even mine!*

With her spirits at their lowest ebb since her arrival, she clenched her fists and forced herself to make her way up the hill to the milliner's. It was necessary to control her emotions in order to face her mother with reasonable calm. And she had to be calm; she didn't want to reveal by so much as a sigh that anything untoward had happened.

But indeed it *wasn't* fair that fate had put her to this torment a second time. Not only was she forced to face this renewed evidence of Max's licentiousness, but she had to decide if she ought to *do* something about it. *Dash it all,* she thought miserably, *now I must truly face the most difficult question of all: Must I tell Belinda?*

Eighteen

A GOOD NUMBER of the inhabitants of Bath were already parading round the Pump Room when the Hazeldine ladies arrived there the next morning. The room resounded with cheerful noise. The voices of the patrons, mixing with the strains of the orchestra (seated in the musicians' gallery at the west end of the room, where they were playing a spirited rendition of a Bononcini gavotte) reverberated from the walls and the high ceiling. But Jan, befogged from the effects of a sleepless night, found the clamor dispiriting.

Hiding her unhappiness behind a forced smile, she left her mother to sip the waters in the company of Aunt Nettie, while she joined Harriet, who was seated with Lord Liggett near the Tompion clock. Harriet was questioning his lordship about places of interest in the vicinity of Bath. "Have you heard that there are caves nearby, Liggy?" she asked. "I would dearly love to explore a cave."

"Oh, y-yes," the stammerer replied, all the while casting glances of doglike adoration in Jan's direction. "W-Wookey Ho . . . Ho . . . Hole."

"Wookey Hole? Where is that?"

"Just twen . . . twen . . ." The poor fellow reddened apoplectically in his effort to respond, but the harder he tried the more difficult it was for him to get the words out.

"See here, Liggy," Harriet said kindly, "there's no need to strain yourself so. Not on my account, anyway. I've plenty of time."

"Time?" Lord Liggett echoed, not understanding her meaning.

"Yes. I think you're in so great a hurry to speak that you push too hard. Take a deep breath and tell me slowly. As I said, I've plenty of time."

Lord Liggett pulled at his elegantly tied neckcloth and, as she suggested, breathed deeply. "Caves at Woo . . . Woo . . ."

"Slowly now, Liggy, old fellow," Harriet reminded him, patting his hand encouragingly. "Wookey Hole. There are caves there. I understood that. Is it far from here?"

Lord Liggett shook his head. "Only twen . . . twenty-two miles. South. No more than a two . . . two-hour ride." He sighed in relief at having managed the reply.

Harriet beamed at him. "There, now, that was splendid. Wasn't it splendid, Jan?"

"Yes, it was," Jan agreed, also smiling at the fellow's boyish pride in his accomplishment. "Splendid."

"We should go to Wookey Hole," his lordship ventured, enunciating slowly. "Outing."

"An outing?" Harriet's eyes widened. "That's a marvelous idea, Liggy! An outing to see the caves! Let's arrange it at once! And you, Liggy, must help me." She jumped eagerly to her feet as she spoke, but because she was looking back at Liggy and talking at the same time, she tripped over her feet and pitched forward clumsily. She would have fallen flat on her face had Lord Liggett not leapt up and caught her in his arms in the nick of time.

Harriet clutched his neck tightly. "Oh, *Liggy!*" she gasped gratefully.

Jan jumped up, too. "That was very quick thinking, my lord," she said in sincere admiration as she took Harriet's arm and assisted Lord Liggett in setting the girl on her feet.

Lord Liggett reddened in pride. "It was n-n-nothing," he mumbled happily. To have earned Miss Hazeldine's admiration was his idea of bliss.

Harriet, once upright, did not give another thought to her little pratfall. She had no intention of permitting the slight (and, to her, commonplace) stumble to deter her from her goal. As soon as she'd regained her equilibrium, she sent

Lord Liggett off to enlist those of his friends who might be interested in joining them in their outing, while she and Jan, aware that no expedition could be launched without parental consent, went looking for their mothers. Fortunately, they found them sitting together near the pump. Lady Hazeldine and her sister had been joined not only by Lady Coombe and Mariella, but by Mrs. Kendall and Sir Eustace. Harriet announced without preamble that she'd come seeking her mother's permission to organize a trip to the caves at Wookey Hole.

"Very well, my dear," Lady Coombe said indifferently, "so long as there isn't any expense involved."

"But Lady Coombe," Nettie objected in horror, "you can't be serious. *Caves?*"

"Heavens, Lady Briarly, there's nothing wrong with caves," Harriet argued, and she launched into a heartfelt defense of her plan. She had not gone very far, however, when Lord Liggett arrived with Belinda, the Brett girls, and Jack and Mary Grindsley in tow. They'd all been informed of the purpose of the gathering, but not everyone was enthusiastic about the idea. "Caves?" Belinda said with a shudder quite like her mother's. "I'd be much too fearful to step inside them. If we have an excursion, it should be to someplace above ground."

"Rubbish!" declared young Jack, tossing his head so violently that his tousled Byronic locks bounced. "Nothing so very frightening about caves."

"Except the dark," Lord Liggett pointed out. "But if we carry can-dles, there's no dan-ger." He enunciated each syllable with deliberate precision.

"Liggy! Good heavens!" cried Belinda, so shocked at this veritable outpouring of words from Lord Liggett's lips that she failed to defend herself. "What has made you so positively oratorical?"

Everyone else turned toward him in amused surprise. Lord Liggett, basking in the light of this momentary attention, reddened and gave a modest shrug, but he couldn't resist throwing Harriet a triumphant little glance as soon as the others turned their attention back to the subject of exploring caves.

William Coombe, who'd slept late, wandered in to the circle at that juncture and, after listening to Harriet's summation of the discussion, merely laughed. "*You,* Harry? In a *cave?* I've never heard anything so jinglebrained. You'd be the first to fall off a promontory or into an underground river. If anyone should be kept out of caves, it's Harriet Coombe."

Harriet's eyes flashed furiously. "Of all the insulting things you've ever said, William Coombe—" she burst out.

But Sir Eustace, ever the smoother of ruffled feathers, intervened. "There's no reason to be fearful of cave exploration," he said pleasantly, "if we all stick together, and if we don't venture too far from the mouth."

"Hear, hear!" seconded Harriet, beaming at Sir Eustace with such grateful enthusiasm that Jan's hope of a match between them was reborn.

"But I've heard it said, Sir Eustace," murmured Mariella fearfully, "that there are *bats* dwelling in caves. What would we do if we encountered one of those horrid creatures?"

Thus began a hot debate that effectively divided the group into two warring camps—those who wanted to explore the caves on one side of the battle lines, and those who wanted to visit abbeys or castles ("or anything above the ground," as Belinda put it) on the other.

Max, who'd spent the morning riding, entered the Pump Room at that moment. As soon as he was spotted, he was encircled by several of the crowd and immediately besieged to take sides—the below-grounders pulling at him from one direction and the above-grounders from the other. While Belinda and her friends jabbered at him excitedly, his eyes sought Jan's, as if he were instinctively seeking her opinion. She met his look for a fraction of a moment, but then dropped her eyes, angry at herself for feeling so glad to see him, and angry at him for appearing so upstanding and admirable when he was, underneath, nothing but a lecher. How could he appear so clear-eyed, so blameless, so untroubled? There he stood, handsome and manly in his riding clothes, surrounded by a crowd of admirers, looking as if there were absolutely nothing on his conscience. Yet all the while he was keeping his "fancy piece" in a hideaway right here in Bath, under their very noses. It was revolting.

Max knew Jan well enough to sense her disapproval. Something was wrong; he could tell it from the tightness of her mouth and the set of her jaw. He felt his chest clench in immediate response. Had he committed some iniquity, some act of knavery or wickedness that had incurred her displeasure? He was not aware of anything, except perhaps a tendency to show too much interest in her. In fact, he had been taking himself to task for days now for his too-great enjoyment of her company. *But confound it,* he reminded himself firmly, *her moods are no longer my concern.* The trouble was that old love-feelings died hard. In his case, anyway. He sighed inwardly. If he had a grain of sense, he would leave Bath until she was gone from the place.

Meanwhile, however, he forced himself to attend the problem at hand. He listened to both sides of the debate and then came forth with a suggestion. "How about the caves at Cheddar Gorge?" he asked after he'd heard all the particulars. "They are only five miles further than Wookey Hole, and the gorge offers both caves and above-ground sights. Those who didn't wish to explore the caves could tramp up the gorge. The view from the top is breathtaking."

That idea had much to recommend it, and soon it was generally accepted that a visit to Cheddar Gorge was the answer to everyone's objections. Excitement mounted as one after the other in the circle, even the older ladies, expressed a desire to join the expedition. Except for Jan, who demurred when her turn came. "I'm afraid I won't be able—" she started to say.

But her mother would have none of it. "I shan't go if you don't," Celia Hazeldine said to her daughter in a firm undervoice, "so if you don't wish to spoil my pleasure, let's have no more of that!"

Unable to object, Jan acquiesced with an obedient shrug and subsided into silence.

Plans quickly began to take shape. The expedition, to be made up of sixteen "explorers," would set forth in two days. They would require, Max and Sir Eustace estimated, at least three carriages and a couple of outriders. The men spoke of warm clothes, stout shoes and the necessity of carrying candles, flint and rope. The ladies babbled happily about baskets of cold meats, cheese, fruit and wine. By the time the group separated at noon, all the details had been worked out.

"I'm very grateful to you, Lord Ollenshaw," Harriet whispered to Max as the group parted at the Pump Room entrance. "If it weren't for your suggesting Cheddar Gorge, this entire excursion might not have come to pass. Thanks to you, everyone in the group is delighted."

Jan passed by at that moment, and Max caught another glimpse of the troubled, wary look in her eyes as their glances met. *Damnation,* he swore inwardly, *what the devil is it she thinks I've done now?*

Jan turned away abruptly and, grasping her mother's arm, hurried her off down the street. Max looked after them for a moment before turning his attention back to Harriet. "I'm sorry, Miss Coombe, but I was momentarily distracted. What did you just say?"

"I said, my lord, that thanks to you everyone is absolutely delighted to be going. Everyone!"

He gave Harriet a wan smile and tipped his hat, but his eyes turned once more to the still-visible Jan Hazeldine. Even from the back he felt he could detect her dispirited mood. "Well, almost everyone," he muttered ruefully as he strode off down the street, leaving a puzzled Harriet staring after him.

Nineteen

RETURNING HOME FROM the Pump Room that noon, the notorious gossip, Mrs. Kendall, sprained her ankle. The accident came about because she was scurrying up High Street with much too hasty a step. She was so impatient to inform her neighbor (and closest confidante) of her latest discovery that she tripped on a loose paving stone.

The gossip she was so eager to impart had to do with Lord Liggett, who, though a foppish, awkward fellow, was heir to a respected title and a huge fortune and was thus a particularly suitable subject for tea-table slander. Mrs. Kendall failed to notice the loose paving stone because she was rehearsing in her mind just how she would phrase this latest bit of tittle-tattle. ("You know that I *never* take it upon myself to criticize the ways of the nobility," she intended to remark to her crony, "but that idiotish boy is heading for trouble. I observed him carefully today, and it became apparent to me—you know, my dear, what an astute observer I am!—that he's taken a fancy to, of all people, *Jan Hazeldine!* What is wrong with *her*, you ask? Well, my dear, for one thing she's at *least* five years his *senior*. And anyone with half an eye can see how she ignores him in spite of his calflike devotion to her. The boy could have for the *asking* either of the Brett girls or the very presentable Mary Grindsley, but no: the gudgeon has set his heart on the Hazeldine chit, who, even if she were tempted for a *moment* to accept him, would surely change her mind before the nuptials, for everyone knows what a jilt *she* is!")

But this well-rehearsed bit of scandalmongering was not

dispensed that day. Mrs. Kendall was carried on a litter to her home, where she was bandaged and sedated by her doctor and ordered into bed. By the next day, however, she had recovered herself sufficiently to be carried downstairs and installed in her drawing room. There, with her foot elevated and a vial of sal volatile at her elbow should she become faint from the pain, she was able to receive visitors.

Lady Coombe and her two daughters were among the first to pay a call of condolence. Mrs. Kendall received them with a wan smile, but she was soon moved to tears when she had to inform Harriet that she would be unable to join them the next day for the excursion to Cheddar. "I was *so* looking forward to it," she moaned.

Her tears became a flood later that day, when Lady Briarly and Belinda, escorted by Lord Ollenshaw, came to call. Lord Ollenshaw brought a charming bouquet of spring blooms to cheer the invalid, but the floral offering failed to stem the tide of Mrs. Kendall's tears. They were brought forth by the sight of the lovely Belinda, looking delectable in a white-and-pink-striped muslin walking dress and rose-colored bonnet. "Oh, Belinda, my dearest love," the injured lady said weeping, "I am so afraid that I shall have to cancel the ball I had planned for you."

Belinda bit her lip in disappointment, but Nettie Briarly shrugged off the news with cheerful nonchalance. "Think no more of such trivialities," she declared with perfect sincerity. "No one expects you to concern yourself with dances when you are suffering such pain. All we wish is for you to recover as soon as possible. Belinda will have other fêtes."

The butler came in at that moment to announce another pair of callers—Lady Hazeldine and her daughter. Jan and her mother were ushered in, and everyone gaped in surprise at the remarkable coincidence of their having paid their condolence calls at the very same time.

While all the greetings were exchanged, Max noticed, to his chagrin, that his spirits (which had been rather depressed of late and which were even further depressed by this tedious visit) rose alarmingly at the sight of his erstwhile beloved. He wondered if there would ever come a day when he could look at the girl without feeling this little clench—was it pain or delight?—in his chest. In his eyes Jan looked particularly beautiful this afternoon. She was wearing a crisp, wheat-colored gown with huge puffed sleeves and a green sash; a yellow straw bonnet sat lightly on her glowing hair and was fetchingly tied at the side with a wide green ribbon; and she carried, hooked on her arm, a green, beruffled parasol. *Why,* he berated himself, *does the sight of her always tip me a settler?*

The new arrivals made their expressions of sympathy to the invalid, and chairs were rearranged in a circle round the sofa so that all the visitors could sit down to hear Mrs. Kendall's account of the accident. She was more than eager to impart to them an exact, detailed description, from the alarming condition of the paving stones of Bath to the humiliation of being carried home on a litter.

While Mrs. Kendall held forth on the excruciating pain she was suffering, Max's eyes sought Jan's. But the irritating girl would not look up. Her face was shaded by the brim of her yellow straw bonnet (which Max reluctantly admitted to himself was utterly captivating, tied as it was with a fat bow over the ear that faced him), and she kept her eyes lowered on the hands folded primly on the handle of her parasol. From the moment she'd arrived, she had not acknowledged his existence by the merest flicker. He wondered again what it was that had caused this unspoken but icy barrier between them. They had managed, a few days ago, to reach a kind of truce, but now her manner seemed to indicate that war had been resumed.

Mrs. Kendall's recital of her woes dragged on. It was only when her neighbor's arrival was announced that the callers felt free to rise and take their leaves. Mrs. Kendall did not insist very long that they remain, for she'd been wishing all day for an opportunity to indulge in the gossip with her confidante that her accident had forestalled.

The Briarly party and the Hazeldines left Mrs. Kendall's house together and then paused on the doorstep to say their adieus to one another. "We're off to Blackwell's," Belinda told her cousin excitedly.

"Blackwell's?" Jan echoed, trying to keep her mind on what Belinda was saying at the same time that she concentrated on preventing herself from peeping at Max's face.

"The linendraper's on Milsom Street. They've had a shipment of very fine silk, we're told. We need some silk for my—" Belinda giggled and glanced up at her betrothed archly —"for my unmentionables."

"Yes, we must ready her trousseau, you know," Nettie explained. "Why don't you come with us, Celia? You know how we admire your taste. Your advice will be so helpful. And yours, too, Jan. Do come! Milsom Street is only a short walk from here."

Lady Hazeldine looked at Jan questioningly. "Well, I'd only intended to stroll about in the Pump Room, so I have no objection, if Jan—"

"Of course you must go with Aunt Nettie, Mama. But I beg that you all will excuse me. I was not intending to remain with Mama at the Pump Room, you see. I planned to go home to . . . to . . ."

Lady Hazeldine's eyebrows knit in disapproval. "To practice?"

Jan put up her chin. "Yes."

Lady Hazeldine sighed and turned to her sister. "Then you'll have to excuse me, too, Nettie. I don't wish Jan to walk all the way to Pierrepont alone."

Max, rousing himself to sudden attention as he realized that an opportunity for private conversation with Jan had just been offered to him, quickly seized the moment. "I'd be happy to offer my escort to your daughter, ma'am," he said to Lady Hazeldine with a wide, innocent smile.

Lady Hazeldine peered at him suspiciously. "But don't you go with Nettie and Belinda?"

He laughed. "To help them select silk for 'unmentionables'? They surely don't want me hanging about while they do that."

"No, of course we don't," Belinda agreed.

"It's good of you to offer, Max." His future mother-in-law beamed. "It's the perfect solution. Well, Celia?"

"Well, Jan?" Lady Hazeldine asked her daughter, knowing full well that she was making mischief by pushing Jan into this tête-à-tête with Ollenshaw.

Jan shot her mother a furious look from under the brim of her bonnet. "Please, Mama, *do* go with Aunt Nettie. But as for me, I'm sure you'll agree that I'm capable of walking home without escort. I needn't take Lord Ollenshaw out of his way."

"Rubbish," Max said firmly, taking her arm in his. "Let's hear no more gammon from you. If my escorting you home will make your mother feel more at ease, then escort you I shall!" With a self-assured smoothness that told her plainly he would brook no resistance, he tipped his hat to the other ladies and propelled her off down the street.

Jan waited until the others were out of sight before she pulled her arm from Max's hold. "That was rather high-handed of you, wasn't it, my lord?" she accused.

"High-handed, ma'am?" He grinned down at her in benign self-confidence. "That seems a most unfair designation."

"Then how would you designate it?"

"I would call it mere politeness."

"Ha!" She threw him a scornful glare. "Is it mere politeness to . . . to *abduct* me?"

"You are indulging in wild exaggeration, my dear. I am not even holding your arm. You cannot call my simple escort an abduction."

"But I don't wish for your 'simple escort,' and you know it."

"Your mother wishes it. And she's quite right. A proper young woman doesn't stroll about the streets unaccompanied."

"I'm not a green girl, my lord. At my age it cannot be considered improper to walk alone on the streets of Bath. This is not London, after all. Therefore, I release you from your promise to my mother. Please feel free to go about your business. Don't let me detain you."

"You are not suggesting, I hope, ma'am," Max teased, "that I break my word and desert you the moment your mother's back is turned."

"That's exactly what I'm suggesting," she declared with asperity. "I do not require, nor wish for, your company, my lord." She whipped open her parasol and, propping it up on her shoulder, walked quickly away from him.

"Ah, I see we are back to 'my lord' again," he remarked, catching up with her easily. "What's amiss, my dear? I thought we had negotiated a truce."

"The truce did not include a stipulation that we call each other by our given names. Nor was it stipulated that we had to endure each other's company."

"This is the second time this week you objected to my company. Is my company so hard to endure, Jan?" he asked, turning bluntly sincere. "You found it pleasant enough at one time. Not pleasant enough for wedlock, perhaps, but certainly pleasant enough for ordinary social intercourse."

"Well, I do not find it pleasant now."

"I see. That does seem to be a facer." He rubbed his chin in rueful speculation. "Is it a *general* dislike of me, or is there something specific that disgusts you?"

She cast him a speaking glance but did not condescend to answer. She merely strode on, trying to ignore him.

He kept pace with her. "I've sensed a change in you in the last two days. You are not the same as you were in our last conversation. I can feel it. I wish you would be open with me and tell me what it is."

"I don't wish to speak of it."

"Then it *is* something specific. And after I have been so careful to be a near-stranger to you. You cannot accuse me of violating that rule, can you?" He grasped her arm and forced her to break her stride and face him. "Come, Jan, *tell* me. Though it makes me feel a deuced mawworm to admit it, I still care about your good opinion. What have I done to earn your wrath?"

She shook his hand off furiously. "This pretense of innocence is worse than anything!" she exclaimed in revulsion. "You know perfectly well what you've done . . . what you're *doing*!"

"What I'm doing?" His brows rose in bewilderment. "What are you talking about?"

His denial so angered her that it broke her reserve. "Blast it, Max, if we must have it out, I'll say it!" she burst out, snapping her parasol shut and using the handle to poke at his chest. "I *saw* her, you dastard! Right here in Bath!"

"Saw her? Who?"

"And don't try to tell me I'm mistaken," she raged on, the words spilling out of her in a torrent. "I actually humiliated myself by going right up to her and peering into her face!"

"Jan, confound it, who—" With the suddenness of a blow to the stomach, he realized what—*whom*—she meant. His cheeks whitened. "Good God! You can't mean—! Not again!"

"Oh, yes, again! *Again!* Your redheaded doxie, Lady Wedmore!"

Max's brain reeled in confusion. "Are you saying you saw her here in Bath and assumed that I . . . *I* am *keeping her here*?"

"I hope, Lord Ollenshaw," she snapped, "that you don't mean to insult my intelligence by calling my *certainty* an *assumption*."

"Intelligence? Do you call that ridiculous accusation a sign of *intelligence*?" He peered down at her in utter disbelief. "How could you possibly jump to so unwarranted a conclusion and call it a certainty?"

"Because, my lord, it is the only conclusion possible."

"Is it, indeed?" His voice was icy, giving no indication of the storm of emotions beginning to churn up in him. "Did it never occur to you, ma'am, that the lady's appearance on the streets of Bath might be a mere coincidence?"

"*Coincidence!* Surely that excuse must be the last refuge of the guilty," she retorted.

Guilty! The word unleashed the torrent of fury in his breast and sent his blood thundering in his ears. She really believed him capable of such debauchery! How *could* she, when for years he'd patterned his life's behavior on standards that he believed she would have wished? But in her eyes, the mere appearance of the Wedmore woman on the street was enough to convict him! He was guilty! Again!

The rage within him was worse than any he'd ever felt before. He wanted nothing so much as to strike her. To slap her face. To wring her neck. He'd never struck a female in his life, nor even had the urge to do so until now, but suddenly he understood why the brutes in the back alleys of London beat their loved ones. Nothing, he thought, would relieve the furious hurt that welled up in him like grasping her shoulders and shaking the life out of her. Nothing would be so satisfying or so capable of assuaging his fury as the sheer physical joy of swinging out at her with his fists. But all he did was clench them.

"So," she taunted, "you seem bereft of words, my lord. By rejecting your excuse of coincidence, have I left you speechless?"

He stared at her for a long moment, struck with the feeling that this was someone he'd never seen before. Where was the angelic creature whose purity of soul seemed to glow from her eyes? She was surely not the same person as this termagant who stood glaring accusingly at him. Was *this* the girl he'd kept stored away in his heart for eight painful years? Impossible! This was someone he'd never seen before. "No, not quite speechless, ma'am," he said, his face rigid, "although I'll not deign to offer a word in rebuttal of your charge. Your accusation is so degrading to me that I'd find it humiliating to respond. I didn't defend myself the first time you made such an accusation against me, when I had more to lose, so I certainly won't do so now. But what I find most puzzling, ma'am, is how you can hold me in such low esteem. What have I ever done to make you think so little of me? How can you find me guilty on such flimsy evidence? Have you actually convinced yourself that my character is so degenerate that I would keep a mistress constantly at my side wherever I go? Can you really be so contemptuous of my moral fiber that you believe I would be not only faithless to my betrothed but that I'd flaunt my inamorata here in Bath right under her nose?"

Jan suddenly felt uncomfortably insecure. "What else am I to believe, under the circumstances?" she asked defensively.

He shook his head, more in self-disgust than in disgust with her. "I've been living an illusion," he muttered in the tone of a man awakening from a dream. "A damned *illusion*! I believed that Jan Hazeldine had such purity of soul that we ordinary mortals could never be worthy of her. What a fool I was! There is no purity in you—only prudery. The kind of prudery that a spinster develops about experiences she only imagines. That's what you have, ma'am, a spinster's mind. The kind of mind that sees *lascivious shadows under the bed*!"

The words delivered a crueler blow than would have been possible with his fists. She reeled back as if struck. "Lascivious *shadows*?"

"Yes, ma'am. Shadows. Insubstantial wisps that take the shape given to them by the warped imagination of the observer. But let me ask you, ma'am: if the observer sees corruption where there is none, then where does the corruption really reside?"

She drew herself up in trembling wrath. "Dash it all, Max, are you calling me *corrupt*? How dare you! A turn-the-tables-on-the-enemy defense, is that it? What do you think you'll gain by such a cowardly trick? I have been *nothing* if not honorable through all of this! I haven't breathed a word to *anyone*, in spite of the nagging of my conscience to reveal the truth to Belinda!"

"Am I supposed to *thank* you for that, ma'am?" he sneered. "Go ahead and *tell* Belinda! Tell her everything! If she were so lacking in judgment as to believe you, I'd want nothing more to do with her. Just as I want nothing more to do with *you*!" He took three long strides away from her and then paused. "You wanted to rid yourself of my escort, didn't you?" he threw over his shoulder. "Well, you've succeeded. I shall break my promise to your mother and leave you to walk home alone after all. To that much corruption I plead guilty." With mocking, icy formality he lifted his hat and bowed. "Good day, ma'am," he said, and he stalked off down the street without a backward look.

"Oh, my *God*," Jan murmured as she watched him disappear from sight. "*Have* I made a mistake?" If she had, she knew in the depths of her being that it was the worst—no, perhaps it was the *second* worst—mistake of her life.

Twenty

THE WEATHER ON the morning of the day of the excursion could only be called indecisive. The sky looked threatening, but no rain actually fell. Among the fifteen "explorers" gathered at the Churchill Bridge, shortly after nine, indecisiveness abounded. No one was willing to wager so much as a groat on the weather.

Opinions differed widely about the advisability of going ahead. The sky was heavy with clouds, but a lighter gray brightened the southern horizon. Since south was the direction they would take, the optimists among them urged that they proceed. But the pessimists continued to assert that even in the south it would probably pour. Six of them claimed that the sky would possibly clear by noon; another six asserted that very likely a deluge would pour down upon their heads. The rest would not even venture an opinion.

Not surprisingly, the elders advised caution and postponement, while the younger set demanded bravery. "If it comes down wet, we can always climb back into the carriages and return home," Harriet argued.

"If it comes down wet while we are scaling the sides of the gorge," Lady Coombe pointed out, "we shall be drenched before we even reach the carriages."

In the end, however, youthful enthusiasm prevailed. The matter was put to a vote, and only four (Lady Coombe, Sir Eustace, Lady Briarly and Mariella) voted to postpone. But once the decision to go ahead was made, even the naysayers went along with the majority, although Mariella Coombe was heard to mutter that they would all be sorry. It was surely going to pour; she could feel it in her bones.

Three sturdy carriages had been donated for the occasion—Lady Briarly's barouche which seated six, Sir Eustace's phaeton which held four, and Lord Ollenshaw's high-sprung little curricle, which would hold three if their hips were slim. The phaeton and the barouche would be driven by coachmen, but the curricle would have to be driven by one of the occupants. Since Max was to lead the procession on horseback, someone else had to drive it. Jack Grindsley eagerly volunteered to drive the curricle. When Ollenshaw agreed, the boy was beside himself with delight. ("When will I ever again have an opportunity to drive such a magnificent pair of grays?" he whispered excitedly to his sister.) To ride with him, he requested the company of the Brett girls, sensing that they were the ones most likely to be impressed by his adept handling of the ribbons.

Jack was not the only member of the party who was concerned with the seating arrangements in the carriages. Since the drive south would consume at least three hours in each direction, everyone wanted to be seated near a congenial traveling companion. To some of them, the seating was a matter of dire importance. Sir Eustace, for instance, who did not wish to be forced to listen to the babblings of either the Briarlys or the Coombes, made certain that Jan and her mother were handed up into his carriage before anyone else might claim those seats. Jan, who had not given up hope for the match between her friend and Sir Eustace, grasped Harriet's hand and propelled her up into the carriage ahead of her. Then, by seating herself quickly beside her mother, forced Harriet into the place beside Sir Eustace. Harriet was so excited by the prospect of exploring the caves that she didn't care where she sat, but Jan couldn't help noticing that Sir Eustace looked disappointed. Sighing to herself over the lack of success of her matchmaking plans, Jan turned to the window and spent the trip brooding about the strangeness, illogic and unpredictability of love.

But the most disappointed of the group was Lord Liggett, who had carefully planned a strategy to win himself a place beside Jan. In this goal, however, the poor fellow was out-maneuvered by the quick action of Sir Eustace and the equally unexpected ploy that Jan contrived to entrap Harriet. With four already seated in Sir Eustace's carriage, and the curricle also fully occupied, Liggy had to find a place in the Briarly coach. In the end he found himself wedged between Lady Coombe and the sour-faced Mariella. Opposite him sat Belinda, her mother and Mary Grindsley. During the entire twenty-seven-mile ride to Cheddar, the poor fellow had to endure listening to Belinda and her mother talk about wedding plans, while a delighted Mary Grindsley (who, not having discovered in her days at Bath a more promising candidate, had decided just this morning that Lord Liggett would make her a perfect husband) spent the three-hour drive casting him flirtatious smiles.

Thus the three carriages, loaded with passengers and supplies, set out on the Wells Road, with Max leading the procession on his roan stallion and William Coombe, riding a dispirited gelding he'd procured from a local livery stable, bringing up the rear.

It did not rain on the trip south, but neither did the sky clear. Nevertheless, all fifteen travelers alighted in the village of Cheddar in high spirits, either because they'd enjoyed the drive or because it was over. Certainly the view of the limestone cliffs, soaring more than four hundred feet into the air over the narrow gorge, was enough to excite them. "Such sights," Harriet declaimed rhapsodically, "seem designed by nature just to take our breaths away!"

After a light luncheon at a nearby inn (where they sampled the local cheese but drank the wine they'd brought with them), they divided into the above-ground and below-ground groups. Belinda, Nettie, Celia Hazeldine, Lady Coombe and Mariella declared for the climb up the gorge, while the rest of the party chose to explore one of the many caves that a meandering underground river had, through the centuries, carved out of the stone.

However, before they set out in their different directions, Nettie Briarly noticed that not one gentleman had chosen the above-ground group. "Don't you think we ought to have at least one gentleman in our party?'' she asked her sister nervously.

"Nonsense," Celia answered firmly. "Why do you think a male escort is necessary?"

"Suppose we lose our way . . . or one of us twists an ankle like poor Mrs. Kendall?"

"Lady Briarly is quite right," Sir Eustace said. "I wouldn't think of permitting you to climb up the gorge without escort. I'll be happy to go with you."

"No, Sir Eustace," Max objected. "You're the one who, along with Miss Coombe, most vehemently declared for the caves. *I'll* join the climbers."

Sir Eustace stubbornly insisted that he did not have an overwhelming desire to explore the caves; he would be just as content escorting the ladies on their climb. But when Max used the argument that his bride-to-be was among the climbers and that he should therefore be permitted to accompany her, the Baronet surrendered to what was unarguably a higher claim. Thus Max went off up the gorge, while Sir Eustace led the below-grounders to the mouth of what was reputed to be the largest of the caves.

William Coombe distributed candles to everyone in the group while Sir Eustace reminded them of the dangers of wandering off on their own. "We should always stay in full sight of each other," he warned, "and keep one hand on the rope that Lord Liggett is tying to that tree."

While Liggy carefully knotted one end of the long rope they'd brought with them to a tree near the mouth of the cave, Sir Eustace lined the others in single file and took the coil of rope over his arm. Each one of the cave explorers was to keep one hand on the rope while holding a candle in the other. Sir Eustace explained that he, at the head of the line, would unwind the rope as they went.

Amid much excited laughter, they went in. The air inside the cave was much colder than outside, and their breaths were immediately caught in their throats. Once they'd gone a few steps from the mouth, the darkness of the cave overwhelmed them. Even the light of their nine candles was not enough to penetrate the blackness of the huge cavern in which they stood. They felt, rather than saw, the enormous size of the cave; the echo of their hushed voices reverberated against walls that seemed great distances away. The sounds of the cavern were eerily strange. Not only could they hear the roar of the river as it roiled over its stony path somewhere below them, and the frightening whir of wings flapping high above, but their own slightest noises—the scrape of a shoe against a rock, a frightened cough from the throat of one of the Misses Brett, the plash of water falling from a weeping stalactite— echoed and reechoed through the rocky passageways until they became unrecognizable, thunderous booms.

As their eyes became more accustomed to the gloom, it became apparent that they were moving along a wide ledge that edged a crevasse. Somewhere down within the fissure the river flowed, but they could not see how far below them it was. "Keep close to the wall," Sir Eustace said uneasily. "This ledge seems to be narrowing down."

They kept moving slowly ahead, sometimes gasping as their candles lit a stalactite or an unexpected outcropping of rock. Once Mary Grindsley screamed in fright as a bat came whizzing toward her head. William, who was right behind her in the queue, waved the creature aside with a swing of his hat. For this act of bravery he earned the girl's immediate adoration. "Oh, Mr. Coombe," she gushed, "I've never seen *any-thing* so courageous in my life!"

William preened but muttered a modest, "Not at all."

"No need to car-ry on," Lord Liggett said bluntly. "Bats are ve-ry ti-mid."

"Good for you, Liggy," whispered Harriet, who was right in front of Liggy in the line. "Your speech is getting better every day."

The ledge took unexpected dips and rises, so they had to concentrate on their footing as they moved along. When the path suddenly veered sharply to the right, they didn't know what to expect. Was this a bridge over the ravine? And if so, was it safe to cross?

Sir Eustace made the rest of the party stop and wait as he moved gingerly forward, carefully aiming the candlelight on the passage ahead of him before taking a step. But when he rounded the bend, he shouted happily for them to follow. The other members of the party hurried after him and found themselves suddenly in a much smaller chamber. Here the ground below their feet was solid and free from any frightening crevasses. Their nine candles threw sufficient light for them to see the hundreds of stalactites and stalagmites that filled the space. They gasped with delight, for the sight was like some unearthly landscape one comes upon only in a dream.

It seemed safe to wander about more freely here, to let go of the rope for a moment or two and go off to look more closely at the odd formations of rock or the larger stalactites. The atmosphere was not so fearful here. The noise of the river was fainter, and their own sounds did not echo with quite so much resonating power. Yet their whispers could be heard distinctly by someone standing at the opposite wall. It was a chamber of wonders, and it delighted them all. Their laughter came more freely. There were cries of "Oh, come, see *this*!" and "Did you *ever* see the *like*?" After a while, however, Harriet, the intrepid explorer, urged Sir Eustace to press on.

"I don't think we can," Sir Eustace pointed out. "We've about reached the end of the rope." There were one or two groans of disappointment, but when the Baronet suggested that it might be wise to start back, most of the party agreed with his judgment. Harriet, who was utterly fascinated with this new experience, and William, who was still elated by having performed the bravest act that Mary Grindsley had ever seen, urged adamantly for the exploration to continue, but when Sir Eustace pointed out that the candles were almost half-consumed, they finally agreed to abide by the wishes of the majority.

They lined up in single file again for the trudge back. Sir Eustace took his place at the front, assigning William to bring up the rear. He was to hold the end of the rope and to recoil it to keep it taut as the distance to the mouth of the cave grew shorter. Mary, who had found in William a new candidate on whom to pin her marital hopes, squeezed in place in front of him. Jan, following Harriet and Liggy, found herself right before Mary, third from the last.

They moved along without incident, feeling the rope pass under their hands. Then Harriet tripped when the ledge made a sudden decline, causing everyone to gasp in terror. But Liggy, in front of her, turned about deftly, caught her up under her arms and set her to rights. "Oh, *Liggy*," Harriet gasped in relief, "you saved my life! I could have fallen down the ravine!"

"That was not only brave of you, my boy," Sir Eustace said over his shoulder as they continued to inch along, "but very quick."

"Yes, very!" Harriet agreed with heartfelt enthusiasm. "You may not talk quickly, Liggy, but you certainly *think* quickly!"

No one could see Liggy blush with pride. William, however, did not enjoy having his reputation for bravery usurped. "Haw, haw!" he mocked. "Told you Harriet was not one to visit caves!"

The words were no sooner out of his mouth when a gust of wind, emanating from some mysterious source, swept over them and blew out five of their nine candles. The Brett girls screamed, and even Jan felt a constriction of fear in her chest. But Sir Eustace, urging them to be calm, halted the line until the candles were relit, and then they moved forward again.

"I wonder where the wind came from," William said to Mary. "I think I noticed an opening in the wall just a step back. I'll wager a monkey the draught came from there."

"You're not suggesting," Mary giggled, "that you want to take a *look*, are you?"

"Yes, I am," he said, eager to reestablish his reputation for courage. "Here. Hold this rope for me for a moment."

"Wait," Mary said, excited by the prospect of a romantic adventure. "Let me come with you. Here, Jan, hold the rope." And she thrust the end of the rope, coiled in several loops, over Jan's arm.

Jan looked over her shoulder in startled alarm. "Mary!" she exclaimed. "Where . . . What are you *doing*? Sir Eustace said we shouldn't go off!" But her candle revealed only a dark emptiness behind her. "William!" she called sharply. "Come back here at once!" But no one answered.

She turned front, where a moment ago Liggy had been closer than an arm's length ahead of her. Now she could see only a length of rope disappearing into the shadows. The group had all moved forward out of her line of vision. "Liggy! *Wait!*" she cried. But there was no answer from that source either.

Her heart constricted in absolute terror. How had she suddenly found herself all alone? *"William! Mary!"* she shouted, her fear making her voice shrill. "We are *losing* the *others*! Come *back* here!"

There was a fearful fluttering of bats' wings. The echo of her voice reverberated above her, the sound rolling about in the heights of the chamber like high-pitched thunder, distorting itself so greatly that the words were indistinguishable. But even if the party ahead of her couldn't make out the words, they must surely have heard the cry. Why weren't they answering? "Oh, God!" she said in a terrified whisper. "Am I deserted?"

"Jan, is that you?" came William's voice behind her. "Come here and see what we've found!"

She felt a wave of relief. She whirled round, but she could not see him through the gloom. "William? Where *are* you? Don't you realize we are losing the others?"

"Never mind that," he said, the light of his candle suddenly appearing visible to her. "We've discovered an adjacent cavern. There's a whole honeycomb of caverns, actually. Come and see!"

"Have you taken leave of your senses, William? The others are out of earshot already!"

His face, smiling broadly, was now visible to her. "No need to take a pet, my dear," he said, condescending in his new-found bravery. "So long as you have the rope, we are perfectly safe."

She felt an overpowering urge to box his ears. "Dash it all, William, you are acting like a child! This is the very thing we've been warned against. I don't feel *at all* safe. Where is Mary? Please, William, get her at once! I want to go back!"

"She's waiting in the other cavern. Don't you want to take a little peep at it?"

"No, I don't," Jan snapped. "I want to catch up with the others. Will you go to fetch her or shall I shout her name and wake up all the bats?"

William shrugged. "I'll get her." And he disappeared into the shadows again.

Jan tried to remain calm while she waited, but it seemed hours before she saw his candlelight again. When his face appeared, it was no longer smiling. "I can't find her," he muttered nervously.

"*What?* Oh, *no!*"

"What shall we do?" he asked, all vestiges of his vaunted bravery gone.

"We'll have to find her, of course," Jan said, her voice stronger than her feelings. "Here, take the rope. We'll unwind it as we go, so we can be sure to find our way back."

William took her hand in a tight, clammy clutch and led her a short distance back to where he'd discovered a small opening in the wall they'd been hugging. The opening was so low that they had to stoop to enter. On the other side was a cavern so small that William had to stoop. The light of their two candles revealed irregular stone walls shadowed with crevices that might or might not be passages to other chambers. There was no Mary to be seen. "Where *can* she have gone?" William asked, a frantic edge to his voice. "I told her to stay right here!"

Jan urged herself to be calm. With William becoming agitated, *someone* had to remain composed. "You said there was a honeycomb of caverns. Might she have gone to explore one of them?"

"I suppose so, but there are so many. See all those dark shadows? I think that each one of them is an opening to another cave. We couldn't possibly search them all! I don't know where to begin—"

"Wait! I've an idea. She has her candle, has she not? Perhaps if we darken this room, we'll see the glow of it."

"You're not suggesting we blow out our *candles*!" William exclaimed, horrified.

"No. Just one. And we'll shield the other with our hands. Perhaps that way it will be dark enough."

The suggestion worked. They saw a dim glow in an opening just to their left. Hiding within a niche no larger than a cupboard, a terrified Mary was huddled. When she saw William's face in the opening, she fell into hysterics. "William! Oh, *W-William*," she wept, clutching him about the neck, "I thought you'd l-left m-me behind to *d-die*!"

"*I* left *you*?" William exclaimed in annoyance as he helped her out of the little space. "It was *you* who left me! Why on earth did you ever climb into that hole?"

"A b-bat came at me. An enormous, *horrible* b-bat. I just c-climbed in there to h-hide."

"They why didn't you come out again?"

"I d-don't know." The frightened girl clung to him, weeping into his neck. "I th-thought I could s-see you . . . or h-hear you when you c-came back . . ."

He was too upset himself to wish to comfort her. He tried to loosen her grip on him, but she would not let go. "Then why didn't you answer before," he demanded querulously, "when I came back and shouted for you?"

"Stop badgering the girl, William," Jan said. "It wasn't her fault. Sound plays strange tricks in these caverns. In some places, one hears water dripping from far off as if it were right nearby, and yet, in others, one can't hear shouts from someone close by. And in that little hole her candle probably blinded her. Let's not dwell on it any more. Come, William, take hold of the end of this rope and let's start back. The others must have discovered by now that we're missing. They'll be frantic."

But with Mary clinging to him like a leech, William could not handle the rope. She would not let go until he promised he keep a tight hold of her hand. Thus he, with Mary clutching his arm like a lifeline, led the way, while Jan brought up the rear, coiling the rope as they went.

As they inched along the ledge, holding onto the rope that Jan tried to keep taut by steadily coiling it round elbow and shoulder, she began to wonder how far they were from the cave's entrance. The candles had only a couple of inches of tallow left. What would happen, she wondered, if their candles burned out before they reached the mouth? She was just about to suggest that they blow out two of the three candles to conserve them when Mary screamed. "Look!" she gasped. "The *rope*!"

She was quite right to scream. The ledge they were moving on swerved slightly to their right, but the rope angled sharply off to the left. The light of their candles made only a small circle, but it was wide enough to see that the rope led *right over the crevasse*!

"How can that *be*?" William asked, distraught. "The others couldn't have gone over the ravine, could they?"

"Not unless they all turned into bats," Jan replied with a brave attempt at a laugh, while inside she wondered miserably how many *more* pitfalls lay in their path.

She and William tried to discuss the problem logically, while Mary had another fit of hysterics. They reasoned that the rope, being pulled in a straight line while the path they were following was full of twists and turns, could thus be pulled over the ravine. Perhaps it had caught on a rock or a stalagmite somewhere out in the darkness. They pulled and tugged at it in an effort to see if they could loosen it, but it would not budge. After a few moments Jan suggested that they ignore the rope and continue to move along the ledge without it, hugging the wall instead. "After all, that's what we did on the way in," she argued.

But William did not like leaving the security of the rope. "Why don't I go back a few yards and pull on it? Perhaps a different angle might loosen the deuced thing."

"I don't see how—" Jan began.

"*No!*" screamed the overagitated Mary, throwing her arms about his chest and hanging on him like a drowning swimmer. "I w-won't let you l-leave me again!"

"But Jan will be with you," he pointed out.

"No!" the girl repeated, sinking down and clutching him about the knees. "We'll *die* here! I know we'll die here!"

William, trying to raise her to her feet, looked over at Jan helplessly. "Can you reason with her?" he begged.

"It will be better if you stay with her. If you insist on it, William, I'll go back a short distance and try to pull on the rope myself."

He did insist. Jan, who would have continued along the ledge if she'd been on her own, did not feel sure enough of herself to argue further. Uncoiling the rope, she inched her way back until she could no longer see their lights. "Now?" she shouted.

Although the roar of the river was deafening, she thought she heard an answering assent. Grasping the rope with both her hands she pulled on it strongly. There was another shout from the distance. "Harder!" she thought he yelled. She widened her stance, planted her feet as firmly as she could on the rocky ledge and, grasping the rope so tightly in her hands that it seemed to be cutting into her flesh, she pulled with all her might.

Something gave, and she tottered back, falling against the wall in a shower of pebbles and small stones. The rope seemed to flip from her grasp as if it had a life of its own and, with a snap, whipped over the edge of the ledge and disappeared from her sight. A gasp escaped her, the sound reverberating against the walls and transforming itself to the whine of an unhappy wind. The candle flame flickered so agitatedly that she feared she would lose it altogether. But she and the flame both managed to right themselves. "William!" she cried. "I've lost the rope."

But no answer came to her over the roar of the water. For a moment she stood immobile, catching her breath and thanking God that she hadn't catapulted over the edge of the ravine as the end of the rope had probably done. Then she began to think about what to do next. William would probably expect her to try to look for any part of the rope that might still be lying on the ledge. Well, she supposed she could try. She tied up her skirts, got down on her knees and crept along the ledge, feeling along the edge of it for the rope. She felt her silk stockings tear at the knees, and she was sure her hands were bleeding. "Blast you, William Coombe, for getting us into this fix!" she cursed under her breath.

After a while, she began to realize the futility of what she was doing. Her candle was becoming frighteningly small, and the rope had probably dropped too far down in the chasm to be found again. She would be faster and safer if she got to her feet and edged along the wall. She obeyed that instinct, moving along the ledge more swiftly than before. Perhaps losing the rope was a blessing, she thought. She was freer without it. But she knew in her heart that it was naked fear that propelled her on. Ironically, fear was making her brave.

She believed she should be seeing William's and Mary's light any moment now, but moment after moment went by and she saw nothing ahead but darkness. After a while she realized that she must somehow have missed them. But how could she have done so? She'd followed the same wall, hadn't she? Where on earth were they? Where was *she*?

She raised her candle higher and saw with horror that she was in another, smaller chamber. How had it happened? Had she edged into an opening in the wall without realizing it?

Her chest clenched in despair. She shouted William's name, but even as she did so, she knew the cry would not be heard in the main cavern. She had to find her way out to the ledge. But how was she to get out? The candle did not light much of the area, and she could see no opening. She simply had to feel her way along. But which way? Forward? Back?

Frozen in indecision, she had a moment of intense panic. Mary had cried that they could die. The girl was right. It was quite possible that they—that *she*—could die right here! She could die, and her body would lie undiscovered in this cavern for years and years. Even forever, unless, in some distant future, an explorer might come upon her dried bones. Never had she experienced a more fearful moment than this. *Oh, well,* she thought, trying to calm herself, *at least I know I've reached rock bottom. Things cannot get worse.*

And then her candle went out.

Twenty-One

THE ABOVE-GROUND party had climbed less than halfway up the cliff when it began to rain—at first a few light droplets, then a drizzle, and then, just as they'd turned to head down the path toward shelter, a downpour. "I told you so," muttered a disgruntled Mariella.

Huddling under the nearest tree, the ladies searched among their possessions for protection. Belinda had a parasol more suitable for sun than rain, but since it was better than anything Lady Briarly carried, she insisted that her mother take it. This act of generosity prompted Max to insist that the girl take his coat to hold over her head. Lady Coombe and Mariella both had shawls, which they raised over their bonnets. Celia Hazeldine's bonnet had so broad a brim that it served her as an umbrella. And so, inadequately protected though they were, the group emerged from the shelter of the tree and started their wet way down.

A turn in the path revealed a vista they had not noticed on their way up. It was Nettie, peeping out at the view from beneath her parasol, who saw it first. "Look," she exclaimed, "you can see the mouth of the cave from here! And, see, our cave explorers have emerged already."

"Yes, look at them!" Belinda said excitedly, stopping to take in the view without being in the least dismayed by the rain. "You can even recognize them, although we're so high above them we can only see the tops of their heads. There's Harriet. You can tell by her bonnet's being askew. Harriet's bonnet is always askew. And look, there's Liggy, running about like a beheaded chicken.''

Lady Coombe surveyed the group below from beneath her already-damp shawl. ''They are more fortunate than we. They'll be in the carriages in no time, while we shall be drenched through by the time we—''

''I don't see Jan,'' Celia Hazeldine said, suddenly tense. ''Does anyone see Jan?''

Max came up behind her. ''I don't see her either. I wonder . . .''

''There's William, just coming out now,'' Mariella pointed out. ''Look, Mama, there's a girl positively clinging to him. Who—''

''That's Mary Grindsley,'' Belinda chuckled. ''I do believe Mary has shifted her aim from Liggy to another target.''

''Vulgar chit,'' Lady Coombe muttered.

''But do you see *Jan*?'' Celia repeated, peering down through the rain anxiously. ''Where *is* she?''

They could see the others swarm about Mary and William like carrion beetles attacking a dead worm. Max drew in a gasp of breath. ''Something's gone wrong,'' he muttered, his lips whitening. ''Can you ladies manage on your own? If you stick to the path you'll be fine. I'm going to take a short cut through the brush.''

Without waiting for an answer, he swung round and plunged down the side. Celia ran a few steps after him. ''Max?'' Her eyes were distended in panic. ''You don't think she's . . . *lost*!''

He turned and looked up at her. ''If she is, I'll find her,'' he swore before crashing off through the shrubbery.

Down in the gorge, he found William nervously relating to Sir Eustace what had happened. Mary had already fallen to the ground in a swoon and was being attended to by the Brett girls. Harriet, distraught and on the verge of tears, was nevertheless trying to keep Lord Liggett and Jack from rushing hurly-burly back into the cave. ''I want to find her as much as you! *More!*'' she was crying. ''But we must make a plan first.''

Max, pausing to catch his breath, stood listening to William's account. What he heard made him grit his teeth in fury. He wanted to smash the craven fellow's jaw with his fists. Sir Eustace, too, was shaking with anger. "Are you saying," he asked William in dismay, "that after sending Jan back with the deuced rope, you didn't wait for her to return?"

"I waited a while. But Miss Grindsley was shrieking hysterically. What could I do?"

"What you could have done, you mawworm," Max snapped, "was to ignore the hysterics and use your head! Even if you lacked the will to go the few steps back to look for Jan, you could have stayed where you were. Didn't it occur to you that we would be coming to find you?"

"We were already preparing to go back with new candles," Eustace added.

"I didn't think there was any use in going back *or* waiting," William said in sullen misery. "I think I . . . heard her fall."

Max grabbed him by his neckcloth in white-knuckled fury. "You damnable blockhead," he swore through clenched teeth, "don't even *think* it!"

Harriet burst into terrified tears. "It's my fault more than William's," she wept. "If I hadn't wanted to explore—"

"Let's not waste time finding fault," Sir Eustace muttered, too upset to be kind. "We must, as you just said, make a plan. It's so damnably dark in there. I'm afraid the few candles we have left won't be adequate."

"Torches," Max said tersely, dropping his hold on William and shoving him aside. "We need torches. You, Grindsley, find us a few dead branches. Thick ones. And you, Miss Coombe, tear up your petticoat. We'll bind the strips of cloth to the tops of the torches and burn them. That'll give us a brighter flame than the bare wood. Quickly, now. We have no time to waste."

While Jack and Harriet fashioned the torches, Max, Sir Eustace and Liggy conferred on how best to mark their passage through the cave. William's defection had left them with no clear starting point, and although Sir Eustace remembered the twists and turns their route had taken (and drew them for

Max on a rough map), he could not say at what point on the route Jan had become separated from William. William was asked to circle the probable area, which he did with a shaking hand.

"I want to come with you," Jack said when he brought them the finished torches.

"No, thank you, my boy," Max said. "Liggett, Merriot and I are enough to keep track of. Besides, we need you to run up the gorge path, there to your left, and make sure the climbers get down safely. As for you, Coombe, if you can shake yourself from your stupor, take these ladies out of the rain to the carriages."

But Harriet refused to go back to the carriages. "Let me wait here, please, Lord Ollenshaw," she begged. "Jan may need me. I'll stay just inside the mouth. I won't move, I promise."

Max nodded. Then the three men lit their torches and went inside.

Somewhere far within, Jan stood leaning against the rocky wall of the black chamber, frozen into immobility. *Think,* she told herself firmly, *think!* It wouldn't do to succumb to panic. She had to behave in a sensible fashion to survive this ordeal.

Of course I shall survive, she told herself. Sir Eustace would come looking for her any time now. And surely Max, when he discovered she was missing, would join the search. Max would not let her die.

But if the cave was as honeycombed with chambers as it seemed, how would he find her? What could she do to lead the searchers to her? Shouting had proven to be ineffective. She and William had found Mary by her candle, but she, Jan, had no candle left. If she could edge her way back to the ledge they would certainly come upon her, but in the pitch blackness it was too dangerous to move. She might fall into a crevasse to her doom. It was safest, she realized, to remain right where she was.

She leaned against the wall, which was clammily cold and rough, and slid slowly down until she was seated on the ground. She shivered with the cold. Drawing her legs up, she pulled her skirts over them and hugged her knees. The sound of the water was somewhat fainter here, but the rustle of wings above her head was chilling. If any of the bats flew down about her face, she was afraid her heart would stop in terror. No, she mustn't think of the bats, she warned herself. She mustn't let herself think of *any* of the horrible possibilities of her situation. She must concentrate her mind on Max, who would surely come to rescue her. She remembered, with a pang, that only yesterday she'd despised him. He was a rake, a lecher, a liar—all the characteristics for which she had nothing but contempt. Yet she felt no contempt for him now. At this moment all she felt was an overwhelming yearning to look at his face once more. She didn't care about anything else. Besides, there was one thing in his character that she was certain of, and that was courage. He would not be afraid of the caves; he'd search them from top to bottom until he found her. He would not let her die in this black hole. She didn't know what made her so sure of him, but she was.

Despite this reassuring certainty, however, the minutes crept by like months. Somewhere nearby, droplets of water were falling down upon a stony floor with the regularity of a clock ticking. The *drip . . . drip . . . drip* became so insistent she felt it would drive her mad. It was like a metronome, keeping time. The rhythm was a perfect adagio, as if it were counting out the beat of the third movement of the Mozart B-flat Major Quartet. She smiled ruefully at the sudden thought that, if she had nothing else in this horrid darkness, she still had music. Using the dripping to set the pace, she began to hum the violin part of the quartet's third movement.

She'd gotten about halfway through the movement when she thought she saw a glimmer of light in the distance. Afraid to trust her eyes, she kept on humming bravely. But her heart began to hammer rapidly as she became certain that the light was brightening. Someone was coming!

"Hello?" She tried to shout it, but her voice cracked.

"*Jan?*" The voice—the beautiful, deep, resonant voice—was Max's, and even from the distance she could hear in it a tremor of tentative joy, as if he were afraid to believe he'd actually heard her.

"*Max!*" she croaked. "I'm *here*!"

"Jan!" It was only a breath, but she heard it quite distinctly. "Merriot! Liggett!" he shouted. "This way!"

Jan got clumsily to her feet, but the trembling of her knees made movement unsteady, and she stumbled. She fell against the wall, causing a projecting piece of rock to break loose and fall to the ground with a crash.

Max heard the sound. "*Don't move!*" he ordered quickly. "I'll come to you. Just keep talking. Or hum, if you'd rather."

"You *heard* my *humming*?"

"Amazing, isn't it? I was afraid, at first, that I was imagining it. Or that it was bats. But after a moment I realized that bats couldn't hum Haydn, so I concluded that it must be you."

"Mozart," she said with a choked laugh. Shaking from head to toe in relief, she hummed as she watched the torchlight grow brighter and brighter. At last it burst into the cavern in a blinding explosion. For a moment she couldn't see anything but rays of brilliance, as if she'd looked into the sun, but when she shaded her eyes she could see him. Max, her rescuer.

He was standing just inside the chamber's round opening, not three steps away from her. His face glowed in the amber light of the torch he carried. He was staring at her with an expression that held more awe than joy. "I bargained with God," he said softly. "I promised that if He let me find you alive, I would never ask Him for another gift."

He leaned the torch against the wall and held his arms out to her. She flew into them. "I knew you would find me," she whispered. "I *knew*."

His arms tightened about her. "I wish I'd been as sure. Oh, Lord, I was so terrified! I kept imagining the most dreadful . . ." His voice broke, and he pressed his lips against her hair. She could feel that his arms were actually trembling. It took a moment before she realized he was weeping.

She clutched his lapels and buried her face in his chest. "Hush," she murmured, "hush, my love. It's all over." She reached up and brushed the wetness from his cheek. "I'm safe now."

An embarrassed laugh rumbled out of him. "Yes. Yes, I know."

Sir Eustace loomed up in the opening, his torch throwing another explosion of light into the chamber. But Max and Jan, locked in a tight embrace, did not move or give the slightest indication that they noticed.

Liggy ran up behind the Baronet, puffing hard from his exertions. "Miss *Hazeldine*!" he exclaimed joyfully, trying to push past Sir Eustace into the chamber. "We *f-found* y—"

But Sir Eustace clapped a restraining hand on the younger man's mouth. "Wait a bit, Lord Liggett," he whispered, his eyes fixed on the immobile pair. "I think we should give them a few more moments, don't you?"

Twenty-Two

OF COURSE, THE skies cleared the next day. The air glistened with a crystalline, rain-washed purity, making even the stone facades of Bath's magnificent buildings gleam in the brilliant sunshine as if they'd been scrubbed clean. Despite the delightful weather, however, Lady Hazeldine would not permit her daughter to leave the house. She insisted that Jan remain in bed. She herself had not recovered from the horrible tension of the day before. When Celia had seen her daughter's condition after Ollenshaw had carried her from the cave, she'd burst into tears. The girl's face was black with dirt, her skirts in shreds, her knees bruised, and her hands cut and bleeding. Even though Jan maintained firmly that she was quite well—and that the only reason she'd permitted Max to carry her out of the cave was that all the gentlemen who'd come to rescue her had insisted on it—Celia Hazeldine ordered her to rest in her bed for the whole day following. "You've lived through a most dreadful ordeal, my love," she said, patting her daughter's bandaged hands with motherly tenderness before pulling the bedcoverings neatly in place. "You may not fully realize it, but your nerves were bound to have been affected. I'm not even going to permit anyone to come up and visit you. Not today."

Jan did not object to spending a quiet day abed. With the books she'd taken home from Duffield's to keep her occupied, she would not miss seeing callers—with one exception. "You may keep everyone away, Mama, with my blessing, except

Max. If he should call, please bring him up. I must speak to him.''

Her mother studied her closely. ''To thank him, is that it?''

Jan's eyes fell. ''Yes,'' she said, adding enigmatically, ''that, too.''

Celia shrugged and went off to dress. If Jan did not wish to say more, she would not press her.

The callers began knocking at the door before the morning was half over. Celia had barely changed from her morning robe to a loose-fitting at-home gown of rose-colored camlet and was still braiding her long, graying hair when Beale came to tell her that her first callers, Lady Briarly and Miss Briarly, were awaiting her downstairs. Celia quickly wound the braid into a bun, stuck in a few hairpins to hold it in place, and ran down.

Nettie was in her usual good humor, but Celia noticed that Belinda seemed strangely subdued. The girl kept her eyes lowered throughout the visit, saying nothing at all after expressing her keen disappointment in not being permitted to talk to Jan. Only when they were departing did she open her mouth again. ''I hope, Aunt Cecy, that you will let me see Jan tomorrow. I am very, *very* eager to talk to her.''

Harriet, the next to call, was also disappointed at not being permitted to go upstairs. After relaying greetings from her mother and sister (both of whom had taken to their beds after the previous day's ordeal), she stumbled onto a chair in the sitting room and looked across at Lady Hazeldine with tearful eyes. ''I wanted so much to apologize to Jan,'' she said glumly.

''Apologize?'' Celia asked in surprise as she took a seat beside the girl. ''Whatever for?''

''For suggesting the horrid excursion in the first place!'' She lowered her head and fiddled with the gloves in her lap. ''But I wanted to apologize for William, too. I'm ashamed that he's my brother.''

''Nonsense, Harriet,'' her ladyship said brusquely. ''In the first place, no one with a grain of sense could possibly hold you responsible for your brother's behavior. And in the second place, his behavior was not so very reprehensible.''

''He behaved like a veritable *poltroon*!'' the girl burst out. ''Leaving Jan behind as he did. It was the act of a *pudding-heart*!''

''Now, Harriet, that's not fair. He had Miss Grindsley to think of, too.''

''Yes, so Mama keeps saying. But none of the others—not Liggy, nor Sir Eustace, nor Jack, nor even I myself!—would have exhibited such a lack of courage, or used so little sense.'' She twisted her gloves together as tightly as if she were imagining she had her brother's throat between her fingers. ''And what's worse, your ladyship, is that he's run back to London. The lily-livered cawker didn't even have the courage to come here and apologize to Jan himself.''

Lady Hazeldine leaned forward and patted Harriet's knee. ''Never mind, my dear. Jan wouldn't have wished for his apologies anyway.''

''No, I don't suppose she would.'' She looked up at her hostess with the ghost of a smile appearing on her lips. ''At least he won't have the cheek to torment her with his attentions any more. Jan will certainly be glad of *that*.''

Lady Hazeldine laughed. ''There, you see? Some good's come out of this after all.''

Beale knocked at the door at that moment to announce Lord Liggett. The gawky fellow, dressed to the nines in a light blue coat, an elaborately knotted neckcloth and shirt-points so high and stiff he could barely turn his head, entered bearing an enormous bouquet of spring blooms. His face fell on hearing that he would not be permitted to see Miss Hazeldine, but Celia noticed that Harriet's expression brightened considerably at his arrival. ''I'm sorry to disappoint you, Lord Liggett,'' she said, forcibly pulling Harriet to her feet, ''but here's Miss Coombe, even more disappointed than you. Perhaps you can take her for a stroll in the Parade Gardens and cheer her up. It is too fine a day for moping about indoors.'' And patting each of their backs, she urged them out into the sunshine.

A few moments later, Sir Eustace Merriot presented himself. He too carried an armful of flowers for Jan, but he took the news that he could not see her in stride. Exhibiting not a glimmer of disappointment, he followed Celia into the sitting room and, seating himself beside her on the sofa, engaged her in a quarter hour of pleasant conversation. Even when they reviewed the events of the day before, the Baronet's remarks were calm and even-tempered. "No long-range harm was done, after all," he said in summation of the previous day's debacle, "and our little excursion to Cheddar Gorge will make a subject of lasting fascination for us all to recount in days to come."

Just when Celia was beginning to relax and enjoy Sir Eustace's company, Beale again appeared at the door, this time to announce Lord Ollenshaw. Celia was overwhelmed with embarrassment. How would Sir Eustace feel when he saw that Max was permitted to go up to see Jan when the same privilege had been denied to *him*? Celia felt keenly sympathetic toward him. But she had no choice. "Tell Miss Jan that his lordship has come to call," she instructed the butler, "and meanwhile, you may send Lord Ollenshaw in here to wait."

Max came in to the sitting room and greeted his hostess with an abstracted smile. It was clear that something troublesome was on his mind, but Celia noticed that his brow cleared when Sir Eustace jumped up to shake his hand. The two men smiled at each other with sincere warmth, for a hearty friendship had been forged between them in the crucible of the search through the caves. It is moments of crisis that reveal one's mettle, and in the crisis of the previous day, each had earned the respect of the other. The Baronet had taken due note of Max's quick thinking and strong, effective leadership. Similarly, Max had recognized, and had been quite grateful for, Sir Eustace's quiet courage and dependable steadfastness. The shared experience had led to a shared admiration.

But this morning they had only a few moments in which to exchange greetings before Beale returned with the word that Miss Hazeldine would receive his lordship upstairs. With the crease returning to his brow, Max made a quick bow to Celia, nodded to Sir Eustace and went quickly from the room.

Celia bit her underlip as she watched him go. Then she turned to the Baronet with a sigh. "I am most sincerely sorry, Sir Eustace," she mumbled, feeling her face grow hot.

The Baronet's eyebrows rose. "Sorry? For what, ma'am?"

"For what just happened, of course."

Sir Eustace seemed sincerely bewildered. "What is it that just happened that would make you sorry?"

She gestured toward the door. "That. Permitting Ollen-shaw to go up to Jan after denying you." She sank down on the sofa and lowered her eyes. "You see, Jan made me promise to permit his lordship to see her."

"But, my dear lady," Sir Eustace assured her, seating himself beside her with comfortable aplomb, "there isn't the slightest need for you to apologize to *me* for that. Why did you think you should?"

"Well, surely you must feel you have a stronger right to see Jan than Ollenshaw has."

"A stronger right? *I?*"

"Of course. You are courting her, after all . . ."

Sir Eustace gaped at her. "Courting *Jan?*"

Celia was beginning to find the conversation painful. She got up and began to pace about the room in distress. "You needn't cover up your feelings for my sake, Sir Eustace. I most sincerely feel for you. Your treatment of my daughter has been most admirable, and you don't *deserve* . . ." She paused, took a deep breath and plunged on. "Jan is a very lovely young woman, as I'm sure I don't need to tell you, but she has the reputation of being a jilt, which I'm sorry to admit she quite deserves. I should never have introduced you to her, for even if she should accept your offer—which she might very well do, since she thinks so highly of you—she would not go through with it." She glanced over at him with eyes moist with sympathy for his pain. "She has never . . . she cannot seem to bring herself . . . and you don't deserve to . . ."

Sir Eustace listened to this disjointed speech with considerable astonishment. "I don't know what you're babbling about, my dear. What on earth makes you think I wish to make an offer to your daughter?"

Celia peered at him with an arrested look. "Well, you've

been courting her, haven't you? Taking her to the assemblies, joining her in the Pump Room, escorting her hither and yon about town . . .''

"No, ma'am, I have *not* been courting her." He put a hand to his head in a gesture of confused helplessness. "I must have been handling myself awkwardly indeed if I've given you that impression."

"But this is ridiculous, sir. You've called every day since our arrival, have you not? There hasn't been an occasion, an excursion, a stroll to the Pump Room or a walk through the park in which we have not had your escort. If you don't call that *courting*, then I don't know what you would call it."

"Oh, I would call it courting, all right," the portly gentleman muttered ruefully, "but I was not courting Jan."

"Not Jan?" She gawked at him, feeling thickheaded. "But no one else resides in this house, except . . .''

"Good God, woman," he said in amused impatience. "How can you be so foolishly blind?"

"Do you mean . . . me?" She sank down on the nearest chair, her breath quite knocked out of her. "Are you saying you've been courting *me*?"

He rose from his place and, crossing to her chair, smiled down at her. "From that first day, when your sister introduced us at the pump."

"But . . . I don't understand you. Jan is so beautiful . . . so gentle . . . so elegant . . . so *musical*."

"Jan is everything you say. I might even have wished to court her, if I hadn't seen from the first that her heart was already given, or if I'd had loverly instead of fatherly feelings toward her, or if I had not met her beautiful, gentle, elegant *mother* first."

"But not musical," Celia pointed out dryly.

"No, not musical," Sir Eustace agreed, pulling her to her feet. "One can't have everything."

"This is quite ridiculous," she muttered, holding him off. "You cannot be serious. I'm . . . I'm . . . well, in the first place, I'm older than you."

"A year or two, perhaps. What difference does that make?"

"But . . . good heavens, sir, *please* don't smile at me in that *proprietary* way! I'm not—"

"Must you call me sir? Surely we've come to that state of intimacy that would permit you to call me Eustace. But I interrupted you, my dear. You said 'I'm not.' You're not *what*?"

"I'm not suitable for . . . for courting."

"Then never mind courting. Let's go right to wedlock. I find you eminently suited for that."

"Balderdash! I'm not at all suited for it. You must have seen it. I've grown unwomanly in my widowhood . . . crotchety and domineering and—"

He pulled her close. "Woman enough for me, my dear. So much, in fact, that I'm quite willing to be domineered. The question is, of course, whether you find me suitable for *you*."

"Well, I have the highest regard for you, of course, but . . ."

"But?"

She shook her head. "No . . . no! How can I answer you? Please, Eustace, this is too much for me to grasp. Go away, dear boy. I must have time to recover from this shock. I must have time to think."

"Of course. Take all the time you wish." He let her go and strolled calmly to the door with his usual measured tread. "Will an hour be sufficient?"

She laughed ruefully. "Don't you dare show your face to me until . . . oh, until tomorrow at the earliest! You are a beast to have stirred me up like this. I feel like a green girl."

He looked back at her, his hand on the knob. "You *look* like a green girl." He smiled across at her fondly. "There is no earthly reason, you know, why we shouldn't be very happy together."

She returned his smile by glowering back at him. "I don't know anything of the sort," she muttered, waving him out. "You've never even seen my bad side. I have this tendency to nag, did you know that? And I'm told I have a very shrewish tongue. And—"

"Enough," he laughed, making a hasty withdrawal. "I

won't listen to another word. Besides, nothing you can say will induce me to rescind my offer.''

''And what's most significant,'' she threw at his retreating back, ''is that I hate music! Didn't Jan ever tell you I hate music? I have not for a moment even *considered* taking another husband, but to take another *musician* as a husband would be the *outside of enough!*''

But he'd already gone.

Twenty-Three

MAX PEERED AT Jan from the doorway of her bedroom and winced. "Good God! *Look* at you!" he exclaimed.

She was sitting up against a pile of pillows, looking very small in a huge, canopied bed that filled most of a modest-sized room. The sun streamed through a pair of casements at her left, making a mockery of the little fire that burned in the fireplace in the wall opposite the windows. "Well, I suppose I should have tried to dress my hair," she said to him in embarrassment, "but I didn't think you'd care—"

"Of course I don't care about your hair!" He came across the room in two strides and looked down at her with knitted brows. "Your *hands*!"

"Oh, the bandages, you mean." She slipped her hands shyly under the coverlet. "There's nothing wrong with them, really. Just a few scratches. Mama overdid it with salves and bandages. I'm sure I'll be fine in a day or two. Good as new."

Max sat down on the side of the bed and withdrew her hands gently from their hiding place. "Good enough in a day or two to play the violin?" he asked, holding them tenderly in his.

She gave him a weak smile but withdrew her hands from his hold. "I could play it now, if Mama would let me."

"I'm glad." Relieved, he let himself look over the rest of her, at least the part not hidden by the coverlet. She was wearing a white nightgown with a ruffle of delicate lace at the throat, and her hair, appealingly tousled, fell in a thick brown mass over her shoulders. Her face was paler than usual, the translucent skin revealing with painful clarity a bluish bruise on her left cheekbone. He leaned forward and touched the area around it gingerly. "I could murder your friend William Coombe with my bare hands," he muttered.

"It's only a little bruise, Max. Though I suppose, with my hair in disarray and my cheek discolored and my hands all bandaged, I look a sight."

"Your bruises and bandages only make you seem more beautiful than ever," he assured her, "if that is possible."

She flicked a troubled look at his face. "That brings me to what I want to speak to you about, Max. I think we must stop this . . . this sort of thing. It is not right."

He stiffened. "What do you mean by 'this sort of thing'?"

"I mean paying me compliments like that, and . . . and other things."

"Other things?"

"Yes. Personal things. Intimate things. Even things that are not compliments—like what you said to me the other day when we left Mrs. Kendall's."

"What did I say?"

"You called me a spinsterish prude, I believe."

"Did I?" He got slowly to his feet and crossed to the fireplace. "I'm sorry for that," he said, looking down at the unnecessary fire and kicking the grate with a booted toe.

"No, don't be sorry. It may be that I deserved it. But that is beside the point. What I'm saying is that the conversation that day was much too . . . too *familiar* for people in our circumstances." She paused for a moment, trying to pluck up sufficient courage to go on. "I don't mean to imply, Max, that the improprieties are all yours. Not at all. I've said several things to you, too, that I should not have. I think I'm more guilty than you of behaving too familiarly. Most particularly . . ." She bit her lip in embarrassment. "Most particularly, I'm ashamed of something I said to you yesterday in the cave."

He threw her a level look over his shoulder. "Calling me your love."

"Yes."

The muscles in his jaw tightened, and turning his eyes back

to the fire, he leaned heavily on the mantel. "Yesterday in the cave was exceptional. I hope we can both be forgiven for anything we may have said."

"Yes. So long as neither of us refines too much on the incident."

"*Refines* too much on it?" He gave a bitter laugh. "How delicately you put the problem, ma'am."

"I don't mean to belittle it, Max," she said, troubled. "You must know how . . . how grateful I am!"

"Grateful? What has that to do with anything?" He swung around to face her, his eyes burning. "Dash it, Jan, I think I shall remember those few moments as long as I live."

Tears sprang to her eyes. "Oh, Max! So shall I!"

He took a step toward her, overwhelmed by an urge to sweep her into his arms and carry her off. If only there were a place somewhere . . . anywhere . . . where they could be alone, where the world could be left behind, where he could hold her and comfort her and throw off this tormenting feeling of guilt. But of course there was no such place. He stopped himself after taking just one step. With an act of will, he stepped back and turned again to stare down at the fire.

Jan, awkwardly wiping away at her eyes, did not see his little movement. She only felt a twinge of shame at what she had just admitted. She had intended this interview to ameliorate the effects of those moments in the cave, not make them worse. "See?" she said in a small voice. "We are doing it again."

"Speaking to each other too familiarly, you mean?"

"Yes. We're supposed to be near-strangers to each other, after all."

He drew in a deep breath. "That's what I came to speak to you about, Jan. This business about being near-strangers. It's no longer believable."

Her eyes widened. "What do you mean?"

"I think it's time I told Belinda the truth about us. You see, she is quite upset about . . . about yesterday."

"Upset? Because you came after me in the cave?"

"Because she happened to see my face at the moment I realized you were missing." He ran his fingers through his hair awkwardly, finding this admission difficult to make. "It seems I . . . I reacted too strongly."

Jan threw him a troubled look. "Too strongly?"

He shrugged. "Belinda says I turned pale. Too pale for the modest alarm appropriate for a near-stranger. She asked me point blank if there was something between us."

"Oh, dear!" She winced as feelings of guilt overwhelmed her. "What did you say to that?"

"Nothing. I couldn't bring myself to lie to her, but I couldn't tell her the truth either, since I'd given you my word. So I merely said that I was not in the mood to speak of it."

Jan sighed unhappily. "That was not kind, Max. Poor Belinda must be suffering terribly. And it is all my fault."

"In one breath you say *I* am not kind, and it's *your* fault?" He gave a mirthless laugh. "Neither one of us seems to be capable of making sense. What a deuced coil we've made of things!"

"It *is* my fault, Max," Jan insisted, determined to make him see that, at least in the matter of Belinda, he had done nothing amiss. "I was wrong to ask you not to tell her about us. But it's not too late. We must tell her at once."

"Yes," he agreed.

"Let me do it, Max," she pleaded. "Since it was I who made you lie in the first place, let me be the one to tell her the truth."

He raised an eyebrow. "The truth?"

She recognized the tinge of sarcasm in his question. "Yes," she answered, raising her chin defensively. "The simple truth. You and I had a brief—a very brief—betrothal, but it happened so many years ago that it can't matter now."

"For Belinda's sake, I suppose that is what must be said," he agreed, starting for the door, "but it can hardly be called the truth. Not even the 'simple' truth."

"I don't understand you, Max. What is not true about it?"

He paused at the door and fixed his eyes on her. "You know as well as I that the full truth is far from simple. But even your simple version is not the truth. Yes, our brief betrothal happened many years ago, but you can hardly claim it doesn't matter now. It matters, my dear. It matters very much. And I'm afraid it always will.''

The words struck her like a blow. She lifted up her bandaged hands as if to ward off the sting of them. They stared at each other for a moment before he strode out of the room and shut the door behind him. Slowly she slipped down under the bedclothes. ''Oh, my dear,'' she wept, turning her face to the pillows, ''what have I done to us?''

Twenty-Four

AN HOUR LATER Jan, fully clothed and with gloves drawn over her bandaged hands, came stealing down the stairs. She was determined to see Belinda without further postponement, but she knew she would not get permission from her mother to leave her bed. Therefore she was trying to slip out of the house without confrontation. She'd managed, thus far, to reach the bottom of the stairs without making a sound. Now if she could just unlatch the front door . . .

"Going out, Miss Jan?" came the butler's voice behind her.

She wheeled about. "Beale!" she gasped. "Where on earth did you come from?"

"From the kitchen, Miss. I thought I heard something. You are *not* intending to go out, are you? I'm certain her ladyship would not approve."

"Then don't tell her," Jan retorted firmly. "Step out of my way, Beale."

"Not until I have her ladyship's leave to do so," the butler said, planting his rotund bulk squarely in front of her. "She gave strict instructions, before she went up for her nap, that you were to be left *in your room* undisturbed. 'Undisturbed' was her very word."

"Never mind about that," Jan said, puzzled. "Did you say Mama went up for a *nap*? How is that? She *never* naps."

The butler permitted himself a shrug. "That's what she told me. 'I am going upstairs for a nap,' she said, 'and I want you to see that both my daughter and I are undisturbed until dinner time.' ''

"That's very strange. Was she feeling unwell?"

"She seemed quite well to me, Miss Jan. In high color, I thought. Perturbed, though. Quite perturbed."

"Really?" the girl prodded, frowning worriedly. "Perturbed about what?"

"I'm sure I couldn't say, Miss. Her ladyship didn't confide in me." He lowered his voice to a conspiratorial whisper. "But I did hear her arguing with someone in the sitting room."

"Mama, arguing? With whom?"

"With Sir Eustace, Miss."

"With Sir *Eustace*?" Jan shook her head in disbelief. "That's quite impossible. You must be mistaken, Beale. Sir Eustace is too good-natured to argue with anyone. But never mind all that now. I'll go into it later, when I've returned from my errand."

"But, Miss Jan, you *can't*—" Beale objected, trying to block her way again.

"Don't be a gudgeon, Beale," Jan laughed, seizing him suddenly by his shoulders and whirling him round like a top. "I'll be back within the hour and slide right back into bed. Mama will never even miss me." And as the butler tottered about trying to regain his balance, she slipped out the door.

Belinda, looking red-eyed and unkempt, led her cousin into the Briarly downstairs sitting room and shut the door. "I know what you've come to say, Jan Hazeldine," the young girl burst out, her voice shaking. "You want to tell me that Max has f-fallen in love with you and wants to b-break it off!"

"Heavens, Belinda," Jan exclaimed gently, "whatever makes you say something so foolish? Come, sit down here beside me so we can talk about all this properly."

The girl, with head lowered and lower lip protruding in a childlike pout, came with sullen reluctance to the sofa. "You needn't treat me like a child," she muttered, refusing to sit. "I know what I saw with my own eyes."

To Jan, the words had a painfully familiar ring. She had said the same sort of thing to Max after she'd seen him embracing Lady Wedmore. And, irony of ironies, she found herself giving the same answer to Belinda that Max had given to her. "Can you not conceive, Belinda, of a circumstance in which there is more—or less—than meets the eye?"

"No, I can't," Belinda answered with the same closed mind that Jan had had all those years ago. "I could see in his face, yesterday at the gorge, that he was in love with you. When he realized you hadn't come out of the cave with the others, he turned absolutely ashen."

"Are you sure that meant he loves me, Belinda? Might he not have felt the same white-faced fear if it had been *you* lost in the cave? Or Aunt Nettie? Or even a mere acquaintance, like Mary Grindsley?"

"You are trying to confuse me," the girl said tearfully, sinking down on the sofa and reaching in her sleeve for a handkerchief.

"I know you're confused, my love. And that confusion is all my fault. But that's why I've come to see you. To clear up the confusion."

"I d-don't know what you m-mean," the girl said, flicking a moist, dark-eyed look of bewilderment to Jan's face.

"I'll explain. I'll explain it all. But I must begin at the beginning, not with yesterday. Do you remember, Belinda, when Mama and I first came to Bath, and you sat down beside me and described your beloved to me?"

"Yes, of course I remember."

"Well, that day was the first day I'd ever heard the name of your betrothed. Aunt Nettie had not mentioned his name in any of her letters to Mama, you see. So when I realized it was Max, I was . . . very surprised."

"Yes, I seem to remember that. You said you knew him slightly."

"Yes, I did say that. But it was . . ." She clenched her fingers nervously. "It was a lie. I knew him better than just slightly. In fact, I knew him quite well."

"Quite well?"

Jan had to drop her eyes from Belinda's. "*Very* well. We had once been betrothed."

"*Betrothed?*" The word was neither a gasp nor a scream but a bit of both.

"You mustn't make too much of that, my dear," Jan said soothingly. "It was eight years ago, and it wasn't much of a betrothal. I think it lasted all of four hours. The matter has only grown in importance because I didn't admit it to you right away, as soon as you told me Max's name."

Belinda blinked, trying to take it all in. "Why *didn't* you tell me right away?" she asked, her underlip trembling in petulant offense.

"I don't know. It was terribly foolish. Perhaps it was because I was so completely taken by surprise. Or because I was afraid it would cause embarrassment between us. Or because I thought you might make too much of it and feel hurt. A dozen silly reasons. And then, I made an even worse mistake. I convinced Max to keep silent also, for the same silly reasons. He was reluctant to do it, of course. He didn't want any dishonesty between you. It was all my fault, truly."

"Confound it, Jan, what exactly are you telling me?" Belinda put a hand through her tousled curls and jumped up from her seat. "Let me be certain that I understand all this." She stood squarely before Jan, hands on hips, and glared down at her cousin with an angry intensity that was suddenly not at all childlike. "Are you telling me that *my Max* is one of your *jilts?*"

Jan was taken aback. "Well . . . yes, I suppose . . . you could put it that way."

"You jilted the *Marquis of Ollenshaw?* You must have been mad!"

"I wouldn't say that, exactly, Belinda," Jan mumbled, disconcerted by the girl's reactions. "We didn't suit, that's all."

"Didn't *suit?* You said the betrothal lasted four hours. How can you have discovered *in four hours* that you didn't suit?"

Jan gaped at her. *How,* she wondered, *has this eighteen-year-old chit managed to twist the direction of this conversation out of my control?* "Well, you see I . . . we . . ." Realizing that the girl was, somehow, intimidating her, she drew herself up stiffly. "We *admitted* after four hours that we didn't suit. We both knew long before that we were not . . . not alike."

"In what way, not alike?" the young girl demanded.

"You can guess, can't you, Belinda? He was a Corinthian, in love with sport. I was in love with music. We had nothing in common."

"You evidently had enough in common to become betrothed." The words were like a denunciation.

"Heavens, my dear," Jan said, trying to smile, "you sound like a barrister in a court of law, interrogating the accused. I know I'm guilty of not being entirely open with you, but I'm not on trial, am I?"

But Belinda ignored the reproach. She was busily pacing about the room, following intently some other train of thought. "Do you know what I think, Cousin Jan?" she asked suddenly, wheeling about and confronting Jan again. "I think you want him *back*! That's it, isn't it?"

"Belinda!" Jan gasped, shocked. "You can't be serious."

"Yes, I see it all now. You learned the identity of my betrothed and immediately began to plan how to wrest him away from me."

Jan, bereft of speech, could only gape at her.

"It was a good little plan, too," Belinda went on, her voice becoming more and more shrill with each new accusation. "I see it all quite clearly now. You convinced Max to keep this significant information from me so that you could engage in secret little meetings to talk about it, and exchange secret little looks behind my back, and have secret little jokes at my expense."

"Belinda, you *can't* believe I could be so . . . so calculating!"

"I *do* believe it. In fact I'm beginning to believe that the whole incident in the *cave* was calculated! You lost yourself *on purpose*!"

Jan stared at her in astonishment. "On *purpose*?"

The girl's full lips trembled with emotion. "You, Jan Hazeldine, are a heartless *wretch*! You lured him into those caves just so you could throw yourself into his arms when he saved you!''

There was just enough truth in what the girl said to keep Jan from slapping her face. She *had* thrown herself into Max's arms, that much at least was true. But as for the rest—well, it was too ridiculous an accusation to respond to seriously. ''You can't mean what you're saying, Belinda,'' she said quietly. ''You're overset by what I've told you. Perhaps we shouldn't say anything more until you've had time to think about it . . . and grow calmer.''

''I don't *need* to think about it! You can't have him, no matter *what* tricks you choose to employ! Do you hear me, Cousin Jan? You *can't have him*!''

Jan could hardly believe her eyes and ears. This was not the sweet-faced, charming, innocent girl the world recognized as Belinda, but a spoiled, overindulged child throwing a tantrum. ''But Belinda, my dear, *listen* to me. I am *not* trying to wrest Max from you. Even if I were, he would not permit it. Max is not the sort—''

''I don't care what sort he is! He is *mine* now, and I won't give him up no matter what! All your plans and ruses were all for naught! So there!'' And, livid with rage, her lips in a more sullen pout than ever, she flounced from the room.

Jan sat immobile for a long while after Belinda stormed out. The temper tantrum she'd just witnessed revealed an aspect of Belinda's character that Jan had never suspected was there. Was Max aware of it, she wondered? If he were not, shouldn't he be warned? But then, she'd never warned Belinda of certain aspects of *his* character for fear it would be meddling. Why then should she meddle on Max's behalf? If she did, Belinda would be quite justified in suspecting her motives.

As for her motives, what were they? Was Belinda so very wrong after all? Didn't she, deep inside, want Max back? She still loved him; she'd known that for years. But she'd rejected him long ago for what she suspected were serious flaws in his character. Weren't those flaws still there? Or was she wrong about that, too?

It seemed evident that she, Jan Hazeldine, was a complete

failure at character evaluation. She'd misjudged Belinda, certainly. She'd misjudged Harriet and Sir Eustace, at least insofar as estimating their likelihood of feeling an attraction for each other. She may very well have completely misjudged Max. And since she'd just realized that Belinda's hysterical accusation—that she, Jan, wanted Max back—had some truth, she wondered if she'd even misjudged herself!

It's too bad, she observed to herself as she walked slowly from her aunt's house back to her own, *that one can't read human character as one reads a piece of music.* Music was so clean, so precise, so beautifully honest. That, at least, was one thing she understood. She could never misjudge her violin.

Twenty-Five

BY THE TIME she arrived home, Jan knew what she had to do. There was no question about it; she had to leave this place. Max was betrothed to Belinda Briarly, for better or worse, and there was nothing she, Jan, could do about it. It was not her affair. Max had ceased to be her concern eight years ago. If now he'd unwisely shackled himself to a spoiled brat, it was his own doing, and he'd have to contend with the problem his own way.

She hurried up the stairs to her mother's bedroom and burst in without knocking. She found her mother sitting at her dressing table staring at herself in the mirror, a pastime she'd never before known her mother to engage in, but Jan was too upset at this moment to note the oddity of it. "Mama," she announced loudly, "I'm going home to London. Tomorrow."

Startled by the girl's sudden appearance, Celia gasped, her hands flying up to her breast. "*Jan!* What—"

"No, dearest, don't try to talk me out of it," Jan went on heedlessly. "You, of course, may remain here for Nettie's little celebrations if you wish. I'm quite capable of making the journey alone."

"Heavens, Jan, what *is* all this?" her mother asked, turning away from her mirror in alarm. "Bursting in here and speaking in that stentorian way. You made me jump!"

"I'm sorry, Mama. I didn't mean to startle you. I suppose I was a bit fortissimo, but I just wanted to tell you *firmly* what my plans are."

Celia frowned. "*Tell* me? Not *ask* me? Am I now no longer your mother?"

Jan, feeling suddenly abashed by her rash behavior, knelt down beside her mother's chair and threw her arms about her. "Forgive me, dearest. I'm quite beside myself. I've just returned from Aunt Nettie's, where I endured a most unpleasant interview with Belinda."

"Returned from *Nettie's*?" Celia peered at her daughter in bewilderment. "How can that be? You were *supposed* to be in bed!"

"Don't be cross with me, Mama. I thought it more important to have a talk with Belinda than to stay cooped up in my room."

"Very well, I won't be cross. I shall try to remain calm. Here, come sit down beside me on the bed so that we may be comfortable while you enlighten me on what was so important to tell Belinda."

She rose from her dressing table and led her daughter across the room to the bedstead. There they perched side by side on the bed. Celia took her daughter's still-gloved hands in hers while the girl related the gist of her conversation with her cousin. She gently removed the girl's gloves while she listened, trying to keep from letting the tale upset her. But when Jan repeated Belinda's accusation that Jan had lost herself in the cave on purpose, Celia lost her temper. "The little cat!" she exclaimed. "I'd like to slap her face."

"I know it was a wild accusation, Mama," Jan said thoughtfully, "but in a sense I don't blame Belinda for losing her head." She lowered her eyes guiltily. "I handled matters badly from the first. By keeping the facts from her, I gave Belinda sufficient cause to distrust me. And what has pricked my conscience even more is the feeling that perhaps she's *right* in believing that I want to steal Max away from her."

Celia gave her daughter a troubled look. "*Do* you, Jan?"

Jan dropped her head in her hands. "How have I become so despicable?" she murmured tearfully. "I'm such a *weakling*. I know I have no right to wish him back, but I do love him so!"

Celia reached up and smoothed Jan's hair fondly, her heart

constricting within her in pain for her daughter. Nevertheless, she spoke with firm disapproval. "I don't understand you, dearest. You jilted Max eight years ago because you felt you did not suit. Now you think you want him back. Why? Has he changed so much since then? Or is it you who've changed?"

Jan lifted up a tear-stained, agonized face. "Oh, Mama, I don't know. I've lost all capability of making judgments. I don't know *anything* any more."

Celia sighed helplessly. "Well, dearest, the question is hypothetical, in any case. Max is Belinda's now, as much as if they'd already taken vows. A betrothal is as binding as a wedding if the female of the pair wishes to keep it so."

"I know. That's why I must get away from here, Mama. It will be for the best all around. Max will no doubt be relieved. And Belinda obviously no longer wishes to see my face. As for me, since I'd feel nothing but pain at seeing Max in her company, I shall be better off in London. So, please, dearest, give me permission to go home."

"Of course you have my permission. I should have taken you home days ago, when you first asked me." Celia got up and began to pace about the room, her brow wrinkled in concentration. "We shall leave at daybreak tomorrow," she said at last.

Jan, who'd been resting her forehead against the bedpost wondering how she was to face her grim future, looked up abruptly. *"We?"* she asked. "But . . . you don't have to accompany me, Mama, if you don't wish to. Aunt Nettie may take offense if you leave so soon."

"If she does, she'll get over it." She rubbed her temples with her fingers for a moment as if soothing away a troublesome thought, and then she smiled at her daughter. "Don't worry about it, my love. I *want* to go home with you." In the few moments of pacing, Celia Hazeldine had made up her mind about her own situation as well as her daughter's, and she now spoke with energetic firmness. "The timing may be as fortuitous for me as it is for you. If I stay, I may be tempted to . . . to take a step in a direction I never intended to go."

Jan blinked at her in confusion. "What do you mean, Mama?"

"Never mind," Celia said, walking briskly across to the bellpull and ringing for her maid. "It's a long and ridiculous story which I have no time to relate now. Don't just sit there gaping, my love. Bestir yourself! We must pack."

Their coach departed the next morning, but not quite on schedule. There were too many details that had to be seen to before Lady Hazeldine and her daughter could leave. Besides the packing, they had to give detailed instructions to Beale about the disposition of the household furnishing, the subleasing of the house, and the transportation of the servants. Coaches and horses had to be arranged for, portmanteaus and boxes had to be loaded, letters had to be written. Celia had to write to Nettie, and Jan had to write to Harriet. Neither of those letters was easy to write, for the true reason for their abrupt departure could not be given, and convincing excuses are hard to concoct for persons who are not given to falsehood. The writing of the letters consumed more time than they bargained for.

But the most difficult letter for Celia to write was the one to Sir Eustace. For several hours she convinced herself that it would be best to run off to London without leaving him a word of good-bye. After all, she reasoned, there had not been any promises exchanged. But after she'd retired, she found she could not sleep. She became troubled, imagining how his face would fall when he arrived at her door and learned she was gone. It was not right to hurt him so. She rose from her bed in the wee hours of the morning and went to her writing table.

She tried, with many scratched-out lines and crumpled sheets, to express to him her misgivings about matrimony in general and about his proposal in particular, but she found the task difficult. "I am too old to learn new ways," she wrote and discarded. "You are too young for me," was penned and similarly abandoned. "I am not of a temperament to adjust to a second marriage," she began, and then threw it away. "I am, after all these years of widowhood, too set in my ways to . . ." But she didn't finish that either. "You surely can find someone more attuned to your tastes," she wrote on a clean sheet, but that was another failure. And so was "There is for you someone somewhere more gentle in spirit," and "I am become a testy old biddy. . . ."

But none of these phrases suited her. They were all true—or partly true—but somehow they rang false. They seemed like weak excuses rather than strong reasons. After several attempts, she dispatched merely a brief, innocuously formal note. *Dear Sir Eustace*, she wrote.

> *Please forgive me for not being able to give you my answer in person, but urgent matters require my immediate return to London. I thank you for your very flattering offer, but after careful consideration I find I must decline. With every good wish for your future happiness,*
> *I remain sincerely yours,*
> *Celia Hazeldine*

It was ten in the morning before they finally departed. Both Jan and her mother were moodily silent as their carriage set off down Pierrepont Street. This brief visit to Bath had had a profound effect on both of them, and their feelings were stirred by this last glimpse of the Abbey tower disappearing behind them and the Parade Bridge looming up just ahead. Jan stared out of the window, wondering if she would ever lay eyes on Max again, and if the awful ache inside her would ever fade away. At that very moment, she caught a glimpse of Max himself, walking down Grove Street in her direction. It was as if he'd materialized out of her thoughts. Her heart began to hammer in her chest. *Stop the carriage!* she wanted to cry. *It's Max!*

But before the words could leap from her brain to her tongue, she saw that he was not alone. He was with a lady. Belinda, Jan supposed. But a closer look revealed that it wasn't Belinda. Jan gasped when she saw that the woman had red hair. *Good God*, a voice within her cried, *it can't be true! I'm imagining things.*

But it was true! Max was right there on the street in front of her, engaged in earnest conversation with Lady Wedmore!

Jan gasped again in utter revulsion. He was *keeping* the woman in Bath after all! And to *think* that she, the supposedly clever Jan Hazeldine, had lately become convinced by his innocent declarations that she'd been *wrong* about him! She'd actually been hating herself for mistrusting him . . . for having harbored unwarranted suspicions . . . for believing the evidence of her own eyes! He'd called her a spinsterish prude, and she'd let herself wonder if it were true. What a *fool* she was! Love certainly made one blind.

But perhaps it was a stroke of luck that she'd caught this glimpse of him. She hated him now! She hated him more than she'd ever hated him eight years ago. Never again would she give a moment's thought to him, to his *cher amies*, or even to the spoiled chit he was about to take to wife! Let Belinda have him! They deserved each other!

"Jan? *Jan!*" It was her mother, pulling at her arm.

"Wh-what is it, Mama?"

"You *gasped*. What is it, my love? Did you see something dreadful out there?"

"No, Mama," the girl answered, burrowing into the cushions and shutting her eyes. "It was nothing. Nothing at all worth speaking of."

Twenty-Six

MAX, AS HE approached the Hazeldine house on Pierrepont Street, did not notice the Hazeldine carriage trundle by. He remained absorbed in his conversation with his companion until he knocked at the door. When Beale answered his knock, Max was startled at the butler's appearance. The fellow was in his shirtsleeves, and a large green apron enveloped his bulk. "Oh," Beale exclaimed in surprise, "Lord *Ollenshaw*!"

"Good morning, Beale," Max said. "I know I am not expected, but will you please tell Miss Hazeldine I'm here." He glanced down at his companion, and his lips turned up in a tiny smile of self-satisfaction. "Tell her that I've brought Lady Wedmore to see her. Be sure you say it just that way. *Lady Wedmore*."

"I'm afraid, my lord, that I can not do so. Miss Hazeldine has gone."

Max blinked at him, his smile dying abruptly. "Gone? What do you mean, gone?"

"I mean departed, my lord. For London."

Lady Wedmore gave a little snort, but Max ignored it. "How can that *be*?" he asked the butler. "I saw her just yesterday, when she was confined to bed, remember? She said nothing to me then about leaving."

"It was a last-minute decision, I believe, my lord. That's why I'm still packing things up. Everything was arranged in a great rush."

"Are you saying that Lady Hazeldine's gone as well?"

"Oh, yes, my lord. Both of them."

"Good God! Tell me, man, is something wrong? Miss Hazeldine has not become ill, has she? I was *afraid* she might feel some ill effects from that deuced excursion!"

"Oh, no, my lord, it's nothing like that. Miss Hazeldine was quite well, I assure you. And her ladyship too."

"Then why . . . ?"

"I'm sure I couldn't say, Lord Ollenshaw. But her ladyship did send a note to her sister. You might inquire there. I'm sure Lady Briarly has more information than I have."

Max sighed and turned away. "Yes. Thank you, Beale. Good day."

Lady Wedmore followed Max down the front steps, her flounced skirts swishing. "So, my dear, you are too late," she said, amused.

He threw her an abstracted glance. "Yes. Eight years too late."

"Eight years?"

"I should have done this eight years ago. If I made her face you *then*, the confrontation might have made a difference."

She cocked her head, studying him. "Then why didn't you?"

He shrugged. "I didn't think of it then. I didn't think of it until yesterday, when you and I passed each other on the South Parade."

They walked down the street in silence. After a while Lady Wedmore put a hand on his arm. "You know, Max, I would be willing to go to London and see her. I'd be glad to do it, if you provided a carriage and took care of my, er, little expenses."

He shook his head. "No, thank you, ma'am. That would be an excessive effort for what amounts to little more than a whim."

She looked at him with raised brows. "Are you saying that you took the trouble to bring me here just for a *whim*?"

"I'm afraid so. I'm feeling very foolish about it now." He took out a small box from his pocket. "Here, my dear. A little trinket to thank you for your time this morning. Shall I see you home?''

''No, it's not necessary. I'm only going a step away, to Milsom Street.'' She opened the box, and her eyes widened to see a little diamond pin. ''Max, my *dear*!'' she exclaimed in delight. ''This is most generous payment indeed.''

''Think nothing of it, ma'am. Good day.'' He tipped his hat to her and set off in the opposite direction.

She looked after him pensively. ''Max?''

He looked back. ''Yes?''

''I'm sorry this did not work out, my dear. Truly.''

''It doesn't matter,'' he muttered glumly. ''I wanted to have the satisfaction of . . . of . . .'' He sighed and shook his head. ''But even if she'd been home, and even if she'd believed you, it wouldn't have made any real difference in my life. No difference at all.''

The Hazeldines' abrupt departure surprised Sir Eustace Merriot, too. His valet was shaving him when Celia's note was delivered. He pushed the fellow aside, jumped up from his chair and, with his face still covered with lather, broke the seal and ran his eyes quickly over the brief message. Then he read it again. Then he sank down on his chair and groaned. The valet tried to tilt his master's head back so that he could proceed with the shave, but Sir Eustace thrust his hand aside. ''Damn it, man, get out!'' the Baronet swore. ''Get out and leave me alone.''

The valet took himself off, shaken. Never before, in the more than twenty years that he'd been dressing Sir Eustace, had the master ever raised his voice. ''It must 'ave been the note ye brought 'im,'' he confided later to Sir Eustace's butler. ''I 'ave no idea wha' in blazes could 'ave been in it to turn the master so stiff-rumped, but whatever was in that note 'ad to be somethin' mighty brummish. 'E looked like 'e'd been kicked in 'is puddin'-basket!''

Nettie Briarly, too, was upset by her note from Celia. ''Will you look at this?'' she exclaimed to her daughter, tossing the note to her across the breakfast table. ''Celia and Jan have gone home to London! And without giving us a *word* of warning!''

Belinda, who'd been poking at her coddled eggs with a dispirited lack of appetite, perked up at once. ''Jan? *Gone?*'' She snatched up the note eagerly.

''Yes, gone!'' Nettie's mouth shaped itself into a pout not unlike her daughter's. ''And without even *calling* on us to say good-bye!'' Shaking her head in offended distress, she picked up the teapot and began to pour herself a cup of tea. Tea, she always found, was the most soothing brew in times of stress.

''They *are* gone!'' Belinda murmured, a smile curling her full lips as her eyes ran over her aunt's missive. ''How lovely! How *absolutely* lovely!''

''Be*linda*!'' Nettie froze in the act of pouring. ''How can you *say* that? They are our closest kin! And now they won't be here for your parties and balls.''

''I'm glad they won't. I *hate* and *despise* Genevra Hazeldine!'' She took a hearty mouthful of egg and then calmly added, ''Look out, Mama, or you'll spill your tea.''

Nettie lowered the teapot, her eyes wide in astonishment. ''Belinda Briarly, have you lost your mind? What are you *saying*? You always *adored* your cousin. She is the most gentle, loving, beautiful, thoughtful girl in the world. We've always said so.''

Belinda tossed her head scornfully. ''I, for one, will never say so again. If you wish to know the truth, I've changed my mind about her.''

''But, my love, *why*?

''Because, Mama, your gentle, loving, thoughtful niece has been trying to steal my Max away from me!''

''Steal *Max*?'' Nettie couldn't believe her ears. She gaped at her daughter as if she'd never seen her before. ''That's ridiculous! It's the most ridiculous thing I ever heard. Why on earth would Jan want to steal Max? She threw him over *years* ago.''

Now it was Belinda's turn to gape. ''Mama! How on earth did you know that?''

''I've known it from the first. I have an excellent memory,

and I recalled, when you first met Max, that he was Jan's first jilt.''

"Then why didn't you *tell* me?"

"What was there to tell? It wasn't important."

"Not *important*? My own cousin was once betrothed to my husband-to-be, and you didn't think it was *important*?''

"No, I didn't. It was ages ago, after all. And it wasn't made much of even then. Cecy didn't even remember his *name* when I first mentioned it. So how can it have been important?''

Belinda slammed down her fork in impatience. "But what if my dear cousin changed her mind? What if she decided, after she saw that *I* wanted him, that she'd made a mistake in jilting him? Well, Mama? Would you consider it important *then*?''

"No, I would not," Nettie declared, rising in magisterial dignity from her place and glaring down at her daughter. "And I do not like the impatient tone you're taking with me. I am your mother, not your abigail.''

Belinda's underlip began to jut out in a pout. "I didn't mean to sound impatient, Mama. But I want to know why you think it's so impossible for Jan to have changed her mind. She hasn't found herself anyone else in all these years—just a few nobodies only worthy of jilting—so isn't it possible that Max looks better to her now?''

"It may be possible," Nettie granted, though she felt a surge of distaste for her daughter's words and demeanor. "It may even be probable. But it is no concern of yours.''

"No concern of *mine*?" the girl screeched. "How can you *say* that, Mama?''

Nettie came round the table and lifted her daughter's chin. "Look at me, Belinda, while I speak to you. I am older and more experienced in these matters than you, so mind what I say. You and Max are *promised* to each other. Pledges have been exchanged and banns read. He and Jan are both too honorable to behave in any manner that would be unfaithful to those pledges or disloyal to you. Max has always behaved in an exemplary manner and has shown you countless signs of his affection. If you are so foolish as to distrust your intended bridegroom, then perhaps you don't deserve him.''

Belinda's pout became pronounced, and she began to whimper. "But, M-Mama, you don't *understand*! It isn't Max, it's *Jan*!" She thrust her mother's hand off and turned her eyes away. "Jan's been up to all *sorts* of evil tricks, trying to win him back. Lying to me, and having secrets with him, and purposely getting herself lost in the cave so that he would have to f-find her!''

"Purposely getting lost?" her mother exclaimed in disgust. "You cannot be so lacking in common sense! You are going too far, my girl. You *cannot* believe that anyone with a head in working order would purposely get lost in a cave. That is risking *death*! Anyone even *slightly* acquainted with Jan would know that such stupidity—and such deviousness— would be completely foreign to her nature.''

Belinda wheeled about in her chair and glared up at her mother. "How is it, Mama," she burst out sullenly, "that you are so quick to take Jan's side against mine? You could be mistaken in her, you know.''

Nettie sighed. "You shame me, Belinda, you really do. Just ask yourself this: if Jan *were* trying to steal your betrothed, would she run away from Bath and leave the field to you? But she's gone, isn't she? Gone away for good. How do you explain that?''

Belinda slumped down in her chair, scowling. "I don't know. For all I know she has some other scheme up her sleeve.''

Nettie threw her arms up in disgust. "I've heard all I care to on this subject," she declared, turning to go to the door, "but if you have a grain of sense left in your head, you'll not repeat any of this rodomontade to anyone else. Certainly not to Max.''

She stalked to the doorway and then paused. Shaking her head, she looked back over her shoulder at her beautiful, sulking daughter. "When you act like this, Belinda, do you know what sometimes occurs to me? I don't like to admit it, my dear, but sometimes . . .'' She expelled a deep, lingering sigh. "Sometimes I think I spoiled you.''

* * *

There was one more Bath resident who was devastated by
the news of the Hazeldines' departure: Lord Liggett. While
Nettie and Belinda were agonizing about it over their breakfast table, and Sir Eustace was venting his spleen on his valet,
Harriet Coombe was imparting the information to Liggy in
the Pump Room. They had met near the Tompion clock,
where Belinda's circle often gathered, but none of the others
had yet arrived.

Liggy's face fell on hearing the announcement. Jan, his
first and only love, was gone! He was stricken. He turned
pale and sank down beside Harriet on one of the Pump Room
benches, groaning pathetically. "Oh, Harry," he gasped, "I
think that my h-heart is bro . . . bro . . ."

"Slowly, Liggy, slowly," Harriet reminded him. "Take
even breaths."

He breathed. "Broken!" he managed.

"No it's not," Harriet assured him. "One's heart can't
break over a love that never was."

He stiffened angrily. "What do you mean, ne-ver was?"

"You and Jan hardly exchanged twenty words during the
few weeks she was here."

"What have *words* got to say to any-thing? I *loved* her!"
He turned his head to Harriet—an awkward movement be-
cause of his high shirtpoints—and studied her face intently.
"Don't you be-lieve I loved her?"

"No, I don't," Harriet said flatly. "It was an infatuation,
that was all."

He blinked in earnest cogitation for a moment. Then he
turned again to his companion. "Are you s-sure, Harry?"

"Yes, I am." Harriet patted his shoulder comfortingly.
"Love is more substantial than the mere admiring of someone's face, you know. There must be spiritual involvement,
too, and a . . . a sharing of thoughts and feelings, a sense of
. . . of oneness."

"Really?" He pondered her words for several moments.
"Do you think that *I* can e-ver . . . ?"

"Of course. Why not?"

"Well, I have this diffi . . . diffi . . ."

"Difficulty expressing yourself?"

"Yes." He threw her a grateful look for helping him.

"That won't matter, Liggy. You are getting better every day at expressing yourself. And when the right girl happens along, you won't need many words."

"But *what* girl, Harry? I don't know many young la-dies."

"Well, what about one of the Misses Brett?"

He threw her a look of horror. "They are ninny-hammers," he said bluntly.

She looked at him proudly. "Yes, they are, aren't they? But see how well you said that? Ninnyhammers. Such a long word, and you didn't even stumble over it. I *told* you you were improving."

But he was more interested in the subject of young ladies than speech improvement. "Who else is there?" he prodded.

"For you to fall in love with? Well, there's always Mary Grindsley. She's had her eye on you from the first."

He shook his head. "She has her eye on any-one who's eli-gi-ble."

"Liggy!" Harriet squealed with laughter. "You're quite the knowing one! I didn't think it of you."

"Just because my tongue is slow doesn't mean my br-brain is slow," he pointed out.

"Right!" she agreed, slapping him on the back. Then she sat back against the bench and folded her hands in her lap. "Of course, there is one other female candidate you might consider," she said, lowering her eyes primly.

"Who?" he asked eagerly. "Who?"

She threw him a laughing glance. "You clunch. *Me.*"

Twenty-Seven

LADY HAZELDINE PERMITTED her daughter the luxury of five full days of uninterrupted violin playing. She knew how much the girl was suffering, and she was willing for Jan to get what solace she could from her music. But after five days, Celia Hazeldine could bear no more. She marched upstairs to the music room and demanded that her daughter cease and desist. Enough was enough!

By this time, the London household had been restored to its normal state. Beale and the other servants had returned from Bath, the dust covers had all been removed, the kitchen was in full operation, the bills had all been paid, and the invitations all answered. The London season was in full swing, and her ladyship informed her daughter in a tone that was decidedly fortissimo that it was time to resume living.

Jan knew what her mother meant. The words "to resume living" simply meant that she, Jan, would have to resume the endless search for an eligible suitor. It did not matter to Lady Hazeldine that her daughter hadn't the heart for it. The girl didn't know what was good for her. "The best cure for a wounded heart, my dearest girl," the mother insisted, "is another love. And the sooner you find one, the better."

Thus the unhappy girl was dragged on yet another round of dinner parties, routs and balls, but never for a moment did the gaiety of the crowds, the elegance of the surroundings, the brilliance of the conversation, or the energy of the dancing free her mind from its gloomy contemplation of what had happened at Bath. After a week of what seemed to her pure torture, Jan decided that the time had come to rebel.

She chose the time for the actual skirmish after she'd been brought home from the opera by the fellow her mother had chosen as her newest suitor. He was a pleasant-looking young man named Robert Fassenden, with an easy drawl, a confident manner and a fortune of fifteen thousand a year. Any girl (as her mother had pointed out on the evening of their first meeting) would think herself lucky to snare him. There was nothing wrong with him, really. Nothing but a sniffing laugh, a pair of furtive eyes and a tendency to begin every other sentence with *Egad*.

Celia had made sure that Jan received him when he paid three morning calls in one week. The girl was also forced to accept his escort for a ride in the park and a visit to the Elgin marbles. By that time, she was begging her mother to let her discourage his attentions. But Celia would not have it. "Give the fellow *time*," she insisted. "Perhaps you won't notice those tiny flaws once you've gotten used to him."

"But, Mama," Jan had pointed out, "if he continues to court me, he'll begin to take for granted that I favor his suit, and then, when I reject him, the world will call it another jilt!"

But her mother had not taken the objection seriously and had compelled Jan to accept Mr. Fassenden's escort to the opera. It was a dreadful evening, during which, egad, the fellow talked entirely and incessantly about himself. When the evening was over, Jan came storming home with her eyes blazing and rebellion in her heart. But since her mother was already fast asleep, the rebellion had to wait.

Jan had to cool her heels and her temper until almost eleven the next morning, when her mother at last decided to rise from her bed. Celia Hazeldine floated downstairs in a ruffled robe and slippers, her braided hair flapping in a long tail behind her. "Good morning, my love," she sang out in cheery greeting to her daughter, and she disappeared into the morning room for breakfast.

Jan held her fire until she'd given her mother time to consume her tea-and-toast breakfast, and then, bursting into the morning room with the explosive energy of a cat just released from prolonged captivity, the girl launched her attack. "Mama," she declared, *molto* fortissimo, "I am calling a halt. I'm too old to be subject to a mother's orders. I am declaring my independence. I shall henceforth decide for myself what gentlemen may call on me, or what invitations I wish to accept. And one thing I've made up my mind about is that I shall never again allow myself to be courted. I have *done* with all that, do you hear, Mama? Done! You must accept the fact that I am now, and shall remain, a spinster. And if you can't accept it, I shall pack a bag and remove myself to . . . to *Timbuktu*!"

"Good Lord, Jan," her mother said, dumbfounded, her teacup frozen in air halfway between her saucer and her lips. "What's come over you? What on earth did that nice Mr. Fassenden do to cause you to fall into such a taking?"

"That 'nice' Mr. Fassenden is a *clod*! After procuring a box right in the center of the opera house and supplying me with a superb pair of opera glasses, he made me miss the first act by dragging me out to the lobby to exchange pleasantries with his friends, he whispered nonsense in my ear throughout the second and third acts, and he fell asleep—and snored!—through the fourth. You know how I love the *Fidelio*, yet I didn't hear a bit of it!"

"Genevra Hazeldine, you're putting it on much too rare and thick," Celia said, unmoved by her daughter's tirade. "A man doesn't have to like opera to make a satisfactory husband." And turning back to the little round table where the remains of her breakfast still lay, she calmly lifted her cup to her mouth.

But her daughter could not be calm. *"Husband?"* she cried, aghast. "I'd rather *die*! I've never known such a bumptious coxcomb. The man is completely wrapped up in his own concerns. He talks in a steady stream, never even pausing to take notice of my reactions. He spoke for fully three-quarters of an hour about the great number of blue bloods on his family tree. Then he went on about the number of young ladies who are pining away for him in hopeless but unflagging adoration. I tell you, Mama, your Mr. Fassenden's tastes are vulgar, his opinions unsound, his attitudes toplofty, his manner egotistical, his—''

''Yes, yes, I see,'' her mother interrupted dryly. ''You admire him so much that you're at a loss for words.''

''Admire him?'' Jan snorted, the strength of her feelings overwhelming her sense of humor. ''I have more admiration for . . . for *William Coombe*!''

One corner of Celia's mouth turned up in a lopsided, wry smile. ''Then you are saying, my love, that I should not rush to order wedding flowers and champagne. Is that the gist of this fanfaronade?''

''I am saying, Mama,'' Jan retorted (although her mother's attitude of tolerant amusement did much to weaken the force of her attack), ''that you should not expect me to accept an offer from *anyone*. I am a spinster, dearest. That's all there is to it. The only man I've met in years who was at all acceptable was Sir Eustace Merriot, and even *you* agreed that he was not right for me.''

Her mother's half smile faded. ''Did I say that?''

''Yes, of course you did. Don't you remember?''

''No. I only remember saying that he was not right for Harriet.'' She looked up at her daughter with a troubled crease in her brow. ''I hope, my love, that you aren't serious about Sir Eustace being 'acceptable.' You wouldn't really wish for an offer from him, would you?''

''No. Not really,'' Jan admitted, realizing with depressing certainty that she couldn't accept an offer from *anyone*, no matter how admirable, while her heart was in thrall to a licentious rake.

The older woman sighed in relief. ''I *hoped* you wouldn't, my dear, for Eustace Merriot is not . . . for you.''

Jan sat down at the little table and studied her mother curiously. ''I don't understand you, Mama. You push suitors at me who are completely impossible—like Fassenden—and yet when we mention someone like Sir Eustace, who is one of the finest gentlemen of my acquaintance, you seem reluctant to consider him.''

Celia put a nervous hand to her forehead. ''But there's nothing to consider, dearest. He didn't make you an offer.''

"That's true. He didn't. But I suppose he might have done, if I'd encouraged him."

"No, I don't think he would have," Celia argued, picking up a spoon and stirring the tea in her cup in uneasy abstraction.

"No?" Jan raised her eyebrows curiously. "That's a strange thing to say. Why don't—"

A tap on the door interrupted her. It was Beale. "A gentleman to see you, Miss Jan," he announced. "It's Sir Eustace Merriot. From Bath."

Celia's hands flew to her hair, but Jan, who burst into laughter at the coincidence of the announcement, did not notice. "You may tell him to come in, Beale," the girl said to the butler.

Celia wavered between a desire to dash up to her room to dress her hair and an urge to discover why Sir Eustace had asked to see Jan instead of her. "Did Beale say Sir Eustace asked for *you*?" she inquired of her daughter.

"Yes, he did. Why should that surprise you?" She fixed a puzzled eye on her mother. "Do you realize, Mama, that whenever we speak of Sir Eustace, you suddenly become odd? What's—"

"Never mind that now," Celia said nervously, starting from her chair. "I must not be discovered in this state of undress."

But she was too late to make an exit, for Sir Eustace stood in the doorway. Celia sank down in her seat in chagrin, and before Jan's startled eyes, a blush suffused her cheeks.

Sir Eustace gave her ladyship a stiff bow and a curtly polite "Good morning, ma'am." Then he turned to Jan with a smile. "And how do *you* do, my dear? I bring you all manner of greetings from your friends in Bath."

"How good to see you, sir," Jan responded. "What brings you to town?"

"Nothing extraordinary. I never intended to spend more than two months in Bath, and that time expired three days ago. I am now installed in my rooms in Cavendish Square. But I must beg your pardon, ladies. I seem to have interrupted your breakfast."

"You didn't interrupt mine," Jan assured him. "I break-fasted hours ago."

"I'm the one who's the slugabed," Celia said, lifting up her chin as if challenging him to find fault. "It is but one of the many bad qualities of mine of which you are unaware."

Jan, who found her mother's words and tone inexplicable, threw her a bewildered glance. But then, remembering her manners, turned back to the Baronet. "Won't you sit down, Sir Eustace, and take a cup of tea with us?"

"No, thank you, my dear. I stay but a moment. I only came to tell you about a small chamber orchestra of which I am a member. All amateurs, of course, who gather to play for our own pleasure. I wondered if you'd care to play with us. You needn't fear that you'd be the only lady present. We have a Miss Deerwood who plays the cello, and sometimes Lady Fitzsimmons joins us with her harp. And there are several ladies in the group who come to listen. If you are agreeable, I would be honored to escort you to our meeting on Wednesday next. We'll be playing Vivaldi."

Jan's face brightened at once. "Oh, I'd *love* to! Mama, may I?"

"Why do you ask?" Celia muttered sourly. "Didn't you just declare independence of your mother? Do as you wish."

Jan blinked at her mother in bafflement. This crotchety manner in front of a guest was completely unlike her. *"Mama!"* She gulped, appalled.

But her mother was not looking at her. Celia's eyes were fixed on the Baronet. "I notice, sir, that you do not ask *me*," she said to him accusingly.

"Ask *you*, your ladyship?"

"To be among the listeners."

He frowned down at her. "I have good reason for the omission, ma'am. For one thing, I seem to remember your telling me that you don't care for music. And for another, I do not think it manly to persist in pressing a suit once it has been rejected."

Jan gasped. "A *suit*?"

Celia, ignoring her daughter, rose up in offended dignity and glared at her visitor. *"Be* manly, then! I would not wish you to persist in your suit any more than I would enjoy going to hear your deuced chamber orchestra perform.''

"Are you *both* demented?" the bewildered Jan croaked. "*What* suit?''

"Don't trouble your head about it, Jan,'' the Baronet said tightly, turning his back on Celia and bowing over the younger woman's hand. "I shall call for you Wednesday at seven. Is that convenient?''

"Yes, sir. Quite convenient,'' Jan mumbled in utter confusion.

"Good day, then.'' He turned to Celia and made his second bow, a much more formal one than the one he'd given her daughter. "And good day to you, too, ma'am,'' he said, his eyes taking a lingering look at her in her tousled dishabille.

In spite of her determination to brazen out this scene without revealing her discomfiture with her appearance, Celia's hand came up to smooth the sleep-tangled braid that had fallen over her shoulder. As soon as he saw the gesture, Sir Eustace's expression brightened. He gave a small, almost reluctant smile. "I must admit, ma'am, that I, too, would sleep till midmorning if, when I got up, I could look as charming as you do.'' And with another quick bow he was gone.

"*Mama,*'' Jan cried, crossing the room to her mother in two quick strides and grasping her shoulders. "*Look* at me! What *was* all that?''

Celia laughed. "Nothing, my love. Nothing of any significance.''

"Don't put me off, Mama. Something passed between you two in Bath. What was it?''

The mother's eyes flicked over her daughter's face. "I hope you won't be upset by this, dearest, but he . . . Sir Eustace . . . he . . .'' She sank down on her chair and hid her face in her hands. "He made me an offer.''

"*Mama!*'' She knelt down and threw her arms about her mother ecstatically. "How marvelous! How absolutely marvelous! You and Sir *Eustace*! Never in my wildest *dreams* did I—''

Celia peeped at her from between her fingers. "Are you pleased about it, then?"

"*Pleased?* I couldn't be more delighted!" She got up and whirled round the room giddily. "No wonder he never looked at Harriet! He was in love with *you*. Why did I never *see* it?"

"I didn't see it either, until the very last."

Jan stopped her whirling, suddenly realizing there was much that was still puzzling. "But you said he offered," she said, probing. "When did he do that?"

"Not until the day before we left. Until then, I never had an inkling of his intentions."

Jan, her brows knit, sat down at the table. "I am still confused, I'm afraid. What was the meaning of that exchange between you just now? Don't tell me you *refused* him!"

"Yes, my love, I did."

"But *why*?" Jan reached out and took her mother's hand. "Don't you care for him at all?"

Celia lifted her eyes to her daughter's face. "I wasn't sure, at first, but now—can you believe it, Jan?—I think I do."

Jan beamed at her in relief. "That's truly splendid, Mama. He is—"

"I know." Her mother grimaced. "The finest gentleman of your acquaintance."

"Yes. And of yours, too, isn't he?"

"Yes. Yes, he is."

"Then why did you reject him?"

"I don't know, Jan. It was, to use a dreadful cliché, too sudden, I suppose. I hadn't given any thought to remarriage. I hadn't given any thought to Eustace as a suitor for me, since I'd convinced myself that it was you he was courting. When he finally revealed his true feelings for me, I was too shocked to think clearly. All I felt was terror."

"Terror? Of Sir Eustace? There's never been a gentler, less terrifying man."

"I know. But I was struck with the most awful fear of making so radical a change in my life. I was so frightened that I took to my bed. And just at that moment you determined to leave Bath! That's when I decided that running home with you was the best solution for me also. So I wrote Eustace a dreadful note, rejecting him without any explanation at all, and fled.'' She dropped her eyes to her teacup and laughed grimly. ''And now that I've decided that I might wish to accept his blasted offer, the deuced jobbernowl tells me it's *unmanly* to persist in his suit!''

''That's not the problem, Mama,'' Jan assured her with a broad smile. ''If he thinks pursuing you is unmanly, then *you* pursue *him*.''

''Never!'' her mother declared, rising from her chair and stalking to the door. ''That would be *unwomanly*.'' At the door, she looked back at her daughter with a softened expression. ''But if we *should* manage to overcome this obstacle, dearest, are you certain you would be happy with Eustace as a new father?''

''More than happy, Mama,'' Jan said tenderly. ''I know I'll never find a husband I can love, but having a father I can love is the next best thing.''

Twenty-Eight

MAX FELL DEEP in the doldrums after Jan disappeared from Bath. He seemed to lose interest in the city and all its inhabitants. He had not realized how much Jan's mere presence in these environs had enlivened his days. Now she was gone, and the whole world was a duller place. He did not seem able to recapture the sense of contentment that he'd experienced before she came. Things and people that had pleased him before seemed colorless and pointless now.

The dark hours of the night were the worst part of his day. It was then that Jan's face haunted him. He had been certain that he'd recovered sufficiently from the wound of their long-past separation to build for himself a satisfactory life, but seeing her again after all those years, talking to her, even quarreling with her—all these had brought back with painful clarity what he had lost. All he had to do was close his eyes, and he would see her as she'd looked at Lady Briarly's party, when she'd sung her little ballad, her face ethereally lovely and touched with sadness. Or he would hear her voice as he'd heard it in the cave: *I knew you would find me . . . my love . . . I knew.*

Sometimes, to wrench himself free from the crushing vise of memory, he would try to concentrate on the times she'd infuriated him, such as the day she'd accused him of conducting a continuing affair with the Wedmore woman. He could not possibly be such a fool, he berated himself over and over, as to remain enamored of a woman who had so little regard for his moral character. Jan was a narrow-minded

prude in that regard, and in all of the eight years since she
jilted him she never once gave him even the benefit of the
doubt. In her eyes he was, and would always be, a licentious,
faithless, unregenerate libertine. Under these circumstances,
how could he keep on loving her? But even reliving that revolting scene in his mind did not cure him. It only made him
wild, overwhelmed by an urge to pull her in his arms and,
by the force of his embrace, crush some sense into her.

He believed that he would recover . . . in time. He'd done
it before. But somehow he knew that it would be harder this
time. It would take longer. And the contentment he yearned
for might never be completely won. Meanwhile, he'd have to
live through these endless hours of grim, gray agony.

But he would not permit himself to indulge in these fancies
in the daytime. He knew what his responsibilities were. He
had to bury his emotions. He had to live his life in an honorable way, and put a good face on it. His bride-to-be deserved no less.

However, the days were not much easier to endure than
the nights. Belinda was totally preoccupied with brideclothes
and wedding plans and excitement over the forthcoming celebrations in her honor. She was basking in the attention of
her bridegroom, the indulgence of her elders, and the envy
of her peers. Weddings were for the gratification of the bride;
the groom was merely a necessary accessory. Max found little in these prenuptial activities to stimulate him. Belinda's
friends, in whose company he was thrown daily, were rather
empty-headed widgeons whose prattle he endured with teeth-
gritting patience. Lord Liggett, whom he rather liked, was
preoccupied with Harriet Coombe these days, and Sir Eustace, whose companionship had been the only bright spot on
his grim horizon, had returned to London less than a week
after Jan's departure. The best part of his day, now, was the
early morning, when he took out his roan stallion and gal-
loped furiously through the countryside outside of Bath.

Belinda, for her part, was as pert and lively as she'd been
before Jan's visit. Whatever misgivings and fears had been
generated by Jan's presence were pushed out of the happy
bride's consciousness. Life had offered her this dazzling op-

portunity for pure pleasure—shopping, parties, amusements, attentions—and she intended to live it to the hilt. All too soon she would be a housewife, with babies and servants and all sorts of boring matters to contend with, but meanwhile she had no intention of cluttering up her mind with troublesome thoughts that might interfere with her enjoyment of these present delights, delights that her mother warned might be all too brief.

Mrs. Kendall, whose sprained ankle was healing more quickly than expected, decided to hold her ball after all. The cream of Bath society had been invited, and the Pump Room buzzed in anticipation. Belinda's eagerness for the event mounted with each passing day. Her mother had ordered a stunning new gown for her for the occasion and had even taken a diamond-and-pearl necklace out of its hiding place for the girl to wear. For Belinda, Mrs. Kendall's ball was to be, at least until the wedding itself, the highlight of the year.

Max was not insensitive to her feelings. On the night of the ball he presented himself on her doorstep early, dressed in his most impeccable evening attire and carrying a nosegay of the loveliest peach-colored roses (the color chosen only after secret consultation with his mother-in-law-to-be) that Bath could provide. Lady Briarly, swathed in a lavender silk roundgown and a purple turban topped with white plumes, greeted him with effusive warmth, her eyes glowing with approval of his appearance. "Max, dearest boy," she cooed, "you look *ravissant*! If I were a decade or two younger, I would try to capture you for myself, daughter or no daughter!"

"Mama, you are *dreadful*!" Belinda giggled from the top of the stairs. Max and Nettie looked up in silent admiration as the girl came gliding down. From the tip of her silver dancing slippers to the jeweled pin tucked among her glowing curls, she looked breathtaking. Her gown was a simple apricot-colored Pompadour silk with a low décolletage and a row of beading edging the high waist. It was dramatized by a flowing gauze overdress shimmering with silver threads. Her mother's magnificent necklace gleamed against her white

throat, but not as brightly as her eyes. The girl was in top
form, and the sparkle in her eyes showed that she knew it.

Mrs. Kendall's spacious rooms were already thronged with
people when they arrived. Belinda passed among them, ac-
cepting their admiration and good wishes with the aplomb of
a princess. Her cheeks glowed pink with joy. She was the
center of this, her world, and she couldn't have been more
pleased with herself if she'd been born to the purple.

The musicians struck up a waltz, and Max led her out on
the small dance floor that Mrs. Kendall had had cleared in
the center of her drawing room. The two danced alone, the
entire assemblage crowding around the fringes of the floor to
admire them. "It's like a fairy tale," Belinda whispered to
Max as he spun her round.

"Well, I hope it's not *'Cinderella,'* " Max laughed, "for
I don't want to lose you at midnight."

He stood up with her for the next set—a country dance that
brought so many couples to the floor that there was barely
enough room to take proper steps—and then surrendered her
to Jack Grindsley, who, since this was his very first ball, had
dressed himself, for once, in proper style. Max stood on the
sidelines watching the dancing for several minutes until he
saw one of the Brett girls eyeing him. Not wishing to endure
an entire set on the dance floor with her, listening to her
babble about waistcoats (or subjects of equally deep significance), he made a quick escape to the card room, where he
joined some elderly gentlemen in a game of whist. He was
not aware of the swift passage of time until he looked up to
see Lady Briarly standing in the doorway signaling to him.
He excused himself at once and went to her.

"Belinda is a bit upset," Nettie whispered. "I think she
expected you to take her up to supper."

"Good God, is it as late as that? I'll find someone to play
out my hand and take her right up."

"No, no, she's already supped. Mr. Grandon took her. But
the last dance is soon to be played, and I think you should
stand up with her for that, don't you?"

"Yes, of course," he said guiltily. "I'll come at once."

Belinda smiled at him brightly when he presented himself

for the dance, but there was something in her eyes that glittered coldly. She kept the same smile throughout the dance, but she didn't say a word. In the carriage during the short ride home, the silence prevailed. Lady Briarly tried valiantly to make conversation, but Max, aware that a storm was brewing, answered only in monosyllables, and Belinda said not a word.

When they alighted at the Briarly house, he kissed both ladies' hands and endeavored to make a quick departure. But Belinda would not have it. "Do come in for a moment, Max," she said, her voice trembling. "I'd like a . . . a word with you."

"It's late, my love," murmured Lady Briarly, eyeing her daughter with misgiving. "I'm sure whatever you have to say can wait until tomorrow."

"We needn't keep you up, Mama," the girl said between clenched teeth. "I'm sure Max will excuse you." And she swept into the foyer and on down the hall to the sitting room.

Max had no choice but to follow. Poor Nettie Briarly, biting her nether lip worriedly, ran down the hall after them both. One look at her daughter's agitated eyes told her that any attempt she might make to deter the girl from making a scene would only make matters worse. "Very well, child," she said from the doorway, nervously trying to indicate to her disdainful daughter that she should *take care*. "You may speak to Max for a moment or two. But I shall be waiting upstairs. If you have not come up in ten minutes, I shall come down to fetch you. Good night, Max, my dear. Don't keep Belinda too long."

Belinda remained motionless, her back to her affianced bridegroom, until she heard her mother's footsteps on the stairs. Then she whirled round, her underlip protruding in a trembling pout. "*Confound* you, Max," she burst out, "you *ruined* my whole evening!"

"Come, now, my sweet, that can't be true," he said soothingly. "No evening in which you looked so delectable can be called ruined."

"I may have looked delectable, but you weren't there to

see me!'' Tears of self-pity filled her pretty eyes. ''I b-barely had your company for t-twenty m-minutes!''

''I'm sorry, Belinda,'' he said softly, lifting her chin. ''I know I was a beast to forget about taking you to supper, but I promise it shall not happen again.''

''What good is that? It's too *late* for such p-promises.'' The tears spilled over and ran down her cheeks. ''There will never b-be another K-Kendall ball!''

''But there will be many other balls. And you'll have my company for supper at every one of them. Word of honor.''

''Swear it, Max! And swear that you'll stand up with me for all the dances, too!''

He laughed. ''What a little vixen you are! Come here and sit down with me on the sofa so that I can dry those tears.''

She let him draw her down beside him and put up her face to permit him to mop it with his handkerchief, but her lips were still pursed in a pout. ''You do swear it, then?'' she persisted.

''What? To dance every dance with you forever more? I should say not. I'd have every gentleman in England calling me out for monopolizing you!''

''But you'll be my *husband*,'' she said, stamping her little feet on the floor in impatience. ''You have a *duty* to monopolize me.''

''No, I don't,'' he said, keeping a wide smile on his face in the hope of teasing her out of her fit of pique. ''There are rules, you know. No man may dance more than three times with the same woman in one evening, even his wife. Didn't you know that?''

''No, I didn't. I think it's a *stupid* rule. I don't want to dance with anyone but you.''

''That will change soon enough,'' he said, smoothing her cheek fondly. ''When we are nicely settled into wedlock, you'll jump at the chance to flirt a bit with other gentlemen. And there will be dozens of them, I predict, lining up for the chance to dance with you.''

''Really?'' She threw him a suspicious glance while she thought over what he'd said. Then, as the prospect of hordes of eager swains forming queues in eager expectation of claiming her hand for a dance developed in her mind, her petulant expression slowly faded. "Surely not *dozens*," she murmured modestly.

"Dozens," he assured her. Relieved that he'd deflected the storm, he lifted her chin and kissed her gently. Then, releasing his lapels from her grasp, he made as if to rise. "I must be going, my sweet. We don't want your mother to come storming down and ordering me from the premises."

But Belinda was unwilling to let the evening end. Tugging at his sleeve, she urged him back on the sofa again. "Max?" she asked in a shy whisper. "Did you truly think I was delectable tonight?"

"The most delectable creature in the room," he answered promptly.

She edged closer to him and began to play with a button on his coat. "Then why did you run off to the card room? Why didn't you stay and . . . and watch me?"

Max found the question troublesome. *Did the chit expect him to gaze at her in adoration every hour of the day?* he asked himself in irritation. But he immediately regretted the thought. She was very young and inexperienced. With time she would develop enough confidence in herself to be less cloying. "You must learn to know me better, Belinda," he said firmly, taking her face in his hand and forcing her to look up at him. "The first thing to learn about me is that I'm a gamesman. I like all sorts of games. Races, and boxing, and all manner of sporting competition. And cards. I sometimes become so caught up in the game I forget the time. Tonight it was whist. But believe me, my sweet, even though I may seem absorbed in other things, you—your interest, your comforts, your well-being—will always be of first importance to me. Will you try to remember that?"

"Yes, Max, I'll try." She lowered her eyes, fixing them on the button she was twisting on his coat. "But I was wondering . . ."

"Yes?"

Belinda hesitated, as if she were fearful of what she was about to say, but then she plunged in. "Did you get so caught up in a game and forget the time when you were betrothed to my cousin Jan?''

He stiffened. ''I've always gotten caught up in my games,'' he answered carefully. ''And as far as your cousin is concerned, I'm certain she told you that our betrothal was short. The truth is, Belinda, that it was so short I didn't even have time for a card game before it was over.''

But having broached the forbidden subject, Belinda couldn't let it drop. She had to ask the question that had been nagging at her since the day Jan told her of their past. ''Did you . . . *love* her, Max?''

He drew in a deep breath. ''Yes, I loved her. I would not have offered for her otherwise.''

Having picked up the apple from the tree, Eve had to bite it. Belinda, too. ''More than you love me?'' she asked.

Here it is, he thought, his heart sinking. He supposed the blasted question was bound to come up sooner or later. But since it was, this was as good a time as any to face it. Taking both her hands in his, he smiled down at the girl with wry but sympathetic understanding. ''That, my sweet, is the eternal feminine question. Did no one ever tell you that comparisons are odious? My feelings for *you* should be your only concern. If you have an urge to measure those feelings against others, it means that you don't have a deep enough belief in them. So, Belinda my sweet, let me assure you that I would not have offered for *you*, either, if I did not love you.''

The answer did not please her. The pouting look came back on her face, and she pulled her hands from his grasp. ''I suppose you will say that I shouldn't ask if you love her still.''

He sighed. ''I won't say that. It is a natural question, under the circumstances. I can't blame you for asking. The trouble is that I don't quite know how to answer you.''

''And I suppose *that* means that you *do* love her still,'' she pouted.

''That means,'' he said firmly, ''that perhaps there are some things, even between husband and wife, that should be left unspoken.''

''I don't *want* it unspoken! I want to *know*!''

''Then, my dear, know this,'' he said, taking her hand

gently in his and kissing it. "My feelings for Jan, whatever they are, are part of the past. They have no relevance for us today, and you must put the matter out of your mind, just as I must do. *You* are my love, my betrothed, and that is all that matters." He rose abruptly and tried to smile down at her. "And now, before your evening really *is* ruined, we'd better say good night. Come here, my girl, and give me one last kiss before your mother pounces on us."

But Belinda wouldn't budge. She sat looking down sullenly on her hands clasped in her lap. "Jan did this, you know," she muttered.

"Jan did what?" he asked, not understanding her meaning.

"Made this . . . this *breach* between us."

"There is no breach, Belinda. Don't make problems where they don't exist."

"Well, there's a *difference* now."

Max tried to be patient with the girl. "It must seem so to you because of learning so suddenly that I'd been betrothed before. But it was all so long ago, my dear. You must not let the past interfere with our present."

Belinda could not take the advice. She sat there clenching her fists, allowing a venomous jealousy to engulf her. Jealousy is so stingingly cruel an emotion that it demands relief, and the only relief the girl could think of was to lash out heedlessly at the most obvious target. "Jan Hazeldine is a devious, underhanded *witch*!" she spat out.

"Confound it, Belinda," Max snapped, trying to hold his irritation in check. "I don't think this subject should be pursued."

But there was no stopping the girl now. "She's made a fool of you, you know," she muttered. "You think she's so fine and . . . and honest, and perfect in every way, but she's not. She's not at all what you think she is, Max. You may as well know it. If you've begun to care for her again, it's because she *tricked* you into it!"

"Belinda," he said warningly, *"cut line!"*

"I *won't* cut line! She maneuvered you into lying to me, didn't she? And she met you for little, secret talks, don't tell me she didn't! And she always managed to appear on the scene whenever we went anywhere together. And then she arranged to lose herself in the cave, so that you would become terrified for her safety and risk your life to find her!''

Max stared at the girl for a moment, breathing hard. He was reeling from the shock of what she'd said. He felt as if he'd just done ten rounds in the ring and gone down for the count. Could this spitting cat be the sweet, naive, lovable little kitten he'd asked to be his wife? He couldn't believe the change in her. "*Listen* to yourself, Belinda," he sneered, unable to keep his contempt from showing. "Do you know how petty and mean you sound?''

Belinda glanced up at him, and something in her breast quailed at the expression on his face. His mouth was tight, his nostrils distended, and a muscle twitched in his jaw. No one had ever before looked at her with such obvious revulsion. Suddenly she understood that she'd gone too far. But she didn't know how to back away from the damage she'd wrought. She dropped her eyes and pursed her lips in her habitual pout. "I don't care," she muttered belligerently.

"How can such . . . such *tripe* fall from so sweet a mouth?'' He stalked up to the sofa, grasped her by her arms and pulled her to her feet. "Don't you know how foolish, how untrue, how *ugly* your words are? If you really *believe* those outrageous slanders, then you don't know your cousin, you don't know me, and worse than all the rest, you *demean yourself*. Do you understand me, Belinda? You will only degrade yourself in my eyes if you persist in these accusations.''

"I don't *care*!" the girl cried, pummeling his chest with her fists and twisting herself in his hold as if quite out of control. "I won't take back a *word* of what I said! I *won't*!''

"Listen to me, my girl," he said icily, holding her still with sheer brute force. "We are pledged to spend our lives together. If you wish to spend those years in the affectionate contentment that every spouse desires, you'll put everything you've just said forever out of your mind. Your accusations are *simply not true*, and the sooner you accept that fact, the sooner we can purge this evening from our minds and go on from there.'' Then he dropped her back down on the sofa and walked swiftly to the door.

But the sound of her sobs brought him up short. He turned and saw that she had thrown herself full-length on the sofa and was weeping pathetically into the cushions. His shoulders sagged in defeat. He could not walk out and leave her sobbing there. Sighing, he went back to her, sat down on the edge of the sofa and lifted her into his arms. ''Don't cry, my dear,'' he said quietly. ''We are still betrothed, and I have every intention of being a faithful devoted husband to you. But if you place any value on my feelings, you will *never* speak to me in that way of Jan again.''

Just outside the door, in the shadows of the corridor, Nettie Briarly watched the scene on the sofa with a deeply furrowed brow. Her daughter had just demonstrated again how spoiled and immature she could be, and the demonstration did not augur well for a happy marriage. *Something must be done about this,* she said to herself as she backed away and tiptoed down the hall. *Something drastic. And soon.*

Twenty-Nine

JAN MADE CERTAIN *not* to be ready when Sir Eustace came to call for her on Wednesday evening. Not being ready was a crucial part of the scheme she'd worked out to bring the Baronet and her mother into each other's arms. If Sir Eustace felt it unmanly to repeat his offer, and if her mother felt it unwomanly to encourage him, then she, Jan, had to step in and play Cupid.

It was a simple plan, really. All she had to do was arrange for the pair to be forced into each other's company without anyone else present. Human nature would do the rest.

With Sir Eustace due to call for her at seven, this very evening offered the perfect opportunity. She and her mother had dined early so that Jan could be ready for her appointment, but her mother had made no special plans of her own for the evening. "Since you'll be deserting me this evening," Celia had said over dinner, "and will probably sit playing your Vivaldi until all hours, I intend to make a short night of it and retire early."

Jan understood the meaning of that remark. It meant that Celia did not intend to wait up for Sir Eustace to bring her home. Therefore the scheme could not be put into play at the *end* of the evening, but the beginning of the evening might be the perfect time. Jan knew her mother would not retire before nine at the earliest. She also knew that between seven and nine, on evenings when she didn't go out, Celia Hazeldine was as likely as not to go to the small sitting room in the rear of the house and work on her stitchery. Wagering the success of her scheme on the likelihood that her mother would follow that custom, Jan gave Beale strict instructions to escort Sir Eustace to the rear sitting room when he called. "Remember, Beale," she ordered. "The *rear sitting room*. Tell him to wait for me there."

Beale found the instructions puzzling. "The *rear* sitting room, Miss Jan? Wouldn't the drawing room be more convenient? Or even the library? Her ladyship is always saying as how the back sitting room, shabby as it is, is not suitable for guests."

"Sir Eustace won't mind," Jan assured him. "I promise you that."

At seven on the dot, Sir Eustace arrived. The butler, as instructed, led him all the way down a long hallway to the very last doorway. "Miss Jan said to wait for her in here," Beale told him, opening the door and standing aside. The Baronet crossed the threshold and stopped short. "Oh," he said awkwardly on discovering Celia Hazeldine in the room, "it's *you*."

Celia gaped at him over the tiny spectacles perched on her nose (which she had to wear for doing embroidery but which she would rather have died than be seen with in public). "What are you doing here?" she asked in surprise. "Where's Jan?"

The Baronet shrugged. "Not ready, evidently. Your butler told me to wait for her here." He edged embarrassedly backward to the door, but the butler had already closed it.

Celia, knowing full well that Jan was rarely late for an appointment and that the butler never brought visitors to the rear sitting room, began to guess the plot. Her pulse began to throb excitedly. But she kept her expression coolly unruffled. "Then do sit down, sir," she said, whipping off her spectacles and motioning him to the worn loveseat which, with the rocker on which she sat and her embroidery frame, were the room's only furnishings. "I'm sure she'll only be a moment. Jan is nothing if not prompt."

"Thank you," he said stiffly, sitting down gingerly on the edge of the seat. A few seconds of strained silence followed.

When the Baronet realized that Celia had no intention of breaking it, he cleared his throat. "I trust I find you well, ma'am," he muttered.

"Very well," she said sarcastically. "And the weather is fine, too, is it not?"

He glared at her. "Dash it all, ma'am, what *else* is there to speak of? The subject of Bath seems to be prohibited, and your life here in London is quite unknown to me."

"I don't see why the subject of Bath is prohibited."

"Because, ma'am, if we broach the subject of Bath, it would be natural and logical for me to ask you why you ran off, and I don't want to ask that question."

"Why not? Because it touches on the subject of your offer, and any discussion of *that* would be *unmanly*?"

"Not at all," he said, thrusting out his chin in irritated pride. "I avoid the subject only because I'd be bound to call your behavior cowardly, and that would surely set up your bristles. Since I don't care to engage in arguments, I think the subject is best avoided."

"But you see, I would not argue the point, Eustace. I agree with you completely; my behavior *was* cowardly. The truth is that I was frightened to death."

He blinked at her, disarmed by her frankness. With one moment of honesty, she'd made his anger melt away. "Frightened?" he asked, leaning forward. "Of what?"

She lowered her eyes to her embroidery frame and began to fiddle uneasily with the loose threads. "Of the interview we were supposed to have," she admitted quietly. "Of your offer. Of the prospect of marriage. Everything."

"Of *me*, Celia?" A wave of sympathy swept over him, penetrating the wall of protection he'd erected to keep himself from being hurt again.

"Well, *yes*." It was a hard admission to make. She swallowed nervously and went on. "You are the only man since my husband's passing who . . ." She threw him a quick glance, and then, coloring, fiddled even more agitatedly with the threads.

Eustace's heart began to thump like a boy's. "The only man who—?" he prodded.

"Who could coax me to change my life," she blurted out, unable to meet his eyes.

His face lit up with hope. Jumping up, he took the two steps necessary to reach her chair and pulled her to her feet. "Celia Hazeldine," he declared, "if you've cajoled me into being so unmanly as to make you an offer a second time only to refuse me again, I shall *wring your neck*!"

She eyed him worriedly. "Nothing has really changed, you know, Eustace. I am still the same old, inflexible, unmusical, crotchety female I was in Bath."

He pulled her to him. "Isn't it strange? Those are the very qualities I require in a wife."

"In that case, my dear Eustace," she said, throwing her arms round his neck, "I won't refuse your offer a second time."

Much later, as they sat together on the loveseat, her head resting on his shoulder, something occurred to her. "I think we should bestir ourselves and go to tell Jan what's happened," she murmured dreamily.

Sir Eustace bestirred himself just enough to pull his watch from his pocket. More than an hour had elapsed since he'd come into this room. He grinned down at his misty-eyed bride-to-be. "I think Jan knows," he said.

Jan did indeed know. She'd peeped in on them half an hour earlier. One glimpse of her mother's glowing face told her that her scheme had worked. Beaming in delight, she tiptoed out of hearing and left them to their joy. Of course, there would be no orchestra for her tonight, but she felt not the slightest twinge of disappointment. For what she'd just witnessed, missing one night of Vivaldi was a small price to pay.

Thirty

LADY COOMBE AND Harriet returned to London during the following week. Harriet's very first action on her return was to pay a call on her best friend. She embraced Jan with such warmth and excitement that one might have thought the two had been separated for three years instead of three weeks. "Have you heard?" Harriet asked as soon as Jan had helped her up (after she'd stumbled over the edge of the carpet) and ensconced her on the sofa in the front sitting room.

"Heard?" Jan echoed.

"About me!"

"No, I haven't heard a *word*," Jan said, perching on the sofa beside her friend and eyeing her with interest. "Has something happened?"

"Jan, you will *never* credit it!" Harriet crowed. "I'm *betrothed*!"

Jan was dumbstruck. How could Harriet have become betrothed, she wondered, when Sir Eustace (who, in her opinion, had been the only "eligible" in Bath) was betrothed to her mother? *"Harry!"* she exclaimed. *"Who?"*

Harriet giggled in delight at Jan's surprise. "Liggy, of course! Who else?"

Jan was shocked. "Lord Liggett? But, Harry, he's only a *boy*!"

"No, he's not. He's twenty-three. I know that makes him several years my junior, but that doesn't trouble me. He's very mature for his age, you know."

Jan gaped at her.. *"Is* he?"

"Very," Harriet declared with absolute certainty. "You'd not believe how deep he is."

"But, my dear," Jan said, studying her friend's face closely, "this has happened so quickly. Are you sure that you really care for him?"

"As sure as I am that the day will dawn," Harriet said, her face taking on a glow. "And it didn't happen as quickly as you think. I think I fell in love with him the moment I saw him, standing there in the Pump Room in his magnificent blue coat with satin lapels, looking so top-of-the-trees! I know he believed that he was in love with *you*, Jan, but when I explained to him that it was only an infatuation, he recovered very quickly." She threw Jan a worried look. "You don't mind, do you, Jan?"

"No, of course not. How can you ask? Besides, you deserve him for having seen so much more in him than I ever did."

"That's because you were looking elsewhere," Harriet said with sympathetic understanding.

"Yes, I was," Jan admitted, a cloud passing over her face, "fool that I am. But let's not even think about that. This is too happy an occasion to spoil with sour memories."

"You're quite right. No use dwelling on depressing things. Besides, I've barely begun to tell you all the wonderful facets of my Liggy." She leaned forward eagerly and rattled on. "It turns out, Jan, that Liggy's *rich*, with estates in Somerset and Yorkshire and who knows where else! And do you know the *best* surprise?"

"I don't think I can *bear* another surprise," Jan teased.

"But this is one you'll *adore. He plays the French horn!*"

"Heavens!" Jan shook her head in amazement. "It seems that your Liggy has all *sorts* of unknown depths."

"Yes, doesn't he?" Harriet chuckled happily. "Liggy says we are *perfect* for each other. He's quick in body, so he can catch me when I stumble, and I'm quick in tongue, so I can help him when he stammers."

"Well, when you look at it that way," Jan laughed, "it *does* sound perfect." She hugged her friend. "I have a feeling you'll be very happy, Harry," she said sincerely.

They chattered on for half an hour, Jan demanding all the minute details of the courtship, and Harriet only too willing to supply them. Jan was amazed at how wrong she'd been in judging what sort of man would please her friend. Liggy was as different from Eustace as a peacock from an owl, and for Jan to have supposed that her friend would prefer the owl was another instance of her inability to judge people's true natures.

But thinking of Eustace reminded her that Harriet knew nothing of her mother's remarkable courtship. She was just about to relate the details of that romance when Beale tapped at the door to tell Jan she had another visitor. "It's a lady, Miss Jan," he said. "A Lady Wedmore. I put her in the library."

Jan paled. "*Wedmore?* Are you sure?"

"Perfectly sure, Miss. She called on you in Bath, too, right after you left. Came with Lord Ollenshaw."

Jan felt her pulse begin to race. "With Lord *Ollenshaw?*" she asked, her voice croaking oddly. "But . . . he's not with her *now*, is he?"

"No, Miss. She's alone." Beale peered at her with knitted brows. "Is there something wrong, Miss Jan? Shall I tell the lady you're not at home?"

Jan's head was spinning with bewildered speculation. Could Max have really brought his doxy to her door in Bath? And if so, why? And what was the woman doing here now, with Max back in Bath? Had something happened? She got to her feet and put a shaking hand to her forehead. A dreadful possibility was beginning to shape itself in her mind. *Of course!* said a voice in the back of her mind. *What else could it be? Belinda has discovered the woman's existence!*

"Miss Jan?" the butler was repeating worriedly. "Are you all right? Shall I send the lady away?"

"No, no. I'll see her. Tell her I'll be with her in a moment." She turned to Harriet, but her eyes, clouded and abstracted, followed the butler out the door. "Harry, my dear," she said absently, "will you excuse me? Someone's waiting . . ."

"Of course. I have to run along anyway." Harriet kissed

her friend and gathered up her reticule and gloves. "Come and see me tomorrow, Jan, and we'll pick up where we left off." She waved, tripped over the threshold, righted herself and was gone.

Jan, taking only a moment to steady herself, crossed the hall to the library. Lady Wedmore was standing at the window. She was wearing one of the broad-brimmed, high-crowned plumed hats she seemed to favor, and a modish walking dress of green jaconet. She had been looking out at the small garden, now abloom with June roses, but she turned at the sound of the door. "Miss Hazeldine?" she asked, looking across at Jan curiously.

So the creature does not remember me, Jan thought. Aloud, however, she only said, "Yes, I'm Jan Hazeldine. Do you have some . . . some business with me?"

The lady shrugged and approached her hostess. "So you're the one," she murmured, studying Jan's face with approval. "I always said that Ollenshaw has taste."

Jan was disconcerted by the remark. "Do you care to sit down?" she asked awkwardly, feeling strangely ill at ease.

The Wedmore woman, however, was perfectly composed. "Yes, but only for a moment. I am leaving for the Continent this evening, and I have a great deal of packing still to do."

They sat down, Lady Wedmore on a loveseat and Jan on an armchair facing her. Jan took a good look at her face. The woman was older than Jan had hitherto suspected—forty-five at least. But her figure was shapely, and her face still attractive despite the lines around her eyes and mouth. The red hair that peeped out below the brim of her hat was not so garishly red as it once had seemed, and her light eyes glinted with a worldly humor. She had an air of brave self-confidence, as if she'd faced many of life's difficulties and survived intact. Jan could see why men found her seductive. "If you are going abroad, ma'am," she said, "then it must be a matter of importance to have brought you here at such a busy time."

"I'm not sure if it's important or not. When we didn't find you in Bath, Max assured me that the matter was not important at all, but an instinct told me to come and see you anyway." She sat back, crossed her legs gracefully, and smiled at Jan. "I am a great believer in following my instincts."

"You and Max . . . Lord Ollenshaw . . . came to see *me* in *Bath*?"

"Yes. We happened to pass each other on the street one day, and while we were exchanging greetings—we'd not seen each other for *years*, you see—it suddenly occurred to him that you would have some interest in knowing that."

"In knowing that you hadn't seen each other in years?" Jan asked in a choked voice.

"Exactly." The woman cocked her head curiously. "*Does* that information interest you, my dear?"

Jan clenched her fingers to keep them from trembling. "Yes," she admitted hoarsely. "Yes, it does."

"I thought so, though I don't know why it should. If my memory serves, you and Max broke it off years ago."

"That's quite true. He is betrothed to my cousin now."

"Then I really don't understand all this. However, I said to myself that if it was worth his effort to drag me across town to see you in *Bath*, I might serve him a good turn to come to see you here. There are very few people for whom I'd go out of my way to do a good turn, but Max is one of them. I've always been inordinately fond of him."

I'm very well aware of that! Jan said to herself bitterly. But if, as the lady was claiming, she was not being kept by Max in Bath, Jan had no reason to feel bitter. She forced herself to concentrate on the conversation and not let her mind drift off on tangents. "Are you saying, Lady Wedmore, that Lord Ollenshaw *didn't* ask you to pay me this visit?"

"No, he didn't. It was my own idea."

"I see," Jan murmured. But she didn't really see anything. She felt so full of shame and confusion that her brain seemed clogged. "But in Bath you were following *his* suggestion? He took you to my house just so that you might tell me that *one thing*?"

"That I hadn't seen him in years, yes. And that I was living in Bath under the protection of a certain gentleman whom I don't care to name, but with whom I have lived for many years." She smiled across at Jan with a look of placid self-satisfaction. "Max doesn't know it, but it is the very gentleman with whom I am going to live abroad."

"To live?" Jan asked, fascinated. "Permanently?"

"Yes. My 'friend' cannot wed me, you see. For a couple in our circumstances, who live together without benefit of clergy, England is a very stodgy place in which to reside. Life will be much freer for us on the Continent. But Max did not expect me to tell you all this. He only said . . ." She frowned for a moment trying to recollect his instructions to her. "Well, he did add that I should feel free to tell you anything else I could remember about the two of us."

"About you and Max?"

"Yes." The woman leaned forward, her arm falling languidly across her knees. "Not that there's much to tell. Do you wish to hear about it?"

Jan colored. She very much wished to hear about it, but this conversation was so far beyond her ordinary experience that she scarcely knew how to conduct herself. "I would not wish you to . . . to embarrass yourself before a stranger."

"Don't worry about that, my dear," Lady Wedmore said flippantly. "It has been many years since I was capable of embarrassment. As far as Max and I are concerned, I'm perfectly willing to tell you about it. We had a brief *liaison* many years ago. Wedmore was still alive, as I recall, so it must have been eight or nine years ago. Max broke it off. That's all there was to it. I never saw him after that until we met in Bath."

"Forgive me for seeming to pry into your private history," Jan said, unable to stop herself, "but surely, my lady, there was more to it than that."

"No, nothing more, I assure you. Max broke it off with the most unflattering abruptness the moment he fell in love with you. I remember his saying that he could not be false to so pure a creature as his Miss Hazeldine."

Jan stiffened in disbelief. "There's no point in trying to flummery me, ma'am. After all these years, it cannot make a difference, anyway."

"That's *just* what Max said," Lady Wedmore snorted in amusement. "But, my dear, why would I flummery you? You cannot be such a silly chit as to believe that I would bother to call on you on one of my busiest days for the purpose of *lying* about ancient history.''

Jan shook her head. ''*Am* I a silly chit for disbelieving you, ma'am? Then tell me why, if Max broke with you when he fell in love with me, I discovered you in his arms when I went to his rooms on the very night of our betrothal.''

Lady Wedmore's brows rose. ''In his *rooms*? In his *arms*? I don't remember any such—'' She lowered her head in thought for a moment. ''Wait! Yes!'' Her head came up, the plumes of her hat waving from the sudden movement. ''I *do* remember! It was the night Wedmore left me. I was frantically agitated, and I ran to Max to beg him to take me back. The incident was quite humiliating. No wonder I pushed it from my mind. Max was not in the least conciliatory, though I used all my wiles. Then someone broke in on—good God! Was that *you*?'' She stared at Jan, her eyes widening as the import of the story broke on her. ''You didn't—! You poor little *goose*! Did you break with Max because of *that*?''

There was no point in answering. Nor could Jan have answered if she wanted to. Her throat burned with tears she would not permit herself to shed. Somehow Jan got to her feet. Somehow she managed to thank Lady Wedmore for coming and speaking to her with such unprecedented frankness. She even managed to express good wishes to the lady in her life abroad. The wishes were quite sincere. Lady Wedmore no longer seemed as despicable as Jan had once thought she was. The woman was straightforward and courageous, even if she was not very respectable. She was certainly not the vile ''Redmore'' creature Jan's imagination had painted. That image was just another of her misjudgments.

As for Max, she thought as she climbed the stairs to her bedroom, her misjudgments had been monumental. All these years, when she'd thought of him as a lecherous rake, he'd been as honest and upright as he'd claimed. She felt a wave of joyfulness at being able to think of him that way. How lovely it was to be able to see him as the man she'd always wanted him to be! It almost made up for the disgust she now felt for herself. Max had called her a spinsterish prude for seeing lecherous shadows where there were none. She had let those shadows overcome her judgment. What blessed relief there was in learning that her judgment of Max had been wrong!

But for herself there was no relief. The misjudgments were all her own. She had no one else to blame and no one else to help her pay the cost. The price was heavy; she would pay for those misjudgments with a lifetime of regret. And she was about to make the first payment . . . with a long bout of bitter tears.

Thirty-One

AT THE LAVISH dinner party held by Mary Grindsley's mother in honor of Belinda's betrothal, Lady Briarly was the only one who noticed that her daughter was not happy. Since the girl looked magnificent in a dinner gown of blue Persian silk and smiled dazzlingly at everyone who glanced at her, no one but her mother could see the seething turmoil beneath the surface. Even Max, who was trying his best to treat the girl with unimpeachable devotion, did not suspect that a crisis was at hand.

But after Max had deposited his affianced bride and her mother at their house, made his good nights and driven off in his curricle, Lady Briarly confronted her daughter with the blunt demand to be told what was wrong.

"Everything!" the girl declared dramatically, throwing off her wrap, striding into the sitting room and throwing herself upon the sofa. "Your niece Jan has ruined everything!"

"I thought we'd gone over all that," her mother said patiently. She followed the girl into the little room and crossed to the fire to poke it up. "Max has assured you, and I have assured you, that the business with Jan is all in the past. Why must you keep harping on it?"

"Because he keeps thinking of her. I *feel* it!"

Nettie shrugged. "Perhaps he does, my love, perhaps he does. But he will be a faithful husband just the same. There's hardly a man in the world who's reached the age of thirty-five without having had some love affair to remember. Max can't help his memories, you know. Besides, mere memories can't do you any harm.''

Belinda's underlip began to tremble. ''I don't want the man I marry to have any memories except of *me*!''

''Oh, Belinda!'' her mother sighed, shaking her head. ''What a child you are! Isn't it time you realized that the world isn't made to your design? You can't change Max's past. Isn't it enough for you to own his future?''

''No, it isn't,'' the girl pouted. ''I can't *bear* knowing that Max's thoughts are not for me alone.''

''But, my love, that's so foolish! There is no way you can control a person's *thoughts*. All you can do is be a loving wife to him, and in time all his thoughts of other loves will fade. You'll see.''

''I don't care about what will happen in *time*! How do I know his thoughts of Jan will fade? And meanwhile everything's spoilt!''

Her mother sat down heavily in the nearest chair. ''If that is so, Belinda,'' she said, taking a deep breath to give herself the courage to say what had been on her mind for several days, ''then perhaps it is time to consider breaking it off.''

''Breaking it *off*?'' her daughter squealed. She gaped at her mother in horror. ''Breaking it off with *Max*?''

''Why not? You've just said that everything's spoilt. If you truly feel that way, it is in your power to end it. You're not yet wed, after all.''

''But, *Mama*, how *can* you? I thought you were *ecstatic* about this betrothal. This is *Lord Ollenshaw* we're speaking of, not some nonentity without titles or estates. You can't mean it!''

''Good God, Belinda, who cares for titles and estates? Have I ever suggested that I wished you to sacrifice your happiness for an advantageous alliance? I have felt from the first that Max, appealing as he is, is too old for you. If I was ecstatic over your betrothal, it was because I believed it to be a love match.''

Belinda frowned. ''Well, we both seem to have been wrong about that. He doesn't love me—at least not enough—and I . . .''

Her mother peered at her with head cocked. "Go on. 'And you . . .'?"

"And I don't love him enough, either," the girl admitted grudgingly. "At least not enough to endure sharing his heart with my blasted cousin!"

"Then why go on with it, dearest? You are barely eighteen and not even out. You have plenty of time in which to find someone else."

Belinda's pout became more pronounced. "I'll never find anyone else as rich and handsome and important as Max," she muttered.

"But you might find someone you love more," her mother pointed out, her voice taking on a suggestive optimism. "Someone younger, who would have no memories . . ."

"Yes, that's so," Belinda said, her expression softening. "Someone for whom *I'd* be the first love."

"Yes, exactly," her mother said, marveling inwardly at how easily her daughter was being persuaded. "And until you find him, you can be cheerfully breaking hearts all over London. You have no idea how exciting that can be. A girl ought to be permitted to break a few hearts before she's leg-shackled. I was never fully reconciled to the thought of your missing your come-out because of this too-early betrothal. A girl should have a come-out before settling down to domestic life. You are so beautiful and charming, my love, and are bound to take the town by storm. Why should you have to miss that experience?"

Belinda's eyes took on a speculative gleam. "Do you really think I'd take the town by storm?"

"I do indeed. With Celia to help us arrange things and pick out wonderful gowns for you and guide you in choosing the best company, why there's no limit to the opportunities you'd have! You'd be the reigning beauty of the Ton. I'm certain of it."

"Yes, perhaps you're right." Belinda's lips curled up in a dreamy smile. "Even Max said that gentlemen would be forming queues to dance with me."

"And so they shall," her mother promised.

"Well, I shall think about it, Mama," the girl said, rising

gracefully from the sofa and drifting toward the door. "I'll think about it all night and tell you my decision in the morning." She paused and looked back at her mother from the doorway. "If I *do* let Max go," she said, her smile turning wry, "at least I shall have the satisfaction of knowing that his next betrothed will have to share his heart with his memories of *me*!"

Thirty-Two

THE VIOLIN MUSIC that floated down from upstairs was very plaintive. Lady Hazeldine looked up from her embroidery at her husband-to-be with a brow creased with worry. "Does that sound as sad to you as it does to me?"

Sir Eustace, who was comfortably ensconced in the deepest wing chair of the drawing room reading his *Times*, put the newspaper aside and sighed. "Yes, every bit as sad."

"What am I to do about the girl?" Celia asked.

"I wish I knew. But be patient, my dear. Perhaps Jan will slough off the doldrums once the wedding has taken place. When Belinda and Max are finally and irrevocably married, she will see that she must put thoughts of him aside."

"I hope so," Celia said, biting off a thread. "But speaking of that wedding, Eustace, I find it strange that I haven't heard from Nettie. Have *you* received an invitation to the nuptials?"

"No, I haven't. Perhaps your sister doesn't mean to invite me. After all, she doesn't yet know I'm to be part of the family."

"Nonsense. In Bath you were her friend and neighbor. She knows you longer than I do. I'm sure she intends to invite you. And she must surely intend to invite *me*. I should have thought the invitation would have been sent out days ago. If the wedding is to be held in June, as planned, why haven't we heard? June is already half over."

Before Eustace could answer, Beale appeared in the doorway. "Lady Briarly, my lady. And your niece."

"What?" Celia asked with a gasp. *"Here?"*

"Speak of the devil," Eustace laughed.

"Heavens! What are they doing in *London*? Well, don't keep them waiting, Beale. Bring them in!!"

She thrust her embroidery frame aside and bustled across the room just in time to meet her sister in the doorway. "Nettie!" she cried, throwing her arms about the visitor. "What a *surprise*!"

"We were just this moment speaking of you," Eustace said, getting himself from his chair and bowing over Nettie's hand after Celia released her.

"Goodness me, is it Sir Eustace?" Nettie blinked at him over her shoulder while her sister led her to a chair. "What a coincidence that you should be here!"

"Not such a coincidence," he said, handing Belinda over the threshold. "I am here quite often these days."

"Often?" Nettie asked in confusion.

"Every day," Celia laughed, turning to embrace her niece. "Belinda, my dear! You are in even higher bloom than when we saw you in Bath."

Belinda made a blushing little bob. "How do you do, Aunt Cecy? It seems an age since then."

"What do you mean, Cecy?" Nettie demanded suspiciously after everyone was seated. "Why is Sir Eustace here every day? Is something havey-cavey going on?"

"Very havey-cavey." Celia grinned.

"We're going to be wed," Eustace said, too kind to wish to continue to tease. "A small ceremony next month. You are both invited, of course. And, it goes without saying, Max, too."

"Celia!" Nettie clasped her hands to her bosom. "You and Sir *Eustace*? I can't believe it! I thought you wanted him for *Jan*!"

"No, I didn't. He's too old for Jan." She reached across to him and, clasping his hand, smiled fondly at him. "I wanted him for me. And now I have him."

"Well, if I hadn't seen this with my own eyes, I would *never* have believed it. You and Sir Eustace! It's shocking!"

"No, it's not, Mama," Belinda said, clapping her hands

in delight. "It's wonderful! Why don't you stop gasping and wish them happy?"

"Well, of *course* I wish them happy," Nettie said. "It's just so . . . so . . ." She pulled a handkerchief from her sleeve and dabbed at her eyes that began to fill with tears. "So *unexpected*."

"It's your *visit* that's unexpected, Nettie," her sister said, leaning forward and patting Nettie's knee fondly. "If you'd given me some warning that you were coming, I would have prepared you for this."

"We decided quite suddenly to leave Bath," Belinda explained. "Just yesterday, in fact."

"But I don't understand." Celia turned to her niece curiously. "How could you have left Bath at such a time? What about the wedding?"

"Perhaps, my dear," Eustace suggested, "they've decided to hold the ceremony here in town."

"Is that it, Belinda?" Celia asked. "Have you and Max decided to hold the ceremony in London?"

Belinda's smile faded, and her eyes dropped from her aunt's face. "Well, you see—" she began.

"There's not going to *be* a wedding," Nettie cut in, wiping her cheeks and pulling herself together. "That's *our* surprise."

Celia gaped at her. "No *wedding*?"

"We've called it off."

"Good God!" Eustace exclaimed.

"Nettie!" Celia cried. "Why?"

Nettie fiddled with the gloves in her lap. "Belinda is too young to settle down, you see. That's why we've come to town, Cecy. And that's why I've come to you. I want you to help me give the girl a proper come-out. It was a mistake to let her shackle herself before even having a chance to be presented to society. The child has not yet seen anything of the world."

"But . . . how can you just drop in like this and behave as if the betrothal were nothing more than a passing incident?" Celia exclaimed, not permitting herself to think about what this news might mean to her daughter. There was an air of unhappiness shrouding her sister's demeanor, and she could not let herself turn mental somersaults over what might be her sister's misfortune. "Not a month ago, you were both in alt over the betrothal!" she went on. "Belinda could speak of nothing else. And *you*, Nettie, you said Max was everything you *dreamed of* for your daughter."

"Yes, I know," Nettie said, lowering her eyes. "You mustn't think this is a decision we arrived at lightly. We have gone over it and over it. But you see, in the end we realized it would be best to break it off."

"You *both* realized it?" Celia asked.

"Yes. Both of us."

Celia peered at her sister curiously. "I'll do whatever you wish, my dear, and help you in any way I can. You know that." She knelt down and took Nettie's hand in hers. "But why on earth, my dear, have you suddenly decided that a come-out is so necessary?"

Nettie looked down at her sister gratefully. "Thank you, Cecy. I want this to be the most wonderful come-out a girl ever had. I promised her that." She sighed and paused for a moment to collect herself, and then went on. "You see, Max and Belinda are not so well suited as we thought. Belinda is very young and . . . and high-spirited. Perhaps a little too high-spirited to accept the restrictions of wedlock at so young an age. So, as it turns out—"

"As it turns out," Belinda cut in impatiently, "we realized that Max is a bit old for me. He's devastatingly handsome and clever, I grant you that, and he *is* a marquis, but we are nineteen years apart. He doesn't care much for dancing or balls or that sort of thing. He's been a part of society for so long that it doesn't interest him. But I have not. As Mama pointed out to me, I should not be asked to sacrifice my youth. A girl should have time to enjoy flirting, and being courted by dozens of young gentlemen, and have her come-out so that her charms can be admired by the world, and she should not be shut away in wedlock at eighteen, having babies and growing fat and—"

"So you *jilted* him?" came an agonized voice from the doorway. Everyone looked up to see Jan standing there. Her eyes glittered darkly in a face that was chalk white. "I won't *have* it, Belinda Briarly! You can't *do* it to him! It isn't fair for him to be hurt again! Max doesn't *deserve* to have to go through this sort of thing twice! I *won't have it!*"

"But you don't understand, Cousin Jan," Belinda said, rising from her chair and turning to her cousin, her manner all sweetness and smiles. "Max isn't hurt. We were not doing well together after you left. We kept raising each other's hackles every time we talked. And if we weren't actually having words, we were trying hard to *keep* from having them. I was quite beside myself. I went to bed crying every night, until Mama and I had a long talk, and she made me see what a sacrifice I was making of my best years. So I finally realized that there was nothing for it but to jilt him. But I assure you, Jan, he wasn't hurt. He seemed *relieved*."

Jan stared at her cousin as if the girl had lost her mind. "Do you really understand what you've done, Belinda?" she asked incredulously. "You've jilted Max—sacrificed a whole lifetime with a wonderful man—just so that you can have a *come-out*!"

"If you want to know the truth," Belinda retorted, a touch of bitterness creeping in below the smiling facade, "I *enjoyed* jilting him. I never enjoyed anything so much!" She tossed her head arrogantly. "Do you know what I think, Cousin Jan? I think that, before my come-out year is over, *I'll* have jilted even more suitors than *you!*"

Thirty-Three

JAN DID NOT feel sorry for Max for very long. He was well out of his entanglement with Belinda, and since he was far from being a fool, he probably knew it. And if he put to use the brain God gave him, he would appear at Jan's doorstep as soon as his feet could carry him there and offer for her once more. *This time, Max,* she would say joyfully, *there will be no jilts. This time will be right. This time will be forever!*

Every minute of every hour she expected him. Every knock at the door sent her pulse racing. She tried to think of other things, to divert her mind from the expectation of his visit, for in the way that water doesn't boil when one watches the pot, he would not appear while she watched the door. So she took brisk walks, she reread her favorite novels, she visited Harriet, she spent hours in the music room, fiddling desperately. But her mind refused to be diverted.

Three days passed, but Max did not appear. "Are you certain he's in town?" she asked her mother on the evening of the third day, when Celia peeped into the music room to see how her daughter was faring. "Perhaps he remained in Bath."

Celia threw her daughter a look of sympathy. "He's in town, dearest. Eustace called on him."

Jan gulped. "*Called* on him? Oh, God! Did he . . . did they . . . speak of me?"

"No, they didn't. Eustace told him about us—the coming wedding and all—but he did not think you'd wish him to talk about you. And Max didn't mention your name."

Jan put her instrument down and sank upon a chair. "He is not coming, then," she said in despair. "Either he doesn't love me after all, or he thinks I don't love him."

"Then perhaps, my girl, you should call on him and tell him that you do."

"Mama!" Jan was horrified. "How *can* you make so improper a suggestion?"

"You made a similar suggestion to me once, as I recall."

"Perhaps I did, but that was quite different."

"It was only different because you were not the one, in that instance, who was required to take the action."

Jan got angrily to her feet. "Then I will only say to you what you said to me at the time, Mama," she said, stalking out the door. "It would be *unwomanly*!"

Alone in her room, however, Jan did not dismiss her mother's suggestion. Perhaps she *should* call on him. He loved her, she was sure of that. Almost sure. He'd certainly given her several signs of it. The incident in the cave alone . . .

If she went to him, she could tell him that she loved him. Then, if he rejected her, she would at least know where she stood. She could go on with her life without listening at the door for his footsteps.

Of course, it would be most unpleasant to have to endure a rejection. It would be humiliating . . . the worst humiliation she'd ever suffered. But she'd subjected him to the same humiliation. Perhaps it was no more than she deserved, to suffer the same hurt she'd given him.

On the other hand, if he loved her, shouldn't he have come to her? Hadn't *she* given *him* as many signs as he'd given her that she cared? She'd even called him "my love," that day in the cave. And later he admitted to having heard her say it. With that evidence, he surely knew how she felt. So what was the point of going to tell him?

That was it, then. The matter was decided. She would not go. She looked out of her window at the dark sky, feeling utterly miserable. But she'd made the right decision, she told herself in an attempt to strengthen her resolve. It was too late to go out tonight, anyway. A girl alone . . . through the nighttime streets . . .

But in spite of being fully convinced of the soundness of her decision, she found herself reaching for a light shawl . . . running tiptoe down the stairs . . . letting herself silently out of the door . . .

How familiar the route was between her house and his. She remembered every moment of the last time she'd come this way . . . how blissful she'd felt . . . how her feet seemed not even to touch the ground. That was not the feeling she had now. What she felt now was sheer terror.

But her feet propelled her on. Before she knew it, she was in Hanover Square, knocking on his door. The butler who answered the door was the very same. And his words were the same, too. "Bless me soul!"

"Is Lord Ollenshaw at home?" Jan asked, her knees knocking.

"Yes, Miss. But I don't believe his lordship is receivin' callers at this late hour. Who shall I say—?"

But Jan could see a light behind him, coming from the same doorway down the hall. Some instinct—an instinct for self-destruction, perhaps—impelled her to behave in the same way she had once before. "Don't bother to announce me," she said, brushing by him. "I'll find my way."

"I *say*, Miss! You can't—"

But she could. She flew down the hall, wondering what she might feel if a scene met her eye like the one before. Would she wait for an explanation this time? And would she believe it? She hoped she would. She did not wish to spend her life as a prudish spinster, seeing lascivious shadows under the bed.

She paused in the open doorway, her heart beating. He was alone, slumped deep in an armchair facing the fire, one hand hanging down over the arm, an almost-empty brandy glass dangling from his fingers, and a book open on his knee. He was not reading, however. He was merely staring into the flames. He looked unkempt and uncared-for, sitting there glumly in his shirtsleeves, his hair tousled and his shirt half-unbuttoned. The firelight seemed to dazzle his eyes, for he squinted into the flames as one would at the sun. Her heart constricted at the sight of him. She wanted to run to him, throw herself in his lap, smooth back his hair and kiss those dazzled eyes. But the butler trotted up behind her, breathless from the chase, and grasped her arm. "I *say*, Miss," he scolded in highly offended agitation, "you've no right—"

Max's head came up, startled. His eyes widened at the sight of the girl in the doorway. The glass slipped from his fingers and crashed to the floor. "*Jan?*"

"Hello, Max," she said softly.

"I beg your lordship's pardon," the butler panted. "This brazen hussy pushed right past me!"

"Go away, Kemble," Max muttered, his eyes, light-blinded, trying to focus on Jan's face as he got dazedly to his feet, his book following the glass to the floor.

"But yer book, me lord," the butler said, trying to pass Jan in the doorway. "And the broken glass. I'll just—"

"I said go away, Kemble. Go away and don't come back." And he pushed the fellow out the door and shut it with one hand while he pulled Jan to him with the other. "I was *dreaming* you were here," he muttered hoarsely. He peered down at her myopically, as if he were trying to make certain through clouded eyes that it was really she. Then, very slowly, as if still in that dream, he tightened his hold on her and began to kiss her, gently at first and then more urgently, first her throat, then her hair, her eyes and finally her lips. It was a kiss that told her better than any words how he'd hungered for her, and it made nonsense of all her doubts. He loved her, and the wonderful certainty of it made her heart pound like a drum in a victory parade and her blood dance dizzily in her veins.

But as abruptly as he'd seized her, he let her go. He shook his head and drew the back of his hand across his forehead as if brushing away the cobwebs. "Damnation," he cursed, trying to catch his breath, "if I'd had a bit of warning, I would never have—" Fully awake now, he scowled in annoyance and embarrassment at his behavior. "I'm sorry, my dear."

"No need," she said.

He leaned back against the door, staring at her with something like despair in his eyes. "What the devil are you doing here?" he asked when he'd recovered his breath.

She backed away several steps, suddenly shy. "I wanted to . . . to start where we'd left off eight years ago," she said, smiling tentatively. "What I was going to say that night, before we were interrupted, was that my mother approves."

This was some sort of game, he thought, and he didn't like it. "Approves?" he asked, eyeing her warily.

"Our betrothal. She gives us her blessing. Of course, now I suppose we'll have to have Eustace's approval, too."

"Will we?"

"Yes, if a stepfather's permission is required. But I don't think Eustace will have any objections. So we can be wed any time you say."

"Good God, girl," he taunted, unwillingly joining in the game but at the same time curious about what her real purpose was in coming. "Are you making me an *offer*?" Jan's unexpected appearance had to be some sort of lark. Or perhaps he was still dreaming.

"It certainly sounds like an offer to me."

Max laughed ruefully. "Is it because of the greeting I gave you? Do you think you must make an honest man of me? I assure you, ma'am, that it's not necessary to go so far."

"It is not very kind, Max, to make a mockery of a serious offer," she reprimanded gently, his kiss having given her sublime confidence in the eventual outcome of this interview, even if he was being guarded at the moment.

"An offer, eh? A serious offer?" His eyes gleamed with a sardonic light. "In spite of the fact that I am keeping a doxy in a flat in Bath? And don't tell me you've forgotten what you saw in this very room eight years ago."

"As to that, Max," Jan said, lowering her eyes in shame, "I wish to make the most humble apology."

"Oh? And why is that, ma'am?"

She flicked him an uneasy glance. "I had a visit from the lady. Lady Wedmore herself. She told me . . . everything."

"Did she indeed? How very good of her. I shall have to send her another gift."

Jan stiffened. "If you are trying to make me believe you

bribed Lady Wedmore to say those things, Lord Ollenshaw," she snapped, "you may save yourself the trouble. She spoke nothing but the truth to me! I am convinced of that, no matter how you may try to diddle me. I am not a spinsterish prude, although I may have behaved so in the past, and will *never again* believe a *word* against you! So there!"

A grin broke out on his face in spite of his attempt to hide it. He was beginning to think something very nice might be happening here. "As apologies go, my dear, that was very satisfactory. The tone may not have been conciliatory, but the words were delightful." ·

"Thank you. Does that mean you are going to accept my offer?"

"Not so fast, woman. Not so fast. How do I know you won't jilt me again? That is your way, isn't it?"

Jan's smile faded, and her eyes dropped from his. "It was. After the first time, I could never find a suitor for whom I . . . I cared sufficiently."

Max closed the space between them in two strides and pulled her roughly into his arms again, part of him singing with elation and part still holding itself protectively aloof. "Are you saying you care sufficiently for me not to jilt me this time?" he asked. "I've really had quite enough of jilts, you know."

She slipped her arms round his neck. "Did my cousin Belinda hurt you very much, my love?"

He tried not to set too much store by that beautiful appellation. "Your cousin Belinda is a spoiled, pouting, self-adoring brat! She would have made an impossible wife, and I shall be forever grateful to Lady Briarly for persuading the chit to let me go. But that doesn't mean that being jilted, even by a brat, doesn't hurt a man's pride." He took Jan's chin in his hand and tilted up her face. "I am getting too old for these games, my girl. The first blow I received of that sort left a permanent mark. I might not recover from another."

"Is that why you didn't come to me after Belinda released you? Because you thought I might reject you again?"

"I was *certain* you would. You were much too good for

me eight years ago. And I'm not a better man now than I was then. Only older.''

''What fiddle-faddle, Max! Except for the rakish part, which I've already apologized for, I never thought that I was *in any way* better than you!''

Those words were what, for years, he'd longed to hear, but he hesitated to believe them. ''God knows I love you, Jan,'' he admitted, ''even more than ever. But I can think of no reason why you should take me now when you didn't before.''

But she heard surrender in his voice. With joy making music in her breast, she buried her face in his shoulder. ''I shall never stop regretting that I didn't take you before,'' she murmured. ''I've loved you for so long, Lord Ollenshaw, that I'm convinced the feeling is a permanent part of me. It took all my strength to hold you off even when I believed you were a lecherous rake. Now that I know you're not, I'll never let you go again.''

He pushed her away and, holding her by the shoulders, peered intently at her face. ''Do you mean that, Jan? This isn't a momentary aberration of some sort, is it? Or a dream that will disappear in the morning?''

''I mean every word. And it can't be a dream. I've never had a dream in all my life in which I felt so deliriously happy as I do this moment.''

The last resistance inside him gave way. ''I'm pretty delirious myself,'' he said, his eyes alight. ''So delirious, in fact, that I'm going to accept your kind and very sudden offer. We, my love, are betrothed. Again.''

''That's splendid, dearest. Utterly splendid. But see here, Max, how long do you intend to hold me off this way? Are you going to kiss me now, or do I have to wait until I get lost in another cave?''

If you enjoyed this book, take advantage of this special offer. Subscribe now and...

Get a Historical

No Obligation

If you enjoy reading the very best in historical romantic fiction...romances that set back the hands of time to those bygone days with strong virile heros and passionate heroines ...then you'll want to subscribe to the True Value Historical Romance Home Subscription Service. Now that you have read one of the best historical romances around today, we're sure you'll want more of the same fiery passion, intimate romance and historical settings that set these books apart from all others.

Each month the editors of True Value select the four *very best* novels from America's leading publishers of romantic fiction. We have made arrangements for you to preview them in your home *Free* for 10 days. And with the first four books you

receive, we'll send you a FREE book as our introductory gift. No Obligation!

FREE HOME DELIVERY

We will send you the four best and newest historical romances as soon as they are published to preview FREE for 10 days (in many cases you may even get them before they arrive in the book stores). If for any reason you decide not to keep them, just return them and owe nothing. But if you like them as much as we think you will, you'll pay just $4.00 each and save at *least* $.50 each off the cover price. (Your savings are *guaranteed* to be at least $2.00 each month.) There is NO postage and handling—or other hidden charges. There are no minimum number of books to buy and you may cancel at any time.

FREE
Romance
(a $4.50 value)

Send in the Coupon Below

To get your FREE historical romance and start saving, fill out the coupon below and mail it today. As soon as we receive it we'll send you your FREE Book along with your first month's selections.
